CABIN FEVER

Visit us at www.boldstrokesbooks.com

By the Author

Visiting Hours

Bird on a Wire

Across the Dark Horizon

And Then There Was Her

Queen of Humboldt

Swipe Right

Two Knights Tango

Almost Perfect

When It Feels Right

Pumpkin Spice

Cabin Fever

CABIN FEVER

by
Tagan Shepard

2024

CABIN FEVER
© 2024 BY TAGAN SHEPARD. ALL RIGHTS RESERVED.

ISBN 13: 978-1-63679-632-1

THIS TRADE PAPERBACK ORIGINAL IS PUBLISHED BY
BOLD STROKES BOOKS, INC.
P.O. BOX 249
VALLEY FALLS, NY 12185

FIRST EDITION: MAY 2024

THIS IS A WORK OF FICTION. NAMES, CHARACTERS, PLACES, AND INCIDENTS ARE THE PRODUCT OF THE AUTHOR'S IMAGINATION OR ARE USED FICTITIOUSLY. ANY RESEMBLANCE TO ACTUAL PERSONS, LIVING OR DEAD, BUSINESS ESTABLISHMENTS, EVENTS, OR LOCALES IS ENTIRELY COINCIDENTAL.

THIS BOOK, OR PARTS THEREOF, MAY NOT BE REPRODUCED IN ANY FORM WITHOUT PERMISSION.

CREDITS
EDITORS: ASHLEY TILLMAN AND CINDY CRESAP
PRODUCTION DESIGN: SUSAN RAMUNDO
COVER DESIGN BY INKSPIRAL DESIGN

Acknowledgments

There are always so many people to thank when I put out a new book and this time the list feels even longer.

Thank you to Brittany Shanley for letting me interrogate you about your job and how people even get picked to go to trade shows. I've never been so happy to be in service rather than sales!

Thanks, Laura, for introducing me (and by extension Shelby) to the glory of low-calorie wine. Also for being a cool cat and everything you do for the community.

The BSB family is so amazing and I'm so proud to be a part of it. Thanks to Rad, Sandy, Ruth, Cindy, and, of course, Ashley, the most kick-ass editor in the world.

I couldn't do any of this without my Sapphic Lit Pop-Up family. They inspire me and make me laugh and give me a community I need the way I need oxygen. Cade, Louise, Serena, Bird, Rita, Anne, and Nan are rockstars like no other.

What can I possibly say about Cris? She's my heartbeat. When I'm out there, grinding up pavement through rain and snow and horrible Maryland drivers, hundreds of miles away, she's the one I'm always driving home to. She's the light at the end of the tunnel. My whole world. Thanks, baby. There's no one else I'd rather be an indoor cat with than you. I love you.

Dedication

For the medical lab technicians and technologists who save lives every day even though no one knows who you are, what you do, or what you sacrifice. You're all heroes.

Chapter One

"Take it all in, kid. You've arrived."

At thirty-five years old, Morgan Allen didn't think she qualified as a kid and she was relatively certain that no one had ever truly "arrived" by walking into the Joseph A. Floreano Riverside Conference Center in Rochester, New York, but she wasn't going to begrudge Chad his moment of hyperbole. After all, he had been the one who had plucked her out of her mundane and increasingly dissatisfying job in a hospital laboratory two years ago. Rochester might not be glamorous, but it was new. So was the feeling of satisfaction her new job gave her.

The cynical part of Morgan—and that comprised a major part of her personality—knew that Chadwick "But You Can Call Me Chad" Hicks had only suggested she apply because of the generous referral bonus he stood to earn if she got the job. That didn't change the fact that she appreciated his efforts—and his reference. And he had taken her under his wing the minute she was hired.

In fact, she wouldn't be at this trade show at all if it wasn't for her self-appointed mentor. Usually, you had to have the top sales in the country to land a company-paid invite to a big national trade show like this one, but Chad had insisted she come along, and their boss did just about anything Chad wanted. He was good and she could learn a lot from him this week if she accepted that the lesson would come with a large side order of grandstanding.

"Let me show you around," Chad said.

He slapped an arm around her shoulders and puffed out his chest like he was the father of the bride and Morgan did her best not to tumble over from the sudden impact. In truth, he could have been her father. Chad was in his mid-fifties, with dark hair graying at the temples and a bit more gut than he had during his days playing baseball at the University of Virginia. He still had the same ridiculously dark tan that switched abruptly to pale white at collarbone and mid-bicep, and he still had the charm of the big man on campus. Unfortunately, at his age it came off more used car salesman than fraternity bro, but he was genuine and kind and that was rare in the world of medical equipment sales.

As they marched through the convention center's main floor, Morgan kept meticulous mental notes on the layout. The sheer number of vendors was dizzying. Anything and everything one needed to run a medical laboratory was on display, from sub-zero freezers the size and cost of a Buick to disposable plastic pipettes that sold for a few pennies a pound. And no matter what was for sale, Chad seemed to know the person selling it. For over an hour, they wound their way through aisle after aisle, stopping at every table for all the world like they were here to buy rather than sell.

When they finally made it into the rows of analytical instruments, Morgan's interest perked up. She was here to sell her instrument for sure, but she was also here to scope out the competition. Since starting this job two years ago, she'd been moderately successful, but she was losing market share to one competitor in particular and she was eager to meet her rival and discover what was so special about their instrument and their sales team.

"Nick. How've you been? How're the kids?" Chad's voice boomed out, cutting through her distraction.

"Chad. Great to see you, old man." A white man with the squarest jaw Morgan had ever seen shook Chad's hand like he was trying to rip it off.

"Let me introduce you to the little lady who's going to take all our jobs. This is my protégé, Morgan Allen." Chad wrapped an arm around Morgan's shoulder again as he introduced them.

"Nice to meet you, Morgan. You're lucky to have a wiz like Chad teaching you the ropes."

Morgan did her best to listen to Nick wax on about all the times he and Chad had met at events like this and all the ways her mentor was superior to everyone else. Sure, Chad was great and she was learning a lot from him, but she was eager to get to their own table and check out the setup. She'd seen a dozen different table configurations as they'd walked through the room, and she knew which one she wanted for their own table. If she didn't get there soon, the installation team might set it up wrong, and she didn't relish having to move it herself.

Eventually, Chad ran out of chummy things to say to Nick and they finally reached their section of the vendor floor. As soon as they turned down the row, Morgan could see the trademark primary blue and stark white of the Pulsar sign. Every time she saw her company's logo, she felt a swell of pride. This time that swell was matched by the sharp sting of tears forming behind her eyes, so she looked quickly away. It was one thing to be proud of the company where you worked, it was another thing entirely to burst into tears on the floor of a vendor show. Her rival was around here somewhere, and she could not embarrass herself right now.

With the swell of emotion under control, Morgan made a shocking discovery. The Pulsar booth was the only one with a bare table. Apart from the banner and tablecloth sporting their logo, their booth hadn't been set up. A young man in a polo shirt stood behind the table, fiddling with his phone and looking around the room impatiently. That had to be the service engineer assigned to install their sample instrument, and he was obviously waiting for her and Chad for direction. As much time as they'd wasted talking to every single salesperson in the room, they were running out of time before the doors opened for customers. If they didn't get to their table soon, they might be in the embarrassing position of setting up while potential customers watched. That was not the impression she wanted to make.

Just as Morgan turned to walk toward the table and get their display up and running, Chad put a hand on her shoulder. "Morgan, let me introduce you to one of the best saleswomen in the world."

Morgan had every intention of walking away without a word. She was determined to make a splash at this event, and she knew she could if she could just get over to their table and start presenting. The only reason she stopped was that she had only met male sales reps so far this morning and she was starting to crave the company of another woman. There was only so much testosterone she could take.

Turning to meet Chad's newest friend, Morgan nearly tripped over her own feet. The woman currently wrapped in Chad's arm was stunning. She was the definition of petite—short and slim with wiry, almost spindly limbs—but her smallness did nothing to detract from her presence. She had long blond hair, a button nose, and eyes so deeply sapphire blue they could have passed for purple. But the feature that really captured Morgan's attention was her smile. It very nearly encompassed her entire face and was one of those captivating smiles that made everyone want to smile back. She was possibly the most attractive woman Morgan had met in a very long time.

"You're too sweet to me, Chad." The woman turned her smile's full force on Morgan and held out her hand. "Shelby Lynn Howard. Nice to meet you."

"Likewise." Morgan's hand felt big and awkward wrapped around Shelby's.

"Shelby is the best in the game. She's the one stealing food out of my kids' mouths, but she's too sweet to be mad at for long," Chad said.

"It's not my fault. I learned from the best." Shelby wrapped her arms around his waist, her shoulders going up to her ears and her voice pitching up an octave.

The sharp edge of Morgan's interest in Shelby dulled at the obvious flattery. It would have evaporated entirely, but she released Chad quickly and went right back into professional mode so quickly Morgan might have imagined the whole thing. Before she could think too much about it, their small group was joined by another stranger. This time it wasn't a beautiful woman, but a white guy in his thirties who walked with his thumbs hooked in his belt and a smirk on his face that begged to be slapped right off.

"Well, look what the cat dragged in," he said as he shook hands first with Chad, then Shelby.

"If it isn't Joshua Andrews. How the hell are you?" Again, Shelby's voice had changed, this time dropping lower and catching a gravelly edge. Instead of the hugging him like an adoring daughter, Shelby grabbed his hand and shook it low at hip level.

His grin flashed Morgan's way for less than a second before he fell into conversation with the others. The first topic of conversation, introduced by Shelby, was their respective golf games.

Morgan stood in awe, her gaze shifting nonstop between the three of them. If she hadn't seen it for herself, she wouldn't have believed it. The malleability with which Shelby shifted in her conversation between the two of them was mind-boggling. And she was talking to them about golf. Golf!

It was obvious to Morgan what was going on here. Shelby was a Pick Me Girl, trying to ingratiate herself with the men by pretending to be interested in their manly pursuits so she could prove she wasn't like other women. It was such a common tactic of women in business it didn't shock her to see it here, but it was no less disappointing. Of course, Chad's allusion to Shelby's success made Morgan suspect a friendship with Shelby would have been doomed anyway. Shelby was standing in front of the table for their biggest competitor, Ashworth Diagnostics. Apparently, Morgan had just met the rival who was stealing all her market share. And with that penchant for sucking up to men, she could guess why Shelby was so successful.

"So which one of you landed that account at Potomac Shores Hospital?" Joshua asked.

"That would be Shelby, of course," Chad answered.

"No surprise there. That lab director was pretty hot. I knew Shelby would be able to sell her an instrument." The way Joshua said "sell her an instrument" was the way some men said "nail that chick" and the dig of his elbow into Shelby's side only emphasized his obvious meaning.

"Ah, come on. You know I'm not the kind of woman who would flirt on the job," Shelby said.

"No?" Joshua said, a hint of disbelief lacing the word.

"Nah. I waited until after she signed the contract to go out with her."

Shelby's reply earned her a roar of laughter and a high five from Joshua. The whole exchange made Morgan's skin crawl. So Shelby wasn't a Pick Me Girl. It was even worse. She was a Bro Lesbian who objectified women to make herself one of the guys. While Morgan normally associated that behavior with insecure butch women, it was no less disgusting coming from a femme in a tight skirt suit and four-inch stilettos. She had no desire to be friendly with anyone who would act like that.

"Chad, I'm heading over to our booth to get set up," Morgan said.

Neither of the men paid much attention to her departure, but she did catch a look almost like disappointment from Shelby. She didn't care whether Shelby was insulted or hurt or disappointed to miss out on an opportunity to flirt with any woman around. Morgan was not the kind of lesbian who objectified women and she wasn't the type of salesperson who spent more time schmoozing than selling. This week was one of the most important of Morgan's life and she wasn't going to be distracted.

Chapter Two

"It's not that I'm not interested, it's just that I think we deserve a substantial discount given how large our hospital chain is." The man leaned his elbow on the demonstration instrument and smiled so wide he showed nearly all his teeth.

Shelby would have done anything to just slap the guy. He'd been roaming the trade show floor, stopping at every booth and putting on this same routine. Of course, with the male sales reps he hadn't been nearly so forward as he was being now. He seemed to think he was attractive and that would help him win another five percent off the instrument price. Little did he know he was barking up the wrong tree with Shelby. Still, a sale was a sale and this one had the potential to be many sales.

"I'm certain we could work something out. After all, a partnership between Ashworth Diagnostics and Mid-Atlantic Hospital Corporation is a no-brainer, isn't it?" Shelby made sure to hit her North Carolina farm girl accent hard and she even batted her eyelashes a couple times.

"I can definitely see the benefits of a partnership between us." Between the smile and the wink he threw at the end of the sentence, his meaning was perfectly clear.

Shelby had to grit her teeth through the flirting. He was giving strong Gaston from *Beauty and the Beast* vibes, but she could deal with it. It's not like this was the first time a man had made a pass during a presentation. Once she got a commitment to let her do an onsite demonstration at one of his hospitals, she could schmooze the lab director rather than this blowhard. All she had to do was bite back her disgust for a little longer and she would make her sales goals for the rest of the year. Maybe even part of next year.

It took another ten minutes before she could work through his uninventive innuendo and bring the conversation back around to the instrument. She was still doing the doe-eyed thing when they were joined by two women in expensive power suits. He introduced them as colleagues without taking his eyes off Shelby's tits and she found herself having to pivot. These two were clearly no-nonsense types and would not take kindly to her batting eyelashes at their obnoxious colleague.

"Let me introduce you to the Ashworth ID-Flow 1500 PCR analyzer," Shelby said.

As she repeated the benefits of her instrument, the man's attention slipped. That allowed Shelby the opportunity to subtly shift her presentation style. She kept the emphasis on her Southern accent since she couldn't very well drop back to her normal speaking voice with him still present. Besides, there was a certain charm to a Southern woman. Though she'd worked hard in college to train the twang out of her voice, she could slip back into it with ease when the situation called for it.

The changes she made to ingratiate herself to these women were more subtle. She shifted her shoulders back to their normal position. While men usually appreciated a woman who took up less space, she wouldn't win points with these two by hunching her shoulders. The moment she started standing up straight and stopped batting her eyelashes, the women's attention sharpened on her. The guy who had been so wooed by her shrinking violet act was too busy being bored to notice the shift.

Within a few minutes, Shelby knew they were impressed. In a couple more minutes, they were all shaking hands and exchanging business cards. She knew her follow-up email would be well-received, and she took a moment after they left to jot down a couple of notes about the conversation in the notebook she always kept in her pocket. With any luck, she'd only deal with the women in the future so she could be more herself, but the man was an easier sell. Maybe she should stick to working on him, as long as she could keep a table between them at all times, she could make a killing. Shelby made sure to make a note of that even though she hated herself just a little for it.

Once finished with her notes, Shelby looked over to the Pulsar booth across the aisle. She told herself it was Chad drawing her eye. After all, he was something of a father to all of them in the field. But the truth was, she was far more drawn to his attractive colleague.

Morgan had a presence Shelby couldn't deny. Everything from the delicate arch of her eyebrow to the firm set of her jaw was captivating. She wasn't supermodel gorgeous like most of the women Shelby took home, but that very fact was one of the most intriguing things about her. She had simple features that would be easy to miss in a crowd, but everything from her impressive height to her ice-blue eyes was stunning when Shelby studied her. And study her she did.

Shelby guessed Morgan was around six feet tall, white but with a deep tan even now in the depths of winter, with shoulder-length brown hair starting to show strands of gray at the temples. She was slightly androgynous, but not so masculine as to fall outside Shelby's preferred type. But overall, her features had the sort of distinguished air that made her look like a sexy fifty-year-old even though Shelby guessed she was closer to early thirties.

The one thing that really intrigued Shelby, however, was the increasingly hostile looks Morgan had been shooting her way since they met the day before. Even as she thought about it, Morgan looked up and caught her eye. Shelby smiled her most ingratiating smile, but Morgan immediately looked away.

Shelby thought they'd hit it off okay when Chad introduced them, even if Morgan had been a little quiet. Of course, she was probably quiet because of Joshua and his fraternity brother attitude toward everything. Shelby hated Joshua. She'd met him right after she joined Ashworth Diagnostics and she'd been nervous about entering a new field midway through her career. He'd immediately hit on her, and she deflected his attention by coming out as a lesbian. She'd hoped that would scare him off and she wouldn't have to deal with him ever again, but instead he decided she was "one of the guys."

Because she'd been nervous in a new industry and didn't want to make enemies, she'd gone along with it. She'd regretted that decision ever since. Every time they saw each other he'd point out attractive women and expect her to join in on the locker room talk with him. Shelby was great in most social situations, but this one was a disaster. She'd made a misstep early on and didn't know how to break out of the dynamic. She truly hated the guy. Worse, the more often she was around him, the more she hated herself.

It was clear Joshua had disrupted the whole conversation yesterday when they'd all met Morgan. He was probably the only one who hadn't picked up on it, but Shelby was pretty sure he'd ruined any chance she had of making friends with Morgan. Which was a shame because her gaydar was pinging hard and she never met other lesbians at these events. She'd much rather be friends with Morgan than Joshua.

Or maybe more than friends, Shelby thought as Morgan turned one of her rare smiles on a customer who approached her table. How long had it been since Shelby had been on a date? Especially with a woman as instantly intoxicating as Morgan Allen. And Shelby was relatively sure Morgan wouldn't yawn in her face when she talked about her job the way the last woman had. In fact, her eyes would probably sparkle across the table if Shelby brought up limiting cross contamination false positive results in molecular testing.

But Morgan seemed to hate Shelby and there didn't seem to be a lot of chances to sway her opinion. It was probably jealousy. Shelby had been on a hot streak, and she knew a few competitors had suffered for it, Pulsar among them. Jealousy could be charmed away with the right approach, though. If only she had five minutes to talk to Morgan. Sales staff were so busy at these events they barely had time to take bathroom breaks, much less interact with other teams once the customers arrived. The chances of her and Morgan speaking at all in the next few days were slim. Unless, of course, Shelby could corner her during the big closing night banquet Thursday.

As another potential customer approached Shelby's table, she adopted a winning smile and made a decision. She would catch Morgan at the banquet and try to get to know her if it was the last thing she did.

❖

"The Pulsar DNA Expert is a one-touch test with far less room for error at setup."

Morgan had her sales smile pasted on, but the lab director standing in front of her booth was barely looking at her. Perhaps it was a mistake for Morgan to give her the brochure before she gave her sales pitch. All this woman could do was stare at the glossy paper, and Morgan had the distinct impression she was just looking for a price tag.

"Hmm. Interesting." The woman's body language expressed quite clearly that she did not, in fact, find it interesting.

"The single step is of course a bonus for your lab techs. They can set up the test and walk away to focus on their other responsibilities rather than waiting to add additional reagents. They can be assured of more accurate results when they return, adding to their peace of mind."

The woman perked up at this, going so far as to tear her eyes off the brochure and look up at Morgan. "So is this instrument automated enough that it requires fewer users to run?"

Morgan bit the inside of her cheek to keep from growling. She knew exactly what this woman was asking. She wanted to know if buying this instrument meant she could lay off an employee or two. Even though they were one of the only departments in a hospital that turned a profit, labs were always looking to cut staff. In fact, Morgan suspected that the fact they made money was the sole reason the purse strings were pulled tighter. For-profit hospitals were hyper-focused on increasing profits and there was no way Morgan would be a part of stretching already overworked and underpaid lab techs.

"No, I wouldn't say it would require less staff, but it will allow your current staff more time to do their other tasks so they'll be less stressed," Morgan said.

The lab director audibly scoffed before flashing a smile even more fake than Morgan's and moving on to the next booth. Morgan allowed her face to relax and caught herself just in time to stop her eye roll. She'd known from the start she wasn't going to make that sale. The woman hadn't really given her a chance. She reminded Morgan viscerally of her old boss, Hazel, the lab director at the hospital where Morgan had worked since she'd graduated college.

Hazel had the same thinly veiled mercenary attitude toward the lab. She wasn't a scientist, just a bean counter who got the job because she was good at saving the hospital money. She had no idea what lab techs like Morgan did every day, just that the fewer of them she employed, the larger her quarterly bonus. Any time they asked for new equipment, updated technology, or even just a working microwave for the breakroom, she would act as though they asked her to pay for it out of her own pocket. She never cared about their opinions, much less their needs or their work-life balance.

Morgan forced herself to stop thinking about either this lost client or her old boss. Neither of them would have any power over Morgan any more. She could find other clients. Clients who cared about the lab techs who worked for them as much as Morgan cared. She turned away from the crowd milling around the conference center and took two long breaths, blowing them out slowly to center herself. Unfortunately, this did nothing to calm her nerves since it put her directly in the line of sight of the Ashworth Diagnostics booth.

Ever since they met two days ago, Shelby had not stopped trying to catch Morgan's eye. Any time Morgan looked her way—which she could admit was probably more often than she should given her distaste for the woman—Shelby was staring at her. Smiling at her. Once even giving her a conspiratorial wink when a customer marched angrily away from her booth for the great sin of Morgan saying hello.

Morgan had disliked Shelby at their first meeting and that certainly hadn't changed with all she'd seen in the last two days. First, there was the fact that she was the stereotypical salesperson, telling everyone what they wanted to hear rather than the truth. Even from this distance, Morgan could see how she was a completely different person for everyone who walked up to her booth. It was disgusting, really, to see her chameleon act. But it did, at least, explain why she was beating the pants off all the competition.

As soon as they were alone, Chad had confirmed Morgan's suspicion that Shelby was the one winning all the market share in the Washington, DC, area. Stealing, more like, considering that her methods were so clearly unethical. Morgan wasn't sure whether she should be relieved or furious. When Pulsar had first started losing customers, Morgan had blamed herself. She was a lab tech, after all, not a saleswoman. She was sure the drop in sales was her fault. Especially since they were losing to Ashworth Diagnostics, a company with an inferior product in just about every metric.

When the losses continued, Morgan had taken the step of following up with clients, asking what had made them go in a different direction. Time after time, she heard about the wonderful salesperson at the chosen company. How charming she was and how, in some cases, they had made the decision based on trusting the sales team alone. That had felt like another mark against her at the time, but now Morgan understood. Those customers had been hoodwinked by a professional liar. A very good professional liar who would say and do anything to make a sale and Morgan could not stand the thought.

And what was worse was that, after the instrument was installed and Shelby had cashed her commission check, it wasn't her problem anymore. No, it was the problem of the poor lab techs who now had twice the amount of work to process a single sample. The lab techs whose lives would be even more difficult when the crappy instrument their sleazy bosses bought constantly broke down. Not to mention the doctors who had to deal with crappy results from the same crappy instrument. And worst of all—having to deal with the fallout when the results were constantly wrong. How many times had Morgan had to deal with that? The hospital wants to save a few bucks and one company's sales team offers the moon and a few freebies to go with it. Then the techs are stuck in a five-year lease and the lab manager gets a bigger bonus for saving the hospital money.

That sort of shady dealing always put the patients last if at all. And when accuracy wasn't important, things could go seriously wrong, as Morgan knew all too well. Morgan took a deep breath and squeezed the rounded stone in her pocket. She felt the grooves of the carved letters against her palm and closed her eyes for a moment. She didn't have to see the stone anymore to know what it looked like. A flat oval of rose quartz, smooth as satin on all the surfaces except once large face where the word "Strength" had been chiseled into the face and filled with black paint. She had handled it so much in the last three years that the rounded bowl of the G had lost a few flecks of paint. She couldn't bring herself to either fix the letter or let it go. She would carry this stone in her pocket for the rest of her life, paint or not. She owed Gail that much.

The stone reminded Morgan that she had a job to do that was bigger than herself. A job that had real meaning. It was a calling for her and it was slipping away because of a snake oil salesman with gorgeous eyes. And now it was even worse because she had basically worked herself into a lather and her anger wasn't going to sell well in this or any other crowd. She had to get herself under control or she would make everything so much worse.

Just as Morgan was getting a handle on her emotions, Chad sent his potential customer off with a smile and a handshake. He looked around, clearly noting that the crowd was noticeably thinning out.

"Well, the day is just about done and that means your first national trade show is just about done. What do you think about the experience?" Chad asked in his fatherly way.

Morgan wasn't exactly happy about how the week had gone, but she pretended to be for Chad's benefit. After all, it was really kind of him to bring her along.

"Great. Really great. Thanks again for showing me the ropes."

"Nah. I didn't need to show you anything. I told you, Morgan, you've got this well in hand."

"I don't know about that, but it's certainly been an experience."

"The good news is it isn't over yet. In fact, the best is yet to come." Chad had the air of a proud parent handing over a huge present for their favorite child's birthday. The problem was, Morgan seriously doubted she wanted this present.

"Oh really?" she asked, doing her best to sound excited.

"Tonight is the banquet." When she didn't respond to this with the enthusiasm he clearly expected, he continued, "It's a chance for us all to relax and get to know each other better. It's always a good time and I've made friends for life at these banquets."

That sounded like absolute hell to Morgan, and she had no interest in pretending otherwise anymore.

"Oh, thanks, but I think I'll just go up to my room and order some DoorDash. I'm so tired after this whirlwind of a week."

Chad laughed like she'd made a hilarious joke and threw an arm around her shoulders, steering her to the exit. "Oh no, that's not an option. But don't worry, we each get one drink ticket for the cocktail hour and I'm going to buy your second drink."

"I'm not really much of a drinker. Or a mingler."

"You are tonight," he said, leaving no room for argument.

She sighed and agreed, but knew this would be one of the most tedious nights of her entire life.

Chapter Three

Shelby was in her element. Nothing made her feel as good as being good at something, and she was very good at schmoozing. The closing night banquet was where her assets really shined. The sales pressure was off—it was considered bad form to pitch your product here—so she was able to solidify some of the relationships she'd made during the week. Nothing won a potential client over like proving you remembered their name when their checkbook wasn't out. It didn't hurt that a glass of wine added a sparkle to her eye and width to her smile.

Not that she could afford to get drunk tonight. Not like Joshua, who stood a couple of high-tops over, leaning in too close to one of the executives of a major hospital chain and shouting about his golf game. That wasn't Shelby's style anyway. She rarely drank more than one glass a night, especially at an event like this. She didn't need to chase happiness to the bottom of a bottle. She loved feeding off the energy of other people. The way they interacted with each other. The story behind a look or a laugh. A night like tonight beat a bottle of Chateau Lafite Rothschild a hundred times over.

That was Shelby's favorite part of being in sales. Meeting new people. Learning what was important to them. Finding out what made them tick. Hearing their stories. And even better was when she could offer them the right product to make their lives easier. Every day, she learned something new about someone else, and that filled her heart. Yeah, life was pretty damn good for Shelby Lynn Howard right about now.

Her only regret tonight, in fact, was that she was standing here at a high-top table near the bar, sipping her wine all alone. She liked working at Ashworth Diagnostics, but she really wished they would spring to send two sales reps to shows like this. When she'd worked in pharmaceutical sales, cost had never been a consideration. Then again, that's exactly why she'd switched careers. Medical instrument sales might not have as much money, but they had morals, and that's what Shelby needed in her life. Plus, Ashworth wasn't exactly stingy. They sent a field service engineer to set up the display instrument and make sure it was working all week, but those folks were busy with repairs in the area and never hung around to chat. That left Shelby alone at these cocktail hours. She was usually fine being alone in a crowd. With as much as she traveled for work and as long as she'd been single, she was definitely used to eating and drinking alone. Still, sometimes she wished she had someone to share moments like these with. The room was dotted with groups of two or three, chatting and laughing and making Shelby feel uncharacteristically wistful.

"The queen stands alone, looking out across the field of victory."

Chad's voice was as warm and soothing as ever and, when Shelby turned to look at him, his smile washed away her bittersweet thoughts.

"I don't know if I'd call myself a queen, but you've always been too sweet to me." Shelby leaned in to kiss his cheek.

If there was one person in this crowd that she respected, it was Chad. He had a fatherly energy that seeped out of his pores as easily as the smile that always lit his face. He wasn't even that much older than most of the sales folks here, but he was the universally acknowledged elder statesman and even Joshua was respectful around him.

"You remember my protégé, Morgan," he said.

How could she forget? Despite Morgan's coolness to her throughout the week, Shelby had been intrigued by the woman.

She wasn't the best salesperson Shelby had ever seen, but there was a genuineness to her that obviously appealed to many of her customers. And there were sparks of genius when she really engaged in conversation. An excitement about her product that most of them had to fake. Unfortunately, she let her frustrations show when things weren't going her way, which of course made it worse. It happened often enough for Shelby to wonder if it was intentional. When her smile met her eyes and the excitement poured out of her, however, she was captivating, and Shelby had lain awake in bed more than once this week with images of Morgan playing through her head.

"Of course. How was your week?" Shelby directed the full force of her smile at Morgan.

"Educational," Morgan said simply.

Shelby'd had an inkling, and the single-word answer confirmed it. Morgan seemed to be wrapped in a cloak of discomfort. It wasn't quite "I'd rather pull out my toenails one by one than be here" energy, but more on the "I'd rather be doing today's Wordle alone in my room" level.

Chad didn't seem to notice his colleague's lack of enthusiasm, however. He merrily announced that he was going to the bar to get drinks and hurried off, leaving Shelby and Morgan alone. It might've been Shelby's imagination, but she thought Morgan was even more uncomfortable now that Chad wasn't here to carry the conversation. In fact, she appeared to be avoiding conversation with Shelby by refusing to meet her eye, even though they were now alone at this small table together.

This was the problem with feeding off the energy of others. When someone else was anxious or sad, Shelby felt that, too, and it made her twitchy. Particularly when she really wanted a beautiful woman to enjoy her company. Fortunately, her ability to read people came in handy in moments like this. Time to work her magic and make Morgan feel more comfortable with her and this event.

Shelby leaned in conspiratorially and said in a low voice, "These things are always so much work. I'd much rather be sitting in my room right now, snuggled in with flannel pajamas and take out."

Morgan didn't exactly thaw, but her shoulders relaxed a fraction and her eyes finally met Shelby's. Her piercing blue eyes were so light they almost looked gray in the subdued light of the bar.

"I have my eye on the new season of *The Great Pottery Throwdown*, but I guess I'll have to save it for the plane," Shelby said.

Now there was a spark in those blue-gray eyes. Had Shelby surprised her with her interest in such a subdued, domestic reality show? That was all the in she needed. A moment of surprise to make Morgan let her guard down.

"What would you rather be watching right now?" Shelby asked.

For a moment, she didn't think Morgan would answer. She was tightly wound, this one, and it might take more for her to let Shelby in. But she surprised Shelby with a small smile.

"There's a new NASA documentary on my list," Morgan said.

"The one about the Challenger?" Another flicker of surprise and a little bit more genuine interest. Finally, Shelby was making some headway. "I watched it on a trip to a client in West Virginia last week. I thought it was a little harsh, but everyone assumes scientists can see the future, so it isn't a surprise."

"I already watched that one, too. I meant the one about Sally Ride."

Now Shelby was the one ensnared. "Really? I love her! Pioneering woman and a lesbian icon to boot."

Morgan's smile this time was unreserved and radiant. Shelby had to grip the edge of the table to keep from swooning. Morgan really was gorgeous when she opened up. If she had shown that smile on the conference floor a few more times this week she'd be rolling in sales. It wasn't fair, of course, for Shelby to join the jerks who told women they should smile more, but she would do just about anything to see Morgan light up like this more often.

A burst of too-loud laughter from across the room drew Morgan's attention, and Shelby snapped back to herself. Morgan's scowl returned as she glared at the loud group.

"You've been to a bunch of these trade shows." Morgan turned her attention back to Shelby. Her scowl was gone, but to Shelby's disappointment the exuberant smile didn't return. "Is it always like this?"

"More or less. Most of the shows are smaller, regional affairs. The people change but the energy is always the same."

"Sweaty desperation and cheap cologne?"

The sharp edge to Morgan's joke made Shelby laugh unexpectedly. "Heavy on the cheap cologne."

"We were in the elevator with four men on the way down from our rooms. I could barely breathe it was so strong. Can't someone tell them they don't have to use the whole bottle?"

"I know what you mean. It's like chemical warfare," Shelby said.

Morgan actually laughed a little at that. Not a full-on guffaw, but a polite, almost ladylike chuckle. It was adorable and Shelby was happy she'd been nursing this glass of wine. Had she finished one she might've done something stupid like ask Morgan out.

Shelby shot a quick look across the room, confirming that several people still stood between Chad and the bar. Unfortunately, her roaming gaze landed on Joshua and he took that as an invitation to stumble over to their table. And stumble he did, knocking hard into the edge and causing Shelby's wine glass to wobble.

"Ladies. Lovely, lovely ladies. What's up?" Joshua slurred the last words, leering in Morgan's direction.

"Hey, Joshie. Had a drink yet?" Shelby deadpanned.

He turned to her, taking a long moment to focus on her face. As he wobbled back onto his heels and then forward onto his toes again, Shelby worried he might actually tip over. Joshua wasn't known for his discretion or his self-control, but this was by far the drunkest she'd ever seen him.

"One or two. Hey, we should dance. You want to dance with me? Let's dance." Joshua tapped his toe on the ground and twisted his hips in a sloppy, uncoordinated imitation of dancing. Shelby wasn't sure whether she wanted to laugh or roll her eyes, but it was pretty clear from the disgusted twist of Morgan's lips how she felt.

"Sorry, Joshie, there's no dance floor. You'll have to save your moves for another night," Shelby said.

A sharp, unexpected burst of laughter escaped Joshua. "I make all my best moves at night. In bed. With women."

"Yeah, I picked up on the subtle innuendo," Shelby said.

Before Morgan could storm off, a hand slapped Joshua hard on the back in a friendly gesture. Shelby breathed a sigh of relief at the interruption, but she wasn't exactly happy to see it was Eric, Joshua's coworker, pulling him into a one-armed hug.

"How's it hanging, Joshie. You aren't hogging all the good company to yourself, are you?" Eric turned an overly interested smile across the table. "Hey, Shelby. Lovely as always."

In other company, Shelby would have told him where he could shove his false compliments. She'd met Eric when she made the lateral move to selling Ashworth's PCR analyzer during COVID. It was a new instrument for her, but she wasn't wet behind the ears anymore and she hadn't felt the need to cater to his disgusting behavior like she had Joshua. In fact, when she'd turned down his advance by proclaiming her sexuality, he'd made a proposition that she had denied with both words and a report to his manager. He hadn't ever forgiven her for the six months on a performance improvement plan that had earned him, but they had both agreed to be civil in public. Unfortunately, he took great pleasure in tormenting her with excessive politeness which she had to reciprocate.

"Hi, Eric. Have a good week?" Shelby asked.

"Nothing to complain about. How about you?"

"It's been great. Really great," Shelby said.

"I hear Anne Porter took the national sales manager role. You going to apply for her position?"

"Me? Heck no. You know I hate middle management. I'm happy where I am."

"You could do it, you know," Eric said. "You have that political mind."

There it was. Shelby had been waiting for him to make some snide remark or give her a backhanded compliment. He didn't do small talk. He was reminding her that in the case of he-said, she-said, she had been believed and he hadn't. It didn't matter that she'd told the truth and he had lied through his teeth about their encounter.

"You haven't introduced me to your friend." Eric held out a hand to Morgan. "Eric Ferguson, Telnet Diagnostics."

Morgan didn't have a chance to shake Eric's hand—not that she'd made any move to, only proving her good instincts—before Chad arrived at the table. His presence immediately sobered Eric's mood, but Joshua remained oblivious to good manners.

"This is boring." Joshua tried unsuccessfully to pull out from beneath Eric's arm. "We're gonna dance."

"Looks like you've had one too many, Joshua. Maybe you should head up to your room to sleep it off." Chad's voice was calm and authoritative. Joshua's response was neither.

"Maybe you should lay off, Chad. You sound like my ex-wife."

A few heads turned in their direction, including a few that belonged to important customers. Chad didn't rise to the bait and shout back, but his "I'm not angry, just disappointed" look most fathers mastered before their children's teen years spoke volumes.

"If you'll excuse me, I need the ladies' room," Morgan said.

Shelby watched her go with a pang of jealousy. She'd do pretty much anything to run away from this awkward scene, but she knew that would only make everything worse. Joshua would shout after her and it would probably be lewd. Eric would make a joke that wasn't quite as explicit, but it would make Joshua's laugh follow them both to the ladies' room. No, it would be much better if she stuck it out with Chad so they could convince Joshua to calm down.

"Things might be a little too tame around here for you and me," Eric said. "Why don't we head outside? I think I saw a wedding rehearsal in the other ballroom. In the mood for a bridesmaid, Joshie?"

It wasn't exactly the most mature way to handle the situation, but it got Joshua to quiet down and leave the room. The two of them stumbled toward the exit, preening like the pair of obnoxious peacocks they were. Shelby was happy to see the back of them, especially Eric.

"Doubt those boys will ever grow up." Chad sipped his beer and shook his head before turning his attention on Shelby. "And how are you doing, my dear?"

"Just fine. It was a good show, don't you think?"

"One of the best," Chad said.

This was his stock answer, but it was always genuine. Chad was the sort of man who found contentment in everything. He had simple tastes and was inclined to enjoy life for what it was rather than what he wished it could be. That made him a damn sight smarter than the rest of them and Shelby couldn't help but envy him.

"Make a lot of sales?" Shelby asked.

"Enough. I'm more interested in getting Morgan's feet under her. She'll be one of the best, you know. She'll be outselling us all in five years."

"She doesn't seem to be having the best time tonight."

"No, not really her style, but she'll come around." After a quiet moment of contemplation, he smiled at her. "But it is very much your style, isn't it? I know you love these closing events when we all get a chance to know each other better."

Shelby smiled, thinking about how she was getting to know Morgan better. That was certainly a relationship she'd like to deepen, if only the Joshuas and Erics of the world would let them talk in peace.

"You know me so well. I love these banquets. The people, the laughter. It's just such a rejuvenating energy. I wish they had one every night, honestly."

"That might be a little too much for me, but I'd join you at least one or two nights. You know I'm getting too old for partying," Chad said.

"Lies and more lies. You can't be more than a day over twenty-one."

"Oh, don't wish those days back on me. I'm exhausted just thinking about it."

Before Shelby could tease him more, Morgan rejoined the table. She didn't look much refreshed from her trip to the bathroom. In fact, the cold, almost aloof Morgan that had arrived at the party was back. That was to be expected, Shelby supposed, after Joshua and Eric ruined the mood, but she much preferred the warm, laughing Morgan.

"Your amaretto sour." Chad slid the drink over to Morgan.

"Thanks," she said, a clipped note to her voice.

Morgan didn't look at either of them as she sipped her drink and even Chad seemed to pick up on her mood this time. He gave Shelby a shrug just as the doors to the banquet hall opened and they announced dinner.

"If you don't have anyone else you've promised your time to, we'd love you to join our table, Shelby," Chad said.

Morgan shot him a disgruntled look, but didn't say anything. When Shelby agreed to the arrangement, Morgan transferred the look to her for a moment before heading in to their table.

Chapter Four

Morgan watched with trepidation as snow collected on the windshield. With unnerving regularity, the wiper squeaked across the glass, snapping up the flakes and pressing them into the snow already caked on the margins. They pressed into each other, and the ridge of snow looked like tree rings, denoting not years of growth but miles of road. Soon the layers would encroach on the visible surface, shortening the trip of the wiper blades.

"Are you sure it's a good idea to drive up to Buffalo?" Morgan turned to look at Chad, sitting in the driver's seat with a calm confidence she didn't share. "This storm is getting pretty bad."

The snow had started to fall while she slept, and by the time she met Chad in the hotel lobby, there was a solid winter storm brewing. She hadn't been concerned then, but now that she saw the state of the roads she couldn't help worry that a man his age shouldn't be driving in these conditions.

Chad waved his hand as though batting away her justifiable concerns. "This is just winter in the Northeast. Not a big deal."

"It's early November. That's not winter."

"It is up here. Snow starts in October above the Mason Dixon line."

He gave her a cheeky smile, but she couldn't argue. She'd never been this far north. Where she was from winter didn't start in earnest until at least January.

"I still don't think it's a good idea for you to drive all that way alone," Morgan said.

"A little snow isn't going to keep me from a week in Niagara Falls with my wife."

It seemed to her like considerably more than a little snow, especially since the layer cake of ice and packed snow had migrated closer to her line of sight, but she didn't want to nag. It wasn't that long a drive from Rochester to Niagara Falls, and his wife, Cheryl, was already there waiting for him. It's not like he could leave her to fend for herself while he flew home.

By the time Chad pulled the rental car up to the terminal at Rochester International Airport, the deluge was slackening a bit, lifting some of her fears. After they said their good-byes and assured each other they would text to say they were safe on arrival, Morgan made her way into the airport. Tension was palpable inside. The telltale signs of nervous passengers were noticeable, even to a less than seasoned traveler such as herself. A glance at the departures board showed a few flights already listed as delayed. Hers wasn't delayed yet, but she decided right then and there that she wasn't taking any chances. Chad had regaled her with enough travel horror stories for her to err on the side of caution.

After joining the line of passengers checking in for their flights, Morgan pulled up the app for Chad's favorite rental car company. There weren't many options for cars, and all of the one-way rentals were sold out. If her options were limited, she was going to take the plunge. There was no way she'd let herself get stuck in Rochester for the weekend. The town had done nothing to ingratiate her during her time here and she doubted a few days stuck in an airport hotel would change her mind.

A few clicks and she had secured the last of the economy class rental cars National had to offer just in case the worst happened. Sure, they intended her to return it to the same airport she picked it up from, but she would deal with the consequences if she had to drive it home. Better a big fee for dropping a car off at Dulles Airport than getting stuck here. Besides, she was sure it wouldn't be necessary. Her flight would take off as planned and she would cancel the reservation for that car once she was in line for takeoff.

With a worst-case escape route secured, she could relax enough to take in her surroundings. Compared to her home airport, the ticketing area here was shockingly cramped. The line for her airline was the longest, but there were a half dozen other airlines represented here as well, all with similarly choked check-in lines.

The room buzzed with the sounds of a hundred overlapping voices, blurring words into a puddle of sound. It wasn't just the sounds. All of Morgan's senses were assaulted. Flashes of every imaginable color cut across her vision as people hurried past. They carried with them the mingled scents of travel. Coffee and burnt bread and too much cologne hung in the stale air. Some people would be overwhelmed or even frightened by the crush, but in many ways Morgan thrived in chaos. She was a scientist, trained to focus on the minutiae in a sea of distractions. This was like searching for unusual blood cells in a microscope. She could see and sort them all with a glance, blocking out sound as she studied the scene with keen eyes.

Lots of the individuals inching forward between the nylon ropes were familiar to Morgan. Other salespeople were predominant, but there were also a fair number of customers waiting to catch flights home.

A few of Morgan's less scrupulous colleagues were engaging customers in conversation, blithely ignoring the discomfort of their marks. She was surprised to see Joshua had dragged himself out of bed and made it to the airport looking none the worse for wear after his heavy drinking the night before. He was, of course, one of those bothering a customer.

Morgan wasn't surprised to see Eric beside his colleague. The sight of him was less shocking this morning than it had been last night, but she'd had all night to work up a head of steam over his renewed presence in her life. At the party, she'd been too shocked to say a word to him, and he clearly didn't recognize her. Not that she expected he would. A man like him wasn't likely to remember the people he stepped over on his way to a fat commission check. Although he did know Shelby, and it seemed like they were friendly.

"Of course they are," she mumbled to herself. "Two peas in a poisonous pod."

As she shuffled forward, a familiar voice caught her ear. The lab director who had audibly scoffed at her for suggesting that buying a Pulsar instrument wouldn't allow her to lay off workers was in a heated argument with a ticketing agent.

"What do you mean delayed?" the lab director asked, her shrill voice cutting through the chatter.

"Your plane hasn't arrived yet. They were held up by weather in Pittsburgh and we're looking at a two-hour delay."

The ticketing agent's voice held a note of bored annoyance and Morgan wondered how many times he'd explained the weather delays this morning. He'd probably have to explain it another hundred times before his shift ended. Morgan indulged in a little wicked smile as the rude lab director whined and complained and overall acted as though she was the only person in the world who mattered.

A moment later, as the line moved forward and Morgan saw real tears in the lab director's eyes, she chided herself for her unkindness. Perhaps the woman was being overly dramatic, but hadn't Morgan just rented an unnecessary car in the off chance she suffered this same fate? Maybe the lab director had kids she was anxious to see or just wanted a weekend at home to decompress after a long week of social interaction. She might have been rude to Morgan, but she was a human and she deserved kindness.

Morgan was still silently berating herself when she heard a collective groan from the crowd around her. The man in front of her grumbled about a delay. She couldn't quite see the departures board from her location, but she had a pretty good idea what it would say. Sure enough, her phone chimed with an incoming text message a moment later.

Your flight from Rochester to Washington, DC, has been canceled. If you are already at the airport, please locate your nearest airline agent for assistance.

Morgan's stomach dropped as she read the message. As similar notifications were noisily delivered to her fellow passengers, the decision to secure a rental car suddenly felt ten times smarter. The tension that had simmered in the room earlier ramped up and people pressed forward even though the line wasn't moving. The lab director, who had left the counter before her message arrived, charged back to the ticket agent, knocking their new customer out of the way.

"My flight was canceled, you need to rebook me," the lab director said.

"I'm sorry, ma'am, but you'll have to wait your turn."

"It is my turn. You were just helping me."

"You moved on and now I'm helping the next customer." He held out his hand to take the new person's boarding pass.

"I just got an email that my flight has been canceled. Can you rebook me please?" the new customer asked.

"I'm afraid there are no flights available today due to the weather, but I can book you on the next available flight for tomorrow."

It seemed that the entire crowd had been waiting with bated breath for the ticketing agent's response. Clearly, they did not like what they heard. Rather than a collective groan, this time there was a collective bark of anger. The tension in the room snapped as a hundred people simultaneously learned their fate.

"What if the weather is still bad tomorrow?" The customer's voice rose above the din of disapproval.

Morgan didn't bother waiting for the answer. The energy in the room was starting to make anxiety tingle along her nerve endings. Besides, she wouldn't be waiting that long. She just needed to get her refund and then collect her rental car. If she was lucky, the snowstorm wouldn't spread down much past the New York state line. Pennsylvania at the worst.

As the line around her undulated with annoyance, another familiar face appeared in front of Morgan. The nylon roping created several switchbacks, so Shelby stood close by in her place several spots ahead in line. Fortunately, Shelby was facing the ticket counter and talking into her cell phone.

She didn't want to talk to Shelby, not after last night, but she couldn't help hearing her half of the phone conversation. It only took a moment to deduce that Shelby was on the phone with the airline and the news was not great.

"So there is absolutely nothing out of Rochester until Monday? What about Buffalo?... I see... No, I suppose it isn't worth the drive up there if I'll arrive around the same time. Thank you so much for your help," Shelby said.

Morgan couldn't help compare the difference in Shelby's tone to the one the rude lab director used. Shelby's faults were many, but she didn't take out her frustrations over the weather on a call center employee. That was something.

In fact, even as the rest of the passengers' annoyance grew more and more vocal, Shelby's mood remained resigned but upbeat. The line had essentially stopped in place, meaning that Morgan was witness to Shelby's next call. She guessed Shelby was on the phone with her boss, since she explained she would most likely miss their regularly scheduled meeting on Monday. Morgan also couldn't help notice the way thin lines appeared around Shelby's mouth and eyes as she listened to the response. Whoever Shelby was talking to, they weren't thrilled with the news that she would not only miss the meeting, but have to expense a couple more days of hotel rooms to her corporate credit card.

"I did actually try that already," Shelby said, injecting obviously strained cheeriness into her voice. "I checked both this airport and the one in Buffalo. No flights out until Monday. Sounds like the storm is a big one. Can I call you back? I'm next in line for the ticketing counter. I'll keep you informed... Yes, I know the daily meal limits... Yes, and the hotel cap."

Morgan had been so busy eavesdropping and trying to remain inconspicuous that she hadn't realized how quickly the line was moving. Within seconds of ending the call, Shelby was called forward and informed, like everyone else, that there were no flights for at least two days, possibly more.

"Can I rent a car to drive home?" Shelby asked.

"I'm sorry, I can't help you with that. You'll have to go to the rental car agency," the clerk said in a well-practiced monotone.

"Don't bother," said the customer at the next station. "I already checked. They're completely sold out. You can get on a wait list in case someone with a reservation cancels, but the list is already a mile long."

That comment brought Morgan back to herself. How long would the overtaxed rental car company hold her car when there were so many others waiting? Not to mention how bad the roads would get the longer the storm raged outside. There were still a half dozen people ahead of her in line to talk to the airline. All Morgan needed was a refund, not a rebooking, and she could deal with that once she was safe and sound in her townhome in Virginia.

Morgan was as polite as it was possible to be as she pushed through the crowd, but no one wanted to give up their spot in line and they weren't prepared to believe Morgan only wanted out. Pushing her roller bag in front of her like a battering ram, she finally found her way to the edge of the line and ducked under the rope. Following the signage, she made her way toward the escalator, going against the flow of traffic, and finally descended to the ground floor rental car agencies.

If she'd thought the check-in area was chaotic, it was nothing compared to the bedlam that greeted her downstairs. It was clear a large chunk of the crowd was desperate to get out of the airport and the rental car clerks were under siege. While this line was moving markedly faster than the one for the airlines, it still took her a long time to get to the desk.

A white woman with frazzled dark curls and an almost manic gleam in her eye didn't even bother to greet Morgan. "All of our cars are booked and we have closed the wait list until further notice. Your airline can get a hotel voucher and an overnight kit."

"I already have a reservation." Morgan held out her phone, showing her confirmation number.

The woman behind the counter visibly sighed in relief. While she entered the number into her system, Morgan wondered how many times this morning she'd been screamed at by angry customers. While she'd been out of the lab for a while now, she still remembered that feeling. The way she had to put on her armor before making phone calls to certain nurses or mentally prepare herself when she saw the name of the surgeon assigned to her patient. Morgan's hand closed around the stone in her pocket, the pad of her thumb tracing the carved lines on its flat surface, and she took a deep steadying breath. No matter what this woman said—even if she'd given Morgan's car away—she would be a moment of safety for this woman.

"Okay, we have you for an economy car. Reservation for two days. So you'll be returning it here to Rochester Airport tomorrow by noon, correct?"

"That's right." Morgan put on her biggest smile to show she fully intended to return this car. She didn't need this poor, frazzled woman to know she'd be breaking one little rule. It's not like she was stealing the car, she was just returning it to a different airport.

After Morgan signed a couple of waivers and refused the extra insurance, the woman handed her a pair of key fobs strapped together on one key chain and pointed her to the garage.

"Thanks so much for your wonderful service," Morgan said. "Hope things get a little bit calmer around here soon."

The smile she received in return was so grateful and so exhausted it sent a pang straight to Morgan's heart. This woman probably had hours and hours still to go of angry, frustrated customers yelling at her for an act of God, but hopefully she would remember one kind face.

Morgan only took a few steps before stopping again. She reached the end of the counter and tucked herself into a corner out of the way of the doors and the exit line for the car rental company. After pulling out her phone, she put a call through to her top contact. Chad answered on the second ring and she was relieved to hear that his voice sounded far away, mixed with the unmistakable sounds of tires on slushy pavement. So he hadn't picked up the phone, he was using the safer option of taking the call through the car's speakers.

"On your plane already?" Chad asked.

"Sadly, no. All flights out of Rochester are canceled and they aren't expecting any to leave until Monday," Morgan said.

"Tell me you learned from my mistake and ordered a rental car as soon as you saw flight delays."

"I sure did. I think I got the last available one in the whole airport."

"Good for you. I'm glad my tips are sinking in. Too bad for everyone else, though. I'm guessing there are a lot of stranded sales folks stuck in that airport this weekend."

Morgan looked around, noticing as many familiar faces down here as there were upstairs. "Definitely. But that's a good thing, right? Keep them out of the area so there's less competition for me next week."

"Ah, these folks aren't competition. They're just colleagues who work for another company." Morgan grinned at his rose-colored glasses approach to the world. He said, "Mostly I feel bad for Shelby. Her manager over at Ashworth is a jerk. I've worked with him before and he'll never let her hear the end of it if she's not in place and ready to sell, sell, sell Monday morning."

"But she's probably the most successful salesperson in the area. Surely he can't hold a snowstorm against her," Morgan said.

As she continued to scan the crowd, she noticed Shelby tucked against the far wall on the other side of the sliding glass doors. Her phone was pressed to her ear and the same pained expression from upstairs was on her face. She must be calling her boss back and not with good news. Maybe Chad was right about him. Maybe he was being terrible to her.

"A guy like that just likes yelling at his subordinates, especially if they're women. One reason he didn't last long at Pulsar. We don't put up with that sort of nonsense. Anyway, glad you're getting home but don't be reckless. Drive safe and make it home in one piece, okay?"

"I will, Chad. Thanks."

Morgan ended the call but kept her eyes on Shelby. She was pinching the bridge of her nose and looking small and insecure. The change from her demeanor on the phone with her boss compared to her confidence and bubbliness all week was shocking. Morgan rubbed her thumb along the stone in her pocket and looked around.

How many other folks in this room were going to get an earful from a cruel boss? Well, the lab directors and hospital executives would probably be okay, but the sales folks would have less leeway.

As if on cue, her gaze slid to the lab director who had been rude to her at the trade show and also rude to the ticket counter representative upstairs. She had stopped with her multiple suitcases in the exact center of the busy hallway, forcing everyone to swerve around her. She was shouting into her cell phone, raging at someone or another as though she was the only person in the world who had been inconvenienced. Morgan looked back to Shelby, who had made sure she was out of the way and was talking quietly into her phone so as not to disturb anyone. Plus she had been kind to the airline representative, just as Morgan had done with the car rental person. Morgan rubbed the stone in her pocket again.

"Why are you even considering this?" Morgan asked herself.

After last night's performance and her association with someone like Eric, Shelby hadn't earned her sympathy. Still, she was kind enough and she had a jerk for a boss. Morgan knew what that was like and somehow it outweighed the rest. Plus, Chad respected her, so she couldn't be all bad. She shrugged and collected her bags, then headed straight across the room toward Shelby, who had just ended her call.

"Morgan," Shelby said. "Hi. How are you?"

"I got the last rental car," Morgan said by way of greeting.

"Lucky you. I'll be stuck here in this airport all weekend with a thousand of my closest friends." She cut a withering look at the rude lab director who was having an epic meltdown while a line of people waited to move around her down the hall.

Morgan took a deep breath and squeezed the stone in her pocket. Shelby hadn't begged for a ride or even begrudged her luck. That meant something for her character, right? Despite ample evidence that she was less than genuine, she wasn't rude or cruel.

"Where do you live?" Morgan asked.

Shelby looked back at her, her eyebrows rising in obvious surprise. "Alexandria."

Of course. Alexandria was one of the most expensive cities in Northern Virginia. It was hip and in easy commuting distance to Washington, DC, and Morgan couldn't afford to rent a shoebox apartment there. Unlike her town which was twenty miles south, definitely not an easy commute given the notoriously terrible traffic, and containing a very different socio-economic group.

"Alexandria is on the way home for me. I can give you a ride."

Shelby's face went from confusion, to hope, to pure joy in a matter of seconds. For a moment, that spark of interest Morgan felt when they first met flared up again. A smile felt more at home on Shelby's stunning features than the frown that had settled there since their flight was canceled. Then she remembered last night and the lies and games Shelby constantly played, and the spark fizzled.

"I would be eternally grateful," Shelby said.

"Grab your bags. Let's go before the snow piles up too high."

Chapter Five

The drive started off quiet and quickly became uncomfortable. Shelby thrived on human contact and silence in a one-on-one situation wasn't her cup of tea. Getting out of Rochester was easy enough. The airport was a stone's throw from the interstate that took them out of town. There were enough turns that the Waze voice—the sexy British woman's voice Morgan used was also Shelby's favorite—filled the silence.

Once they were on the interstate, however, Shelby started to get antsy. With all the dead air between them, she wondered how she was going to survive a seven-hour drive like this. Longer, probably, because Morgan was driving pretty slowly.

Not slowly, Shelby internally corrected herself. Carefully. Morgan was driving the speed limit, which, given the quickly deteriorating conditions, was the fastest she could expect. In fact, with mountains looming directly in their path, the weather was bad and destined to get even worse.

The Lyft driver who took Shelby to the airport was local and handled the snowy conditions well, but it was just a couple of inches at that point. She'd seen the delayed flights and was surprised. She'd assumed there was worse weather at whatever airports those planes were coming from. As she waited in line to get her boarding pass, however, she saw the snow picking up through the wall of glass behind her. That's when she'd started to get nervous. But she had purposefully chosen an early flight to give herself as much time as possible to account for delays. She had not accounted for cancellations.

The phone calls with her boss were brutal. She'd known they would be. He was not the kind of person she enjoyed working for. Until today, she hadn't been on the receiving end of his condescension or his wrath, but she'd seen it directed at other team members and it made her blood boil. Standing against that wall next to the rental car agencies had been a low point in her career. He'd threatened to deny her expenses for another two days in a hotel and would not accept any excuses for her being away from the district on Monday.

When Morgan had appeared out of the blue with an offer to drive her home, it had been like a gift from God. It had also been wildly unexpected. Of all the people in the world she thought might help her, Morgan was the last one. They had been getting along swimmingly last night while they shared solitary drinks, but dinner had been an awkward affair. Chad had tried gamely to keep the conversation going, but he could only do so much. Morgan had shot daggers across the table at Shelby every time she spoke and had excused herself the moment dessert had been served. Shelby had no answers for Chad when he asked what happened between them. She hoped that, if this long drive gave Morgan the time to air her grievances, it would be at least after they passed the Maryland state line.

Shelby recognized a mental spiral when she was in one and decided it was far too early into the drive for that. She grabbed Morgan's phone to start some music. To her surprise, there was no music app on the phone at all. Not even an old Pandora app still lingering from when that one was cool.

"Wow. How do you survive all the driving we have to do without music?" Shelby asked.

Big mistake. Morgan kept her eyes on the road and her mouth shut, but Shelby could see her hands grip the steering wheel tighter and her body go rigid. Okay, thinking back, the question might have come out like criticism, but honestly why couldn't Morgan give her the benefit of the doubt? Why did she have to assume Shelby was criticizing her?

"I listen to audiobooks sometimes," Morgan finally said. "But mostly podcasts."

"I love podcasts. Do you listen to that one with Glennon Doyle and her wife?"

"I'm more into history and true crime."

"I loved that first season of *Serial*," Shelby said.

Apparently, this was a mistake, too. She actually saw Morgan roll her eyes.

"People who aren't really into true crime have always listened to *Serial*."

Shelby opened her mouth to argue, but Waze spoke up at that moment, telling them to stay in the left two lanes. Morgan turned on her blinker, checked her mirrors, and then glanced over her shoulder to check her blind spot before changing lanes. Shelby couldn't help notice that she was a meticulous rule follower. Sure, the only way to be accident-free in the frantic mess that was DC Beltway traffic was to check for other drivers constantly, but you also had to be decisive and quick. She guessed Morgan missed her fair share of exits waiting for someone to let her in once her blinker was on. No one on the Beltway would do that, especially the Maryland drivers who seemed to exist in a constant state of hyperactive carelessness on the road.

The maneuver derailed their stilted conversation long enough that Shelby decided not to try again. Her only option had been to defend herself, and that would've sounded childish after such a long pause. Instead, she focused on the snow swirling around the side mirror in their slip stream. Even as she watched it dance, the snow fell thicker, the currents now more flakes than open air. How long could this continue before they were in true white out conditions?

"Stay on I-390 for seventy miles," the disembodied voice said through the speakers.

Shelby sighed. Seventy miles on this bleak, deserted highway. At their speed of exactly fifty-five miles an hour, seventy miles sounded like an eternity. She glanced at the bottom of the car's screen to see they had three hundred eighty miles left on their drive. How in the hell were they going to survive this when even the topic of a shared interest in podcasts started a fight?

Things got even worse in a few miles when Shelby realized she had to pee. She'd been expecting two hours in the airport and a quick hour-long flight, all with uninhibited access to a bathroom. She'd had an extra cup of coffee and a glass of orange juice with breakfast because she hadn't expected to be trapped in a car with someone who hated her for seven hours. She tried to ignore the pressure in her bladder for another two miles, but those mountains were worrying her. There wouldn't be many gas stations when they got into that.

No sooner had the thought permeated than she noticed Morgan was a little squirmy behind the wheel. She'd had the same expectations for bathroom access and Shelby guessed she had to pee, too. She also guessed Morgan would be too proud to say anything until it became an emergency. Well, Shelby wasn't too proud. She grew up in an area not unlike this. She knew what would happen if they played this game of chicken, and she hadn't peed in the bushes on the side of the road since she was a teenager. She didn't want to break that streak in a snowstorm.

"Sorry to do this, but I need a bathroom," Shelby said.

As she suspected, Morgan grumbled her annoyance at having to stop, but then surprised her by freely admitting she had to go as well. Shelby grabbed the phone and searched in the driving app for gas stations.

"Well, there's only one option before we hit Pennsylvania one hundred miles away."

"I definitely can't wait that long," Morgan said.

"Me either. Let's take our chances with this one."

Shelby added the Exxon to their trip and Waze took a long moment to recalculate their trip. This one was fifteen miles away, but that was much better than their other options. She congratulated herself on the choice to speak up and tried to think about anything else besides the growing urgency to pee. That wasn't easy as they settled back into not quite comfortable silence.

Shelby almost cried with relief when Waze announced, "In two miles, take exit eight, US 20A west toward New York 256/Genesco."

❖

Morgan was thoroughly annoyed as she pulled off the highway toward the gas station and their unexpected pit stop. Extending her time alone with Shelby was the last thing she wanted. As she would have guessed, Shelby was being falsely chipper and they'd barely started this trip. She wasn't quite sure why she'd been annoyed at Shelby's reaction to her not having a music app. She should have been more receptive to bonding over podcasts because now she'd soured the mood. She'd have to do better if they were going to survive a seven-hour drive.

The Exxon station she finally pulled up to looked like it had yet to enter the twenty-first century. With its peeling paint and decades-old gas pumps, it looked like some of the rinky-dink places she was forced to stop while visiting rural areas of Virginia. It wasn't exactly what she expected from New York, but then again she had never been to this part of the state before this trip.

There were a surprising number of customers inside the gas station, which also had a small cafeteria-style seating area to one side. One of the Formica tables was full of grizzled older men in trucker caps and another pair were leaning against the counter, chatting with the cashier. The moment Morgan and Shelby entered, all eyes were on them. The stares didn't seem to bother Shelby, even as they followed the two of them across the room, but Morgan did not feel particularly safe here. Shelby might pass as a straight woman, but Morgan was far more androgynous and was sometimes asked if she'd entered the correct bathroom in public.

Fortunately, the two-stall bathroom was empty and the door swung shut, protecting them from the hostile stares. Shelby went straight to the far stall, but Morgan took a moment to look over the single, small sink with a rust stain streaked down the back. The stall wasn't much better, but the dinginess was clearly from age, not dirt.

"Not exactly the vibe I was expecting from New York," Shelby said. "But I guess mountains are mountains, right?"

Morgan was surprised that Shelby shared her sentiments, but was annoyed she couldn't even stop talking in the bathroom. Morgan had never been that sort of chatterbox who always went with other women to the bathroom so they could gossip. She decided there wasn't much need to respond to Shelby, so she finished up as quickly as possible.

Shelby waited for her as she dried her hands and they exited the bathroom together. The crowd seemed less interested in them now, with only a few searching stares, and that made Morgan feel marginally safer.

"Why don't we get some snacks for the road?" Morgan said.

"Sounds good. I didn't have much breakfast. Besides, nothing passes the time on a road trip like a bag of chips."

Morgan was shocked to see the first thing Shelby grabbed was a bag of pork rinds.

"Huh. I pegged you as more of the egg white omelet and kale smoothie type."

Shelby laughed and the sound was just short of intoxicating. Morgan tried to shake it off, but she couldn't deny that Shelby was gorgeous when she smiled like that.

"My parents had money, but my memaw was plain old Carolina trailer trash. My summers were full of pork rinds and Vienna sausages."

They ended up with way too much food, mainly because Shelby's haul was heavy on snack food and Morgan's was more prepackaged sandwiches and bottled water. Between the two of them they had enough food for a road trip twice as long as the one they had planned.

With everything safely stowed in the back, within easy reach of the passenger seat, they set off again. Unfortunately, the reception in this backwoods town wasn't great and Waze couldn't load the directions. Just as Morgan was panicking about the prospect of going back into the hostile gas station to ask directions, Shelby pointed out a sign for I-390.

"Head that way. Waze will catch up once we're in a better area," Shelby said.

Morgan didn't like flying off half-cocked, but she knew they were supposed to be on I-390 for another fifty miles or so. It seemed safe to just head that direction. If she could remember what direction they were heading on I-390, of course. But the snow had picked up considerably while they were inside and they really needed to get moving if they didn't want to get stuck here.

The signs directing them to I-390 had them turn onto NY-63, but Waze still hadn't caught up and Morgan didn't remember turning on another road when they came off the interstate. She also didn't remember driving this long. Morgan told herself it was just her nerves getting the best of her—she'd never been great at driving in new places, especially without GPS to guide her. She was also having trouble seeing signs through the thick snowfall, so it was hard to settle down.

"All set, let's go. In two hundred feet, turn right to merge onto I-390 south," Waze barked through the car speakers.

"Shit," Morgan said.

She hit the brakes so she could make the quick turn, but the sedan fishtailed in the slushy snow. Morgan struggled to keep control of the vehicle and watched in dismay as the exit passed her by.

"Shit. Goddamn it. There was no way I could make a turn that quickly," Morgan said.

"It's okay. Don't worry about it." Shelby pointed to their current route on the map, just under the "recalculating" wheel. "This road runs parallel to 390. There will be another exit."

"But how long will that be? Maybe we should turn around?"

Even as she said it, she knew that was a bad idea. The road was two lanes with no discernible shoulder under the piles of snow. The chances they'd get stuck were too high.

"Let's just see what GPS tells us to do," Shelby said.

The smooth confidence in Shelby's voice helped settle Morgan. She was right, of course. There were other options. How many times had she seen accidents when drivers were so intent to get to their exit they made stupid decisions. There was always another way to get where you were going, you just had to be calm and patient.

Sure enough, a moment later, the app finished recalculating, pointing them to an exit in fourteen miles. That was farther than she'd like to go on a surface road that had not yet been plowed of accumulated snow, but she didn't have much of a choice. She gritted her teeth and tightened her grip on the steering wheel. It was only a few miles and then she'd be back on the better maintained highway, headed home to a hot dinner and her own bed.

Two or three miles later, Morgan was feeling more relaxed. This road wasn't so bad. It had clearly been salted before the storm, so she could still see the center line and she could maintain a decent pace. Beside her, Shelby picked up her own phone and started searching through screens.

"Do you mind if I put on one of my playlists? It's nothing too wild or loud, I promise," Shelby said.

Morgan realized she'd not been the most gracious host to Shelby. After all, she'd invited her on this trip so Morgan couldn't exactly resent her presence. Plus, the silence was even getting to her and she knew they needed something to entertain and distract them as the hours ticked by.

"Okay, but I need the directions plugged into the screen and speakers."

"No problem," Shelby said. She started up a subdued, folk singer-songwriter style song. "I can put it into the cup holder. That'll make it loud enough to hear."

"You're using iCup." An unexpected burst of warmth filled Morgan's chest.

"What?" Shelby asked.

"That's what my coworkers called it back when I worked in the lab. You put your iPhone speaker down into a cup and it amplifies the sound to make it louder."

She glanced over to see Shelby smiling at her and quickly turned her eyes back to the road.

"We weren't allowed to have speakers in the lab, but scientists will always find a work-around," Morgan said.

"I didn't realize you worked in a lab."

Waze interrupted with a reminder that their turn was coming up in five miles and Morgan used it as an excuse to stop the conversation. She couldn't help but hear the criticism in the way Shelby said she used to work in a lab. Morgan was used to people dismissing her because she was new to sales. To judge by some people's reactions, you'd think they were hired into sales from the crib. She wasn't shocked to discover Shelby was one of those people.

Shelby was the kind of woman who could make any sale any time because she was beautiful and charming and men hung on her every word. Morgan didn't have the advantage of being conventionally attractive and she would never use it the way Shelby did if she was. She sold her instruments because she believed in them, not because she could make a buck by batting her eyelashes. Morgan knew that she shouldn't let her mind wander down that road. She could feel the stone in her pocket, the weight of it a reminder of what she couldn't focus on while driving in a strange place with bad weather.

That's when she noticed that the little car on the Waze screen wasn't moving anymore. She glanced down at it regularly for the next few minutes and sure enough, the car wasn't moving and the distance wasn't ticking down. They'd clearly lost cell signal again. She glanced up at the top corner and saw zero bars of signal. Worse yet, she had no idea how long ago they'd lost signal and thus had no idea how much farther they had to go before their turn.

Shelby was quietly singing along to the latest song on her playlist and looking out over the scenery. Rather than fill her in on their predicament, Morgan chose to quietly freak out. It wasn't like Shelby could do anything to help and she didn't want to engage in more conversation. That would just leave her more flustered than she already was.

Morgan relaxed a fraction as they entered a small town—just a cluster of houses really—but more than they'd seen in a while. It obviously wasn't a town of much consequence, because the cell signal did not improve and the little Waze car sat resolutely still in the middle of nowhere miles back on their route. Even as the cluster of houses turned into a cluster of businesses, there was no change. Morgan hated to do it, but she had no choice but to fess up.

"So, um, looks like we lost signal again. The directions stopped updating," Morgan said.

Shelby's head snapped around so quickly it looked like it hurt, but she didn't freak out like Morgan was expecting. She took in the stalled virtual vehicle and nodded once in a surprisingly firm manner.

"Okay. I'm guessing we're pretty close to the exit. Let's work together to look for a sign back to 390," Shelby said.

A mile or so later, Shelby spotted the sign. There was a fluffy layer of snow across the top, but it wasn't enough to obscure the road number or the arrow pointing them right. Morgan noted that they had turned onto Route 36, but she had no idea how long they would be on that road before the exit for 390.

"Why don't you pull up the list of directions and see how long we should be on this road," Morgan said.

"Great idea."

Shelby snatched up the phone and went through the obnoxiously long process of pulling up the list of directions. She scrolled through, the phone inches from her nose as she studied the list. Morgan kept glancing over at her as she looked, but she knew from experience the listed directions were frustratingly vague.

"How long were we supposed to be on that last road?" Shelby asked.

"Fourteen miles, I think."

Morgan tried to peek over at the phone, sure she could find the next direction faster if she looked herself.

"Then that was Route 36."

"Yeah. I think so," Morgan said. She looked back at the road just in time to see the exit ramp for 390 pass them by. "Oh shit. We missed it," she said.

"We did?"

Shelby turned around to look behind them as though that would help anything. Annoyance bubbled up in Morgan's chest again. Why had she been looking over Shelby's shoulder instead of looking for a sign? How many times had they said they could just follow signs? If she hadn't been such a control freak, they would be back on the interstate.

Before Shelby could give her hell for missing the sign, Waze finally caught up. As they rolled out of town, it told them several times to make a U-turn, but where in the hell could they make a U-turn? It was a two-lane road and nothing more than unplowed driveways to the right and left. Just as she thought she might scream if Waze told her one more time to make a U-turn, a new, loud rock song came on Shelby's playlist.

"Can you turn that off? I can't hear the directions."

It wasn't until she heard the echoing silence that she realized she'd shouted. Shelby calmly reached down and lowered the volume on the music on her phone, then turned stiffly back to stare out the windshield. It was pretty clear Shelby was mad at her and well she should be. Missing the exit was her fault, but yelling about the music made it sound like she thought it was Shelby's fault. Morgan contemplated apologizing for her overreaction, but it was probably better to just ignore it rather than call attention to her bad mood.

A moment later, Waze cut through the thick tension with directions to continue straight for several miles. Looking at the map, it appeared that they would drive through a state park, then loop around on an access road and drive back the way they'd come. That seemed far better than making a U-turn in the middle of a snowstorm. She could make that happen. Morgan relaxed a little, not realizing until her back hit the seat how far over the steering wheel she'd been.

As they drove through the park, the snow seemed to clear a little. Of course, it might've been that the forest to their left was blocking some of the worst of it, but the road at least had some pavement still visible. Morgan felt safer, so she finally felt able to glance over at her passenger, expecting to see Shelby still sitting stiffly, angry at her. Instead, she was leaned over toward the window, staring up at the falling snow like a little kid. It was endearing enough that she felt bad for yelling.

"You can, um, turn the music back up while we're in the park," Morgan said.

Shelby increased the volume a few clicks and then went back to staring at the sky.

"Isn't it neat when that happens?" Shelby pointed through the windshield at a bit of visible sky between dark clouds. "The sky always looks bluest through breaks in the clouds."

Morgan glanced at the sky, but she could have sworn she heard Waze give her directions. Between Shelby speaking and the increased volume of the music, however, she wasn't sure.

"Did you hear that? More directions?" Morgan asked.

"No, it says to keep going straight for a few miles," Shelby said after glancing at the screen.

Morgan was back to panic mode. That's what happened before, when it lost signal. It gave them an update on how long to drive and then it went brain dead. She didn't feel comfortable on this much smaller, windier road, looking for too long at the screen, but she was pretty sure the car wasn't moving again.

"I thought the turn was coming up," Morgan said.

"It says to go straight."

Morgan noticed a road off to the right that looked like it might be the one they were supposed to turn on.

"I think that's our turn. I'm taking it," Morgan said.

"I don't think that's a good idea. The directions say to go straight."

"I'm pretty sure it lost signal again and we're only going to have so many chances to miss our turn. I'm going this way."

Morgan knew she was being unreasonable, but she was panicking. How had everything gone to shit so quickly? Her tires spun a little as she completed the turn onto the side road, but she didn't care. She needed to get back to the highway. She needed to get out of this car.

Shelby sat silently beside her while she picked her way down this new road. It had not been plowed at all and the snow was picking up again now that they were away from the cover of the trees. As if she needed another obstacle, the road started up a steeper grade than she was comfortable with in these conditions and this car. It was hard to see where the road was going around the hood.

Then suddenly, there was no road beneath her at all. Her tires whined, spinning in open air. Morgan slammed on the brakes even though she knew it was too late. They hung in midair for a heartbeat before the hood tilted down again and she could see the snow-covered ground beneath them. Way too far beneath them. Then she felt the impact and an airbag burst out of the steering wheel into her face. Morgan felt a sharp pain in her neck and then the lights went out.

Chapter Six

When she realized the car had gone over the bank and was falling, Shelby threw her arms up in front of her face. The hood slammed to earth and the airbag deployed, the force of it whipping her hands into her face. She felt the moment when her grandmother's ring sliced across her forehead and also the moment a burst of pain exploded in her right shoulder. She wasn't sure if that was from the airbag or the seat belt, but it hurt a lot. More than she was expecting.

It wasn't just the pain though. When the airbag fully inflated, it covered her nose and mouth, and her panicked breathing was suddenly stifled by cloth. She felt like she was drowning. Suffocating in the unending folds of fabric. A wave of nausea rippled through her, and she fought hard against it. The last thing she needed was to puke all over her favorite traveling sweater. Or worse—choke on it with the airbag blocking any chance of breathing.

That thought had her fighting hard. She pushed and swatted and swam against the airbag, but it was already deflating, giving her room to breathe. Soon enough, she could see the interior of the vehicle around her and her first thought was for Morgan. She whipped her head toward the driver's seat, earning a sharp stab of pain to flash up her neck, but the view distracted her from the pain.

Morgan was clearly unconscious, her body straining against the taut nylon of her seat belt and her neck drooping limply as the air bag fluttered to emptiness. Fear like nothing she had felt in her life flared in Shelby as she desperately sought signs of life. Morgan was so still, so quiet, that Shelby's mind immediately went to the worst-case scenario. The thought that Morgan might be dead brought the nausea back with a vengeance, making Shelby actually heave. She couldn't handle that scenario. It simply could not be true.

Shelby forced herself to be calm, pushing her fears into the tiny box inside her she'd created long ago to store away any weakness. She took a deep breath, then reached out a shaky hand toward Morgan's shoulder. It was warm and soft, and Shelby told herself that was a good sign. She shook Morgan's shoulder, fear making her movements rougher than she'd intended. The first shake had no effect, so Shelby shook her again, this time making Morgan's head loll unpleasantly on her long neck.

Shelby was reaching for her seat belt buckle, intent on dragging Morgan out of the car and forcing her to be alive, when a quiet groan filled the cramped space. The groan sounded more like someone waking up when they didn't want to than a groan of pain, but that might have been Shelby's wishful thinking.

"Morgan?" When she didn't get an answer, she repeated the name, this time with a snap of authority. "Morgan. Wake up."

Morgan's head rolled against her shoulder, this time voluntarily, and she gave another groan. Relief swam through Shelby with enough force to make her dizzy. She had to fight back an ill-timed giggle that she hoped was just shock. Although maybe she was having a mental breakdown, because she couldn't help thinking how cute the sound was. Her mind even played out a scenario of waking up in bed beside an adorably tousle-haired Morgan as she made a similar noise. Rather than dwell on the absurdity of the thought, Shelby shouted at Morgan until her eyes fluttered open.

"What happened?" Morgan asked, her voice thin.

"We crashed. Are you okay? Does anything hurt?"

"Crashed? What are you talking about?"

"The car crashed, Morgan. Listen to me. Does anything hurt?" Shelby did her best to keep hold of her frustration, but the interior of the car was getting colder by the second and she could see snow still falling outside.

Morgan moved first her neck, then her arms one at a time. "Yeah. My neck hurts. And my chest. Actually, I'm pretty sure everything hurts."

"Good. That means nothing is paralyzed," Shelby said.

Now that the air bags were fully deflated and Shelby could look around, she noticed that the car wasn't actually at that steep an angle. She braced her feet and pushed back toward the seat, waiting to release her seat belt until she was sure she wouldn't topple into the windshield. The door was a little harder to open, and when she put one foot outside, wet snow poured into the open top of her low-heeled ankle boot.

"Don't move. I'm coming around to get you out."

Morgan's only answer was a grunt that might have been pain this time, but she did as she was told and stayed in her seat. Stepping fully outside the vehicle felt like walking into a freezer. Shelby was definitely not dressed to be outside in weather like this and the snow pressed heavily against her feet, soaking them through and chilling them to the bone. She wrenched open the back door and grabbed her coat, fat flakes falling onto her neck with alarming speed.

Shelby struggled to get her arms into the coat as she scrambled around the car. She couldn't help noticing how dark it was, but she wasn't sure that was from the sun going down or from the dark gray clouds looming overhead, blocking out the sun. Either way, they needed to find help or shelter immediately. She was already starting to shiver from head to toe.

Getting Morgan out of her seat belt and onto her feet was far easier than Shelby thought it would be. She'd lost consciousness, but it didn't seem to be from any major injury, probably just from the impact with the air bag. While Morgan grabbed her coat out of the back seat, Shelby went in search of her phone. She found it in the floorboards on the passenger side, but the screen was shattered and there was an ominous crunching noise from inside the casing when she tried to turn it on.

"My phone's toast." Shelby fought back both panic and hope. "How about yours?"

Morgan blinked at her a couple of times over the top of the car before diving back in. Shelby kept staring at the spot her face had been. The scene before her was a sea of white on white on white. The snow covered everything so that the smallest undulation of land was hidden. There were trees in the distance around them on three sides, but they seemed so far off with acres of snowy blanket separating them.

Then there was the sound. Or rather the lack of sound. No traffic noise or the distant roar of planes overhead. The only sound was snow falling on snow like the shuffling of papers in an office where everyone else has gone home. Somehow that quiet noise was more frightening than the thought of Morgan dead in the car beside her. Where on earth were they and how on earth would they get out?

Shelby reached up to touch the spot on her forehead that ached. Her fingers came back with a sticky dot of drying blood, but it wasn't much. Neither of them seemed too badly hurt. At least not yet. A few hours exposed to this snowstorm might change that dynamic. The wet and cold seeping into her clothes felt like a clock counting down to their doom.

Morgan stood up, her presence snapping the frightening fantasy in Shelby's mind. "It works, but there's no signal."

The words couldn't penetrate through the fear gripping at Shelby's limbs. "What do you mean? Let me try."

Shelby shuffled around the car and was shocked to discover Morgan handed over her phone. She was clearly dazed, and her docile acceptance of the situation was unsettling. Shelby was used to a Morgan who fought and grumbled. While it could be annoying, it was the Morgan she wanted in an emergency. Still, the ache in her shoulder reminded her that they'd both been through an adventure. Not everyone reacted well to an adventure.

"Mind if I try to make a call?" Shelby asked.

Morgan shrugged, then grimaced at the movement. Rather than investigate further, Shelby focused her full attention on the phone. As Morgan said, there were no bars, but that was a problem Shelby could chip away at. She kept her eyes glued to the screen while she trudged through the snow a few feet to her left. There was no change to the signal, so she turned and fought through the snow a few feet in a new direction. A flicker in the corner made her gasp.

A single bar had appeared for a heartbeat, but it was gone just as quickly. She zigged and zagged, trying to catch the elusive bar, but she couldn't get it back. In a last-ditch effort to find service, she threw her arm into the air to raise the phone. A zap of pain shot through her arm and she cried out.

"What's wrong? What happened?"

Faster than she would have thought, Morgan was at her side. Shelby gritted her teeth and took deep breaths as the pain lessened.

"I'm okay. I hurt my shoulder in the crash I think. I just need a second," Shelby said.

Morgan slipped the phone from her hand and tried the emergency call. They both listened, waiting for the far-off sound of ringing, but it never came. After a long few moments, as cold and dread seeped deeper and deeper into Shelby's bones, Morgan ended the attempted call.

"It's no good," Morgan said.

"But what do we do? How do we get help? Are there bears in New York?" Shelby looked around, now almost more frightened by the prospect of other living things surrounding them than emptiness. Panic made her shout, "What do we do?"

"I don't know," Morgan shouted back. "It's your fault. With your stupid music playing so loud I couldn't hear the directions."

"I turned the music down like you asked. I told you not to turn here."

"Well, I thought it was our turn. I missed the directions while you were talking about the stupid sky."

Shelby's breaths were coming in short, angry bursts, but she couldn't help shouting back. "I was trying to make conversation so we didn't freak out."

"Great job. So glad we didn't freak out!"

Shelby was wheezing now, the shouting and the cold and the panic were gripping at her like angry fingertips. She yanked her coat closer around herself and jammed her eyelids shut, telling herself to calm down. Calm down and think. Calm down and make a plan.

"We need to make a plan." Her voice was surprisingly even. "We'll freeze to death out here."

"We stay in the car. Someone will find us," Morgan said. Shelby was relieved to hear she was speaking calmly as well. Morgan's burst of anger seemed short-lived and that was fortunate right now.

"The car will get too cold," Shelby said. "Without the heater, we can't keep it warm."

"What other option do we have?" Morgan's voice was tight with anxiety.

Shelby opened her eyes. Her breathing had slowed and her fear had finally agreed to stay inside the little box inside her. But Morgan was clearly panicking. Her eyes darted around like a cornered animal and her teeth were already chattering. Shelby knew it was up to her to find a way out. That was fine. Finding a way out was her superpower. It's what she'd always been best at.

Shelby turned slowly in place, scanning their surroundings. The road they'd driven off of disappeared into the distance, the tracks made by their tires already erased under freshly fallen snow. They hadn't passed anything for miles down that road anyway. It wasn't an option. She followed its path up, around the curve they'd driven over. It continued that way, steadily climbing for some time before it disappeared into the stand of trees at least a mile off. They had no idea where it went and Shelby was sure it was not the road that looped back to the main road. It wasn't an option either.

Following the line of trees bisected by the road, she saw nothing but thickly stacked pines and bare limbed oaks. Nothing to indicate civilization that way. The tree line swooped and swerved, sometimes farther from them, sometimes closer, but always a long way off as it circled their clearing. Shelby vaguely remembered that their road had paralleled a state park. Was that on this side of the main road or the other? She supposed it didn't really matter. There wasn't much chance of a Target or shopping mall in the vicinity.

As Shelby scanned, however, something caught her eye. Directly in front of them, as if in a straight line from the crumpled hood of their rental sedan into the woods, was a flickering something. A light? As the wind whipped, the limbs on the edge of the tree line swayed to the right and then, yes! As they swayed back to the left it was clear. Definitely a light. Maybe a headlight? A snowmobile? No. It wasn't moving. Perhaps a porch light then? She watched for another few moments until she was sure that yes, while the light flickered in and out of view thanks to the swaying trees, the light itself was a fixed point.

"There. Look," Shelby said.

"What?"

"A light?"

"What are you talking about? I don't see a light," Morgan said.

"Look straight ahead into the trees. There. Do you see it?"

Shelby turned happily toward her, hope warming her from the center of her chest. Morgan squinted, and Shelby witnessed the moment when she saw the light. A flicker or shock, followed quickly by disappointment.

"It looks really far away," Morgan said.

"So?"

"We can't walk that far. Not in this weather," Morgan said, waving an arm at the snow.

Shelby had finally had it. She was cold. Her shoulder hurt. Her forehead hurt. She honestly wasn't sure why she hadn't snapped before now, but Morgan's stubbornness finally sent her over the edge.

"We either walk to that house in the woods or we freeze to death in this car. I'm going to walk. You do whatever the hell you want to do."

Shelby's shouting hadn't even finished echoing off the frozen ground when she wrenched the back passenger's door open and started sifting through the tumbled articles. She grabbed her computer bag first, thinking that she could email her boss once she got onto the house's Wi-Fi. Next, she went for the snacks she'd picked up at the gas station. The bags of chips and bottles of water had been flung all around the floorboards, but the bag they'd come in was still intact.

Shelby was marveling at the miracle she hadn't been knocked unconscious by airborne Dasani when the other door opened.

Morgan grumbled under her breath as she collected her things, but she had clearly seen that seeking shelter was the only option. Even with the muttering, Shelby did feel a little bad for yelling at her. If her own aching body was any indication, Morgan was probably not feeling her best and Shelby understood her not wanting to traipse off into the wilderness during a blizzard. Still, the longer they waited out here, the more chance something really bad would happen.

Morgan didn't say anything else and didn't look at Shelby, but she marched along willingly toward the light in the distance once they'd shut up the car and collected all they could carry. Everything was going fine until they were nearly to the tree line. That's when the light in the distance flickered out. Shelby had a moment of panic, but fortunately Morgan's gaze was locked on the snow just in front of her feet. Had she seen the light go out, she might've turned right back around. For a moment, Shelby worried it was the right move to go back to the car, but she shook the thought away. It was probably just a motion light on someone's front porch. Or maybe a tree branch blew in front of the light. There was an explanation and Shelby wouldn't give up. It wasn't her style. She decided to do like Morgan and focus on the ground in front of her. That would keep her from worrying too much about the disappearing light.

Unfortunately, that plan made her think about her feet, which felt like cubes of ice after only a few minutes of trudging through the ankle-deep snow. Once they were under the cover of the trees, the snow wasn't quite so deep, but this wasn't a thick forest and there was plenty of accumulation between the sparse trunks. Shelby pushed the cold and the fear and the aches away and kept walking in the direction she had seen the light. They would make it. Everything would be fine once they got to the house in the woods.

If they were lucky, the residents had heard them crash and were heading out to meet them. This whole nightmare would be over soon. Soon they would be safe and warm inside. Shelby formed an image in her head of what their rescuers would look like. They'd be an older couple, looking for peace and solitude in the forest. They would have sweet, wrinkled faces like grandparents in a Hallmark movie. Right now they would be stoking a big fire in their hearth.

It would be one of those massive fireplaces that take up a whole wall, and there would be a big pot of beef stew simmering on the stove. Since they were older, they wouldn't rely on a cell phone that could lose signal out here in the middle of nowhere. They'd have a landline to call for help. Or, better yet, a big four-wheel drive vehicle that could take Shelby and Morgan to safety.

She'd done such a good job of crafting this daydream that Shelby half expected to see a bundled-up elderly couple walking toward them when she looked up. Of course they weren't there, but she spotted something almost as promising. The light was back and much closer this time. So it must be a motion light and something triggered it again. Flicking her eyes to her left, Shelby tried to be subtle as she assessed Morgan. She was quiet. That was probably a good thing after their many tense conversations and shouting matches today, but she didn't look like she was in too much pain. Hopefully she was just working through her shock at the accident and would be halfway polite when they arrived on some strangers' doorstep.

It didn't take nearly as long as Shelby thought for them to get to the light, but when she saw the building it was attached to, Shelby lost all hope for a warm meal and a call for help.

Chapter Seven

Morgan stared at the cabin in disbelief. It looked like a stiff breeze could knock it over, and since the snow was swirling around them, she feared it would, in fact, fall over right that moment.

It was hard to tell too much about the structure, but it was tiny and dark and was clearly abandoned. The walls were wide slats of gray-brown wood siding with nails visible at the seams. Some of the nails were pushing worryingly far out of the wood and some of the boards, particularly the ones along the side dusted with wind-blown snow, were curling away from the structure as though they didn't want to be there any more than Morgan did. The roof hung lower than she would have liked and there were tufts of green moss visible through the snow on some of the shingles. The porch was covered, but the elements had clearly had their way with most of it. The supports did not inspire confidence and several of the floorboards sagged in ominous places. There were three steps leading from the forest floor to the porch and they looked just as rickety as the rest of the cabin. Morgan didn't want to be the first one to test her weight on them, that was for sure.

More concerning than the wear and tear was the air of abandonment about the place. There were two windows flanking the front door and they both had their shutters closed and bolted into place. The storm door glass was fogged, and the welcome mat looked like it was growing into the slats of the porch. She couldn't see how deep the building was from this angle, but there were at least two more shuttered windows on the snow-dusted side of the house.

Clearly no one was at home. In fact, the building reminded her of her of a scene from *The Last of Us*. Even infected zombies would steer clear of this place or risk falling through rotten floorboards. The only thing that looked halfway new or even functional was the motion light clamped to the porch roof just above the stairs. It flickered on and off each time the wind blew a long branch from the nearest pine into its line of sight.

"This feels like a bad idea," Shelby said, her voice just as hesitant as Morgan felt.

"Yeah. It really does." Even as she agreed, Morgan felt the burn of the seat belt across her chest, the ache in her head, and the cold wind cutting through her too-thin coat. "But we don't have a choice. Let's see if we can get inside."

Shelby looked over at her in surprise. Or maybe it was disbelief? Either would fit. Morgan hadn't exactly been the one to focus on solutions today. She hadn't done much more than whine and complain since they'd gotten into the car. She wasn't proud of blaming Shelby for the crash, especially since every decision that led to it had been hers and hers alone. Normally, she would have been frozen by shame and self-recrimination, but Shelby's outburst earlier had snapped her out of her stupor. She couldn't let Shelby do all the work here. She had to be decisive, too. She had to be brave.

Morgan's hand closed around the stone in her pocket for a moment before she reached out for the wooden railing by the stairs. The wood was cold and soggier than she would like, but she was pretty sure it wouldn't fall apart if she put some of her weight on it. She tested each step with her foot, and they all held. The porch might not look like much, but it was actually very sturdy. She took a moment to appreciate how much warmer her feet were already now that they weren't buried in snow. Even more reassuring was the sizable stack of firewood running the length of the porch under the window to her right. It was protected from the elements deep under the porch roof and looked dry.

"There must be a fireplace inside. We can get warm while we wait for rescue," Morgan said.

When she didn't get a response, even a snarky one, Morgan turned to look back at her. It wasn't like her to neglect a chance to talk. Shelby was still staring at the cabin in what looked like shock, but Morgan also noticed she was shivering really hard. She'd spent so much of the day annoyed at Shelby, but now all Morgan felt was concern. Shelby had taken control when she needed to, but she might be shutting down now. Morgan needed to get her inside and warm before she completely fell apart.

The storm door opened, though the hinges protested loudly at being disturbed. The thick wooden front door was locked and there weren't any glass panels in it to break. Morgan moved to one of the windows, but the shutters were bolted from the inside on both top and bottom. Despite how weathered the wood was, the slats were solid and she didn't think she could break them.

Going back to the front door, Morgan tried to ram her shoulder into it, but all she got was a fierce flash of pain from shoulder to neck. She hadn't even hit it that hard, knowing she wasn't likely to break through, but now she knew just how solid that door was. Maybe her first impression of this cabin wasn't quite right. It might look neglected, but it was proving surprisingly hard to break into.

Next, she tried pulling back the welcome mat in search of a key. All she found was a thick line of mud outlining a bare patch of porch. The rocking chair on one corner of the porch was equally bare of keys. The firewood stack seemed an unlikely hiding place, so she only gave it a cursory search. She was about to jump down from the porch to circle the cabin when she heard a clatter from behind her. Shelby was on her tiptoes, running her hand along the top frame of the door and she'd dislodged a key.

"How did you know it was up there?" Morgan asked.

Shelby shrugged and handed the key over. "That's where my grandpa kept the key to his work shed back home. This place looks like a man owns it. Seemed worth a shot."

Morgan held her breath as she fit the key into the lock. What if it didn't work? What if she tried to turn it and it snapped off in the doorknob? She couldn't bear the thought of another disappointment today.

It turned like the lock had just been oiled that morning. There was a crack of hinges separating as the door popped open a few inches. Morgan turned to Shelby and saw the same anxiousness that she felt. They both blinked hard before turning back to the door. Morgan wondered if Shelby was as nervous as she was. Had they finally hit a break or was this just another obstacle they'd have to overcome? Only one way to find out.

Morgan pushed the door open wide and stared into the gloom. With all the windows shuttered, it was dark inside, but she had a feeling the room would be just as depressingly dim with sunlight streaming in. The room was dominated by old, heavy furniture bunched too tightly together for the limited space. There was a small kitchen tucked off to one side with a two-seat cafe table wedged into the corner. A massive stone fireplace and raised hearth took up most of the opposite wall and a hallway disappeared into the gloom directly across from them, promising either a bedroom or a nice place for a serial killer to hide.

Apparently, Shelby didn't share her apprehension. Almost the moment the door opened, she pushed past Morgan into the cabin. Whether she was being brave or foolhardy, Morgan couldn't let her do it alone. Plus, it was still bone-chilling cold outside and her feet were soaked through with melted snow. She needed to get inside and get warm.

With more time to look around, Morgan did see a few things that brightened her mood. First off, the sofa was covered in an old sheet, but there wasn't any dust on the sheet. Garish flowers in colors that reminded Morgan of seventies fashion, yes, but no dust. So the cabin wasn't abandoned, maybe just shut up for the winter. The sheet covering the armchair was also free of dust, though it didn't match the one over the sofa. Clearly these were cast-offs, and old ones at that.

She also noticed a pair of flimsy bookshelves tucked into the corner behind the door. They were crammed full of books and some of them relatively recent. So maybe this place wasn't a hideaway for an axe murderer. Or, if it was, said axe murderer was literate and had a penchant for thrillers and police procedurals.

By silent consent, Morgan and Shelby made their way carefully down the dark hallway. There wasn't much back there. They found a single small bedroom with a double bed and a serviceable bathroom. When Morgan tried the faucet, nothing happened, but they soon found a utility closet with a breaker box and a water main. Morgan was dubious, but both the water and power turned on without a hitch. There were a few ominous pops from the sinks as the air escaped from the pipes, but the water that flowed out after was clean and the small hot water heater clicked on right away. Hopefully, they'd be able to take hot showers in the morning.

While Morgan cleared the water lines, Shelby searched the small cabin for a thermostat. Unsurprisingly, given that this was clearly a summer hunting cabin, they didn't find one. Morgan very much doubted the tiny space would have central heat or air.

"Isn't much warmer in here than it is out there is it?" Morgan couldn't keep the annoyance out of her voice as she rubbed her arms to warm them up.

"At least it's dry and we don't have to worry about the wind. Looks like the storm has really picked up out there."

Shelby made this observation by looking through the still-open front door, which, of course, was letting all that cold air inside. Since she didn't look likely to do anything about the freezing temperature inside, Morgan decided it was up to her.

"I'll start a fire," she said.

❖

While Morgan got busy building a fire, Shelby went into the kitchen to look around. She didn't know the first thing about how to make a fire, but she knew how to scrounge for food. Besides, she needed to move and get blood flowing through her limbs or she might just lose a toe to frostbite.

It wasn't much of a kitchen, really, but Shelby had seen worse. Hell, she'd made do with a hot plate and a mini fridge for a whole year once. This was gourmet compared to that. The first thing she did was open the shutters blocking the tiny window over the sink. It wasn't easy, given that the window was cheap and stuck at awkward angles every time she tried to lift it, but she got to the shutter bolt eventually and closed the glass in a hurry.

The sunlight was fading fast, but there was enough to illuminate the basic electric stove and oven as well as the builder's grade sink and faucet. The water popped and hissed, but ran clear soon enough and all the burners worked on the stove. Shelby's next stop was the pantry, which was well-stocked with dry and canned goods. The soups, veggies, and preserved meats wouldn't exactly make a gourmet experience, but at least they wouldn't starve in the day or two it would take them to be rescued.

The cabinets held a fair number of other treasures. Lots of coffee and tea bags in one and quite a few bottles of cheap whiskey in another. Shelby found a metal kettle like her grandmother kept on her stove and started water for tea. It seemed reasonable to crack open one of the bottles of whiskey while the kettle heated. After her day, she didn't bother with a glass, she just yanked off the lid and tipped the bottle to the ceiling. It burned like the dickens on the way down her throat, but it warmed her far more effectively than pacing the kitchen had.

"You better be sharing that," Morgan said.

Shelby slapped the corked top back into the bottle and looked across the room. Morgan had taken off her coat and blazer and slung them over the back of the armchair. Now she knelt, her forearms on her knees, in a shell-pink button-up with the sleeves rolled up. Behind her a fire was blazing nicely, throwing an orange glow across her features. It was probably the whiskey that made her pulse pound and her gaze travel appreciatively over Morgan. After all, she had done very little to ingratiate herself today. Okay, so she had a pretty face and those eyes were dreamy, but that was literally all she had going for her.

Shelby shook herself out of her alcohol-soaked thoughts. "Of course."

She grabbed a bag of pretzels from their gas station stash on her way and dropped cross-legged onto the floor in front of the fire.

Apparently, she sat too close for comfort, though, because Morgan rocked back on her heels and scooted a foot away before settling. Whatever. Shelby was too cold and too hungry to care about Morgan and her hang-ups. Her butt had barely dropped onto the rug when waves of heat from the burning logs rolled over her skin, making her shiver pleasantly.

"It'll warm up soon," Morgan said, misinterpreting the movement. "This will help."

Shelby held out the bottle and Morgan snatched it out of her hand like she was dying of thirst. While Shelby ripped open the bag of pretzels, Morgan tipped the bottle back just like she had. Unlike with Shelby, the liquor didn't go down smoothly for Morgan. She sputtered and gasped and her eyes watered, but she took a second swig anyway.

"You must be used to the good stuff." Shelby stuffed a couple of pretzels in her mouth. The salt did wonders for her mood, so she offered the bag to Morgan.

"And you aren't?" Morgan said with a skeptically-raised eyebrow.

"You think you know me so well." Shelby paused to wink and take another hit from the bottle. She couldn't help hoping the pink in Morgan's cheeks was due to the wink rather than the whiskey. "But I might just surprise you."

Morgan's eyebrows did a dance that seemed to say she doubted it, but her cheeks were bulging with pretzels. That was probably for the best. They didn't communicate well at the best of times, and cheap whiskey on empty stomachs wasn't likely to improve matters. Mostly because Shelby knew she got a little mouthy when she got tipsy. That was the last thing they needed tonight.

Shelby decided to tread back into safer territory. "There's enough canned food and oatmeal here to last us until someone finds us."

Morgan nodded and glanced in the flames over her shoulder. "Same with the firewood. Thank God it's dry since it's probably the only way we can heat this place."

"Let's not be too eager to thank God for anything."

Shelby hadn't meant to say that out loud, but Morgan didn't seem inclined to comment on it. Morgan had opened the shutters on the windows flanking the fireplace and Shelby looked up, hoping to see the sky. All she could see were trees and darkness. She hadn't realized it had gotten so late, but it wasn't just the mature trees and clouds blocking the sun. Her watch also told her that the day was coming to a close. She was surprised to register disappointment that they probably wouldn't be rescued tonight.

Where had the day gone? It felt like only a couple of hours ago they were dragging their suitcases out of the terminal to pick up their rental car. Of course the ache in her shoulder and the exhaustion that was seeping into her bones along with the warmth of the fire told her that was ridiculous. Still, she'd expected to be found by now. Hadn't anyone heard the crash? Wasn't anyone looking for them?

As though reading her mind, Morgan checked her phone. Shelby knew what news she'd have by the scowl creasing her forehead.

"Still no signal." Morgan looked around at the cabin's walls. "And no landline or Wi-Fi in here."

"That doesn't surprise me. The guy who owns this place isn't the Wi-Fi type."

Shelby's eyes flitted around the room, a fond smile making a drip of whiskey dribble from the corner of her mouth as she drank. She was surprised to see an angry scowl marring Morgan's features.

"What are you talking about?" Morgan asked, and it was definitely anger sharpening her syllables.

Shelby leaned back against the raised hearth and looked around the room.

"I can almost picture the man who owns this place." A fondness for this stranger warmed Shelby as effectively as the fire and whiskey. "He built this place with his bare hands, I bet. He comes up here to get away from the family, sure, but he probably doesn't do much hunting anymore. Maybe he did when he was younger, but now this is just his place to be quiet and alone."

Morgan's scoff was like a bucket of cold water over all those fond feelings. Had Shelby really thought she had a pretty face? Her sneer ruined that image for sure.

"How can you possibly know all that? You've never met him. If it is even a man's cabin," Morgan said.

Shelby was genuinely confused by the remark. Not only because it was unnecessarily rude, but also because Morgan should know all that, too. It was so obvious. Most of selling was knowing how to read people. Picking up on little clues and using them to your advantage.

"We've done better than meet him," Shelby said. "There's nothing so intimate as being inside someone's sanctuary."

Morgan's face was like stone and her stare was as icy as any Shelby had ever seen.

"It's the little things." Shelby was sure that, once she started to explain, Morgan would put the pieces together as easily as she had. Maybe she'd just been distracted by survival and that's why she hadn't come to the same conclusions. "The gun safe in the bedroom closet was empty and the key was hanging in the lock. There was no keychain or adornment on the key."

Morgan just stared silently at her. The longer the silence grew, the more confused Shelby became.

"He doesn't worry about losing it because he never takes it out of the lock. That's why there's no keychain." After another long beat of silence, Shelby said, "Plus the only trophy on the walls is the buck's head over the front door. An avid hunter would have trophies all over the place for their kills."

Morgan's glaze finally peeled away, moving up to the dusty antlers of the deer. She stared at it for a long time, like she was just seeing it for the first time.

"So he doesn't hunt that much, but the bookshelves are loaded down with books. All the spines are broken and some of them are pretty worn down. I can't even read the title of that one. Those are his trophies. He collects books, not bucks."

Apparently, Morgan didn't appreciate her little joke. She was tight-lipped when she said, "That's a lot of assumptions. Doesn't mean you really know the guy."

"Well, sure. I couldn't pick him out of a crowd walking down the street. But if I wanted to sell him something, I wouldn't talk to him about hunting, I'd talk to him about James Patterson."

Oddly, Morgan didn't seem to enjoy their banter as much as Shelby did. She thought they were two professionals, bonding over their work, but obviously not. Morgan didn't even respond, just pushed to her feet and went into the kitchen. While Shelby replayed the conversation in her head, looking for the place she'd said something offensive, Morgan rummaged through the plastic bags containing their gas station snack haul.

"Do you want egg salad or turkey?" Morgan held up a pair of prepackaged sandwiches.

"I'll take turkey if that's okay with you."

"Sure." Morgan came back to the living room with their lackluster dinner. "We'll save the rest for tomorrow."

"Good idea. I don't want to survive too long on Dinty Moore beef stew." Shelby tried to inject humor into her words, but it didn't do much to dispel the chill that had settled between them.

They ate their sandwiches in silence apart from the crackling of the wood fire. They'd both switched to water for the meal, but back to whiskey when they were done. Better to pass the time tipsy since there didn't seem to be any end to the tension.

After a quiet moment with her thoughts, Shelby was startled to see Morgan abruptly stand and strut off into the kitchen. In fact, it was possible Shelby had been dozing a bit. Her hand was at her scalp and she hadn't realized she'd been twirling her hair between two fingers. Morgan came back just as quickly as she'd disappeared, a damp paper towel in her hand, and knelt in front of Shelby.

"The cut doesn't look too bad, but we should clean the blood off at least," Morgan said.

"Huh?"

"The cut on your forehead." Morgan held up the paper towel. "May I?"

"Oh sure. Thanks."

Shelby had forgotten all about the blood on her forehead after the crash. It ached like a bruise more than stung like a cut as Morgan held back her bangs and cleaned the wound.

"I didn't see any broken glass," Morgan said. "How did this happen?"

Shelby held up her right hand, showing off the blue topaz set like a diamond into a sterling silver ring. The ring was like Granny Reeves herself, one shining precious gem attached to something cheap and tawdry. Shelby could see a spot of red on one of the prongs holding the topaz.

"It was my grandmother's," Shelby said. "My grandfather gave her a cheap engagement ring, but she tossed out the cubic zirconia when he died and put in a topaz. They were her favorite. She and I shared the same birthstone."

"It's pretty." Morgan's disinterest in jewelry was clear, both from her brief glimpse at the ring and her own lack of adornment, but neutral was kind enough here.

"She gave it to me when she got sick because she knew my mother would never pass it on when she was gone. We had a very special bond."

Morgan rocked back on her heels and looked Shelby in the eye for the first time in what felt like forever. There was genuine kindness in her soft voice when she said, "I'm sorry for your loss."

"Thank you."

Shelby's heart was beating too fast to maintain the eye contact. Stupid whiskey. Making stupid grumpy Morgan seem gentle after her stupid stubbornness. Shelby's gaze slipped to the open top button of Morgan's blouse and the sight made her gasp.

"Morgan, your chest!"

"Um, what?"

"That looks really painful." Shelby scooted closer to get a better look in the subdued light. "Can you even take a deep breath?"

Morgan tried to look down, but the angle was clearly wrong so she put her hand to her chest just below the hollow of her throat. Her lips twisted into a pained grimace and Shelby reached out, only stopping herself at the last minute.

"Can I take a look? You might need to ice that," Shelby said.

Morgan moved her hand away, and the grimace turned into the most adorably awkward smile as Shelby loosened the first button.

"I'm pretty sure Mother Nature iced me enough. It's okay. Really."

Shelby stopped when she caught a glimpse of the beige lace border of Morgan's bra, but that was enough. There was an angry red slash across her chest, cutting from her left collar bone to the valley between her breasts. Shelby tried not to notice how deliciously round and inviting Morgan's cleavage was, but she was only human after all.

"It's just from the seat belt." Morgan held the loose sides of her shirt against her breasts, keeping it from billowing open, for which Shelby was very grateful. She had an excellent imagination, and she didn't need to feed it any more than she already had.

"Take a deep breath." Shelby snapped back into medical mode. "Does it hurt? Does it feel like there's fluid in your lungs?"

"It hurts but not much. I don't know what fluid in my lungs feel like."

Shelby wasn't entirely sure either, but she could hazard a guess. "Is it hard to take a deep breath? Any sharp pain in your side? Cough onto your palm. Any blood?"

Morgan did as she was told—a miracle in its own right—and shook her head, showing an unstained palm to Shelby. There were pinpricks of burst blood vessels across Morgan's chest and Shelby guessed she would have a wicked bruise soon, but she didn't think there were any broken ribs or internal bleeding. She'd have to keep an eye on Morgan, though. Just in case.

"Do you have a headache?" Shelby asked, remembering the loss of consciousness after the crash.

"My neck hurts." Morgan massaged her shoulder and stretched her neck to both sides. When Shelby grabbed her phone, Morgan said, "I don't have a signal, remember?"

"I'm not making a call, I'm checking your pupils." Shelby turned on the flashlight.

Both Morgan's pupils dilated normally but her eyebrows knitted in annoyance. She grabbed the phone back from Shelby before buttoning her shirt back into place.

"I told you I'm fine." Morgan sat back and sipped her whiskey in silence.

So much for a thorough examination, but Shelby had to admit she was being overly cautious. The crash hadn't been that bad, after all, and she had brushed aside her own potential injuries. Morgan was clearly not the type to be fussed over and Shelby could appreciate that, even if she preferred appreciation to a return to sullen silence. Even her brief mention of her grandmother hadn't elicited any personal stories in return.

It wasn't long before exhaustion threatened to overtake Shelby. Exhaustion and annoyance, if she was honest. She just didn't know why Morgan couldn't try to make the situation tolerable at least. It's not like this was Shelby's dream way to spend a Friday night, either.

Truthfully, Friday nights for Shelby were usually spent the same as any other night. Hunkered in front of her computer until her eyes burned too bad to keep going. This was actually the first night in as long as she could remember that she didn't go back to finish up emails and paperwork after dinner. When had that become her whole life? She'd had friends at some point. She used to hang out with them. Now here she was, finally spending a Friday night drinking and it was so awkward all she wanted to do was go to sleep. Maybe Morgan's mood would improve tomorrow.

"I think I'm going to turn in." Shelby pushed to her feet and Morgan scrambled up, too.

"Yeah. I'm really tired."

"I'll take the couch. You're taller so you should have the bed."

"You don't have to do that." Morgan's scowl clearly communicated that she wasn't saying it to be polite. It was more of a "don't do me any favors" look.

"It's the option that makes the most sense," Shelby said.

"You aren't even that much shorter than me."

"It's really not a big deal, just take the bed."

"If it's not a big deal, you take the bed," Morgan said.

Shelby did not have the energy for some big production, but she really didn't want to lose her temper over this. She took a deep breath. "Let's compromise. We'll trade off. You take the bed tonight, I'll take it tomorrow."

A sensible woman would have accepted the deal and just gone to bed, but obviously Morgan was not interested in being sensible. She crossed her arms over her chest. "I don't think we'll be in the cabin that long. Someone will find us tomorrow."

"Then when they find us you can tell the whole damn world that you were gallant tonight." Shelby's voice held an impatient snap, but at least she kept herself from shouting again.

She'd had it. Everything had to be a fight with Morgan. Everything had to be an insult or an argument and she was over it. Shelby stormed off to the bedroom and slammed the door shut behind her.

Chapter Eight

Morgan realized she was being a bitch, but she just couldn't stop herself from arguing with Shelby. Why did the woman have to be so smug and such a show-off? Like was it really necessary to point out how clueless Morgan was about the cabin? Okay, so she hadn't noticed details or worked out a picture of what the cabin owner's personality was. She had been too busy trying to keep them from freezing to death, thank you very much.

Besides, she wasn't the type of person who immediately put people into boxes based on the books on their shelves or the lack of dead animals hanging from their walls. She didn't see people as puzzles she had to figure out because she wasn't nearly so interested in manipulating them all the time. It didn't matter whether the owner of the cabin hunted or read cookie-cutter best sellers. She treated everyone the same. She was the same person no matter who she was talking to. She didn't pretend to prefer Netflix in pajamas with one person when she would admit she wanted the exact opposite the moment that person walked away. She wasn't the kind of person who would be friends with the likes of Eric Ferguson.

Morgan lay awake far later than she'd intended, staring at the cabin ceiling and listing each and every one of Shelby's deficiencies. The really annoying part was how easily Shelby's face swam into her mind every time she closed her eyes. And it wasn't the face she'd worn the night Morgan had overheard her talking to Chad, confessing that every word she'd spoken to Morgan moments earlier had been a lie. No, it was the far more pleasant, relaxed smile she'd worn while sipping whiskey straight from the bottle in front of a fire and telling the story of her grandmother.

Shelby was gorgeous, Morgan could admit that. But she was that fake sort of gorgeous of supermodels and Barbie dolls. Plastic and vapid with no real personality. Looks without substance. Just the kind of woman Morgan couldn't stand. So she didn't care what Shelby thought of her. But still that flawless smile and those navy-blue eyes chased her into her dreams.

Morgan woke the next morning cold as hell. It might even have been her shivering that jarred her awake far earlier than she'd preferred to wake up. The scratchy faded serape she'd pulled off the back of the couch to cover her last night was no protection against the chill that had returned to the cabin. The sun wasn't yet up and the fire was long dead.

The twinge in her neck and shoulder had escalated to a full-blown ache overnight, making it difficult for her to drag herself off the sofa. Then, of course, there was the way her arms and legs were cramped from having to basically fold herself in half to fit onto the sofa. In fact, having spent an uncomfortable night squished into it, Morgan would now classify it more as a loveseat than a sofa. She hated to admit it, but there was no way she could sleep on it long term. If they weren't rescued soon, they'd have to figure out another option. She wouldn't force her worst enemy—who Shelby might just end up being—into sleeping on it either. While that only left one alternative, Morgan wasn't quite ready to contemplate sharing the only bed with Shelby, so she decided to wait on that thought. If everything went to plan, neither of them would have to sleep in the cabin for another night.

Once she'd sufficiently stretched her limbs and twisted enough to crack a kink out of her back, Morgan set about the task of starting a new fire. She made several trips from the wood pile stacked along the porch, ensuring she had enough fuel to keep the fire going all day.

She still believed they'd be rescued today. Someone was bound to find their rental car, and then all they'd have to do would be follow the chimney smoke and lighted windows. Rescuers wouldn't be able to follow their tracks, unfortunately. The snow was still coming down just as hard as ever and even the footprints they'd left at the bottom of the steps were covered. It would be up to smoke and lights to point out their location at least until the storm stopped and the two of them could venture back out to the road.

The fire started even easier than it had the night before. Thank God she'd paid attention in Girl Scouts all those years ago. Apparently, the same rules applied to building a fire indoors for warmth as outdoors for s'mores crafting. It's not like Shelby had even tried to start a fire. If she'd been alone, she would have been a human ice cube by the time help arrived. But had she thanked Morgan for her fire making efforts? Of course not. Shelby Lynn Howard didn't show gratitude. No doubt she thought she deserved everything she got.

Morgan closed her eyes and slipped her hand into her pants pocket. As she traced the outline of the stone, she reminded herself that she was better than those sort of unkind thoughts. She didn't really know Shelby at all and she shouldn't judge her so harshly. So she didn't know how to make a fire. So what? She had other skills and no doubt they would prove useful on this adventure.

The longer Morgan stood there, calming herself down, the more she noticed an unpleasant reality. She had been into and out of an airport and a backwoods gas station, crashed a car, hiked through a snowy wilderness, built two wood fires, and slept on a couch that was probably older than she was all while wearing the same clothes. She smelled terrible. Her skin felt grimy. Her teeth were in desperate need of a brush and her bladder in desperate need of relief. If she didn't clean herself up soon, she would not be fit company for man or beast. Or even Shelby Lynn Howard.

It was still early—the sun was just peeking through the limbs of the pine trees outside—and the cabin was quiet except for the crackling of the fire behind her. She was pretty sure Shelby was still asleep, so she tiptoed across the room to look down the hall. The bedroom door was still closed. Morgan was thrilled at the prospect of getting the first shower, since she had doubts about the efficiency of the hot water heater. With luck, she could be in and out and dressed again before Shelby woke up.

Morgan eased the door to the linen closet open, ensuring the hinges didn't squeak. It was mercifully silent, and she was equally delicate closing it once she'd grabbed a towel at random off the shelf. She was less delicate with the bathroom door. The urgency from her bladder and the aching proximity of cleanliness made her reckless. She didn't care if the hinges squeaked anymore. Let Shelby wake up. Then she would know her laziness kept her from getting the hottest shower. She threw the bathroom door open with reckless abandon and stopped dead.

The first thing she noticed was the steam billowing out around the door. The second thing she noticed was the shower-tub combination, the curtain wide open. Then she noticed Shelby.

Shelby was standing there, one foot on the mustard-yellow bathmat, the other foot still inside the shower. Steam wrapped around her body. Her extremely naked body. Morgan's mind filled with a sound like the hum of bees. Or maybe it was the rush of blood leaving her brain. Individual images flashed into her brain like waves of an angry sea slapping against her body.

A strand of hair, water making the straw-blond two shades darker than usual, clinging to the curve of her collar bone. A scattering of freckles dotting the slightly pink skin on her chest. The line across the top third of her small, pert breasts where her tan ended and her skin smoothed to creamy alabaster. A bead of water clinging to her hardened nipple. A neatly trimmed, inch-wide column of tight curls that disappeared between her thighs.

Morgan's breath caught in her throat and she couldn't rip her gaze away from those curls. Heat flooded through her and her mouth went as slack as her brain. A throbbing ache like she hadn't felt in who remembered how long stabbed through her core. Never once in her life had she seen such a mouthwatering sight. Part of her wanted to drop to her knees and worship that body, part of her wanted to fold in on herself and melt into the floor.

The towel dropped from Morgan's hand and the sound of it finally kicked her brain back into gear. She spun on her heels until she was facing the linen closet again. Even as she moved, she was conscious of a pang of disappointment the loss of such a heavenly sight evoked. But once she could no longer see Shelby, she was able to think rationally again and her rational mind reminded her that she should not have seen Shelby naked.

"Oh God. I'm so sorry." Morgan stammered through her apology like a tongue-tied idiot. "I thought you were still asleep or I would've knocked. I'm sorry."

Morgan was conscious of the rustling of fabric behind her, but she wasn't sure how she could hear over the roaring of her blood. If the heat pouring off her face was any indication, she was blushing harder than she ever had in her life.

"I couldn't sleep. I was trying to be quiet so I didn't wake you up." Shelby's voice held the same tremor of embarrassment Morgan had heard in her own. "I'm sorry. I've lived alone so long I didn't even think about locking the door."

"No, it's my fault. I should've knocked. I'll just go."

Morgan tried desperately to pull the door closed with her back to it, but something was wrong. It wouldn't shut no matter how hard she tugged at it. She just couldn't figure out why the door wouldn't shut and why she couldn't shove the image of Shelby's deliciously round breasts out of her mind. God, why hadn't she put her towel on before she got out of the shower? Morgan would never be able to see breasts again without thinking about how much she wanted this particular pair in her mouth.

Towel. That was it. She'd dropped her towel when she turned around. It must be blocking the door. She knelt to retrieve it at the same moment Shelby said, "It's your towel. I'll get it."

Morgan knelt and turned, making sure to keep her eyes low so as to avoid another embarrassing eyeful. Unfortunately, Shelby had the same idea at the same moment. Morgan turned around only to be eye level with Shelby's magnificent cleavage, barely contained by a thin towel wrapped beneath her arms.

It had been bad enough to see that incredible body across the small bathroom. Now it was an inch away at most. Close enough that Morgan could smell the heady mix of fresh soap and warm skin.

Close enough that she leaned forward subconsciously, her body drawn in like metal shavings to a magnet.

And then it got oh so much worse. Shelby settled down onto her knees, completing the movement they'd started together, and suddenly her lips were right there. A breath away. Morgan could feel gravity settle against her flesh, like Shelby was dragging her into orbit. Dragging her closer and closer to a collision of two forces so powerful they could rip the very ground beneath them apart.

The moment stretched inside that strange orbit. Shelby's breath stuttered to a halt. Her lips parted, the flesh peeling apart with such sensuality Morgan's heart skipped a beat. For a wild, untethered moment, Morgan was sure Shelby was staring at her lips. Staring with a hunger laced with the headiness of the moment. She was sure Shelby's eyes were fluttering shut in anticipation of a kiss. That her face was tilting ever so slightly to the side so it would better fit against Morgan's.

With the same impossible speed at which the gravity settled between them, it dissipated. Morgan remembered that Shelby pitied her and looked down on her. She remembered that she hated Shelby's fakeness and the thousand faces she showed to the world, each of them a lie. She remembered that they were stuck in a ramshackle cabin in the wilderness with a crashed rental car and no way to call for help.

Before the moment could build again or her mind could betray her, Morgan snatched up the towel and bolted back into the living room.

❖

Shelby stared blankly at herself in the mirror. The rapid rise and fall of her chest strained at the towel tucked haphazardly under her armpits. Her body was still tingling from the intensity of Morgan's stare and the breathlessness of their near kiss. The thought sent another ripple through her body, but she quickly shook it off.

They had not almost kissed. Morgan hated her way too much for that. Didn't she? Sure, there had been an undeniable hunger in her eyes when she'd burst in to find Shelby naked. That hunger had been even more palpable when they knelt on the floor, so close they'd almost touched.

If it had been anyone other than Morgan who'd looked at her like that, Shelby would've made the first move and kissed her, to hell with the awkwardness that would've come from it. Hell, she might even have marched across the room and kissed her when she'd first come in. The way Morgan had examined every inch of her naked body had sparked desire in Shelby that still raged. She had never—not once in her life—been looked at like that. Morgan had devoured her with her eyes. Being the object of that sort of naked lust was a powerful aphrodisiac.

But that was the problem. From Morgan it would only ever be lust. It wasn't Shelby who had inspired that desire. It was just the presence of a naked woman. Any pair of tits could inspire horniness, but that was very different from desire. Morgan hated her, even if the reasons for that were unclear, and, honestly, after the way she acted last night, the feeling was becoming mutual.

It had been years since anyone had been so irrationally unkind to Shelby, and the last time it had come close to breaking her. She certainly didn't want to feel like that ever again. Morgan was the last person in the world she wanted to kiss. Now if only her body would get the message and stop tingling all over.

Shelby just needed to get her own libido under control. She needed a night out on the town to settle her hormones because there was no chance of anything happening with Morgan. That was it, she thought as she snatched up the comb from the sink and attacked the tangles in her hair. She would get back home to DC, get herself a new phone, and then immediately go to Riveter's Cocktail Lounge. She'd find some sexy lesbian who wasn't a jerk to her for no reason and kiss that woman all night long. That would get thoughts of Morgan's hungry stare and her glistening lips out of Shelby's mind forever.

The comb hit a sensitive spot on her forehead, making her hiss in pain. The cut from her grandmother's ring wasn't too bad and it was already healing, but it would certainly be tender for a few days. Hopefully it wouldn't scar, but she'd have to keep an eye on it. The only other area of concern was her shoulder where the seat belt caught her. It didn't have the same sharp pain from the previous day when she moved, but it was sore as hell, and she sure wasn't going to do any intensive yoga any time soon.

Checking that her towel was secure around her, Shelby took a deep breath and then opened the bathroom door. Peeking around the frame, she saw the back of Morgan's head on the couch.

"Bathroom's free," Shelby said.

Morgan didn't turn around, but Shelby knew she must've heard, so she darted into the bedroom and made sure to lock the door. She waited until she heard Morgan's footsteps down the hall and the bathroom door close before turning to the room. They were tight quarters, with very little space to maneuver around.

She laid out yesterday's clothes on the bed and then glared down at them. The slacks were wrinkled and there was a line around mid-calf of both legs that showed where the snow had melted and then dried. The sweater hadn't fared much better and she'd slept in her undershirt. Everything had a smell that she didn't want anywhere near her clean skin. If only she'd thought to grab her suitcase out of the trunk before they abandoned the rental.

As she looked around the room in desperation, her gaze landed on the dresser tucked into the far corner. She'd seen a stackable washer-dryer in the utility room, so maybe the cabin owner kept clothes up here? It seemed practical to avoid having to bring suitcases into the wilderness, and this man was eminently practical. With a shrug, Shelby marched across the room and pulled open drawers.

Shelby smiled triumphantly. "What a guy."

The dresser was full of well-worn but neatly folded undershirts, jeans, and sweatpants. Most everything was hopelessly huge for her, but she was able to pull the sweatpants strings to their limit before tying them tight. It would work for the day and fortunately the only mirror in the cabin was in the bathroom so she wouldn't have to see how ridiculous she looked.

To finish the outfit, she pulled on a white undershirt and an old flannel from the closet. The flannel was soft and thick, like being wrapped in a warm blanket. It was clean, but there was the lingering scent of aftershave or cologne or something that reminded her of her grandfather. The way his hugs enveloped her in his massive arms when she was a little girl. She pulled the fabric to her face and closed her eyes, remembering the wrinkles on his weathered face when he would boop her nose. It always made her feel like the sun his world orbited around.

Shelby opened her eyes and rolled her shoulders, shaking off the memory. She had tucked thoughts of her family away a long time ago, and she wasn't going to dig them up now. It had been bad enough to think of Granny Reeves last night. She wouldn't go there again in a hurry. Closing the closet doors, she noticed the distinct lack of hunting camouflage or blaze orange.

"Definitely not into hunting these days." She cut a glance at the closed bedroom door and the bathroom beyond it.

When she stepped out into the hall, she heard the shower cut off. The water pressure left a lot to be desired, so she probably wouldn't have heard it if she hadn't been standing right by the door. That's probably why Morgan hadn't known she was in there. Before she could get lost again in thoughts of what happened right after she'd turned the shower off not long ago, she took a step closer to the door.

"There's clean clothing in the bedroom closet and dresser," she shouted to be heard through the door. "I'm going to go make us some breakfast."

There was such a long pause between her shout and the response, she almost thought Morgan hadn't heard her. A moment later, however, Morgan shouted her thanks back through the wooden panel.

With that confirmation, Shelby headed into the kitchen to make some oatmeal and check the expiration date on those bottles of apple juice she'd seen in the pantry.

Chapter Nine

Morgan stood alone in the bedroom feeling distinctly strange. She couldn't quite manage to keep her eyes off the bed, knowing that Shelby had slept there the night before. Not that she cared. She wasn't interested in Shelby, of course, but she did see her naked and she hadn't been able to think about anything else since. So where did that leave her? Standing alone in a stranger's cabin, stark naked, staring at a bed where a different stranger had slept the night before. Like an absolute creep. What the actual hell was her life?

She grabbed a fistful of her damp hair and growled low in her throat. Everything had been totally weird since she'd offered Shelby a ride. Why had she even done that? It wasn't the kind of thing Morgan did. Not that she was heartless, she was just focused. Sometimes that focus made her forget.

As she released her hair, Morgan's gaze fell to the stone resting on the quilt at the foot of the bed. She hadn't looked at it in a long time. Every night before bed she would take it out of her pants pocket and put it in the jewelry tray she'd inherited from her grandmother. Every morning she would slide it into her pocket last thing before heading out her front door. She'd done this so often that she didn't think about it, and she never let her eyes linger on it. The stone was for remembering, but she didn't want to dwell.

The stone had started out life in some tacky gift store, no doubt, but it was more meaningful than any other object in her life. Not because of what it was, but who it represented. The paint was more faded now than the last time she'd really taken the time to look at it. That wasn't a surprise. Everything faded over time. Everyone faded over time, too.

Morgan squeezed her eyes shut before thoughts she didn't want flooded in. They'd been so close since the conference center, and she couldn't let them all the way in. If she let them in she would cry, and the last thing she wanted to do was cry while she was stuck in this cabin with Shelby. God knew how Shelby would try to use her tears against her.

With the heat of the shower fully receded from her body, her muscles reminded her that she had been in a car accident. She'd thought her shoulders were tight from sleeping on a tiny couch, but it was abundantly clear the ache was much deeper and more persistent than a poor night's sleep could account for. She stretched her limbs and each small movement sent a new burst of agony through abused muscles. The bruise on her chest looked awful even from the awkward angle of her chin on her chest. But stretching her neck to see it brought a pain like nothing she had ever felt from her neck.

Morgan struggled to move her neck to a more comfortable position for what felt like ages, but every new angle hurt. Everything hurt so badly she felt woozy and had to sit down on the edge of the bed. Was this whiplash? For a moment, she panicked, trying to remember anything from the first aid class she'd had to take right after being hired at the hospital, but it had been so long ago and the pain was clouding her mind. She sat still, trying to let the dizziness pass. After a few successful experiments, she was able to move her neck enough to loosen some of the muscles, but she knew she'd have to take it easy today or risk another battle with the pain.

Blowing out a deep breath, Morgan finally forced herself to focus on the world around her. She needed to get dressed and get breakfast. No doubt someone would find them today, so she needed to be ready to go. She grabbed some jeans that were probably older than she was from the dresser. They were a few sizes too big, but she found a thick belt to hold them up. She completed the outfit with an undershirt and flannel, and was ready to face the world. Or worse, she was ready to face Shelby.

When she entered the living space, it was to find Shelby stirring raisins and condensed milk into a pot of oatmeal. Morgan's stomach growled at the delicious aroma, but that gave away her presence.

"Great timing, breakfast is just about ready," Shelby said over her shoulder.

"Cool." Morgan cleared her throat and squared her shoulders. "I just wanted to say again how sorry I am for walking in on you this morning."

Shelby clicked off the burner and waved away the apology with one single, fluid movement. "Don't worry, it was an honest mistake. Like I said, I'm too used to living alone."

Morgan stamped down her annoyance with the dismissal by squeezing the stone in her pocket. She reminded herself that she couldn't dictate other people's responses. Her therapist kept telling her that. She had to accept what other people had to offer, even if they were too busy scooping oatmeal into bowls rimmed with brown floral print to accept her apology the way she wanted.

"Are you?" Shelby looked up at her, eyes like interrogation spotlights. "Used to living alone?"

The question seemed to come out of the blue and Morgan's brain immediately began to spin. Why was she asking if Morgan lived alone? What business was it of hers? And, mostly, what would she do with the answer when she got it?

Apparently, Morgan took too long to answer or else her racing thoughts were showing on her face. Shelby's smile melted into a clenched-teeth sneer and she slammed the pot of oatmeal on the counter. A raisin swathed in creamy oats jumped up and fell onto the countertop with an unpleasant splat.

"Damn it, Morgan. We're stuck here together, probably for another day." She indicated the windows, all of which showed the snow still falling thick as a curtain, with an angry sweep of her arm. "So we might as well get to know each other. It's going to be a long day if you just sit over there, silently hating me."

Shame flooded through Morgan. Shelby was absolutely right. She was being a brat and she was expecting the worst of Shelby for no good reason.

"I don't hate you." Morgan could hear how timid her own voice was and she couldn't quite meet Shelby's eye.

"Bullshit. You were an ass all day yesterday and it's not like you were super personable at the trade show. I tried to talk to you then and you looked at me like I kicked your dog. So obviously you don't like me."

"We're competitors. Why would I like you?"

"Because we work in the same field. Because we can respect each other and be professional."

When she said it like that, Morgan couldn't quite remember why she disliked Shelby so much. Sure, she didn't like Shelby's style, but it's not like she was a murderer or a drug dealer. She was just a salesperson who was more successful than Morgan. Was that really Shelby's fault?

"Yes, I live alone." Morgan still wouldn't look at Shelby. But hey, old habits died hard.

After a beat, Shelby gave a laugh that seemed to clearly say "I guess I'll take what I can get" and picked up the pot of oatmeal again. Morgan thought it best to just go sit down quietly so she didn't do anything else to make Shelby yell at her.

There were already two places set at the little cafe table, each with a glass of apple juice and a steaming mug of coffee on the placemat. Shelby followed quickly after her, setting a bowl of oatmeal in front of each of them and dropping into her chair. She didn't say anything else, just tucked into her oatmeal, and Morgan followed suit.

She was actually impressed with how good the food was. Morgan rarely ate oatmeal because she hadn't been impressed as a kid. Her mother had made it with water and brown sugar, maybe a drizzle of maple syrup at most. What Morgan remembered was chewy and bland. This was anything but. Maybe it was the condensed milk, but the oats were creamy and the raisins had plumped nicely.

"I wasn't sure if you took cream or sugar in your coffee, so I brought both to the table. It's powdered creamer, but at least it's something." Shelby added a scoop of sugar to her own cup.

"Thanks." It was something, but Morgan decided she needed to try harder. "I drink mine black."

"I wasn't trying to pry when I asked if you lived alone."

To Morgan's surprise, Shelby looked a little embarrassed, and there might've even been a blush on her cheeks.

"It's okay," Morgan said.

Shelby set down her coffee but continued to stare into the mug. "I realized while I was making breakfast that no one is going to miss me. I don't have plans with friends and I don't talk to anyone regularly. When I don't show up at home, no one will report me missing."

Morgan had assumed Shelby would be as popular in her personal life as she had been at the trade show, and she was shocked to discover that wasn't the case. She was going to ask questions, especially about the lack of regular phone calls even to her family, when she realized she was in the same boat. She called her mom sometimes, but not enough that a lack of a call would send up warning bells. She didn't really have any friends after moving a couple of years ago. No one would notice if her car wasn't in her driveway.

"Shit. Me too." Morgan set her spoon down, suddenly not very hungry at all. "No one will miss me until work on Monday."

"It'll probably be Tuesday for me. Not until I miss the area sales meeting."

The oatmeal, which had been filling and warming her nicely a moment ago, turned into a pile of writhing snakes in Morgan's stomach. This was not good. She looked at the windows again. The snow was still coming down hard. Maybe not quite so hard as yesterday, but enough to keep people inside. Certainly enough to keep them from driving a little used road off the beaten track near a state park. Shelby turned to look out the same window.

"By now our tire tracks will be covered." Shelby turned back to look at Morgan, a childlike fear tinging her words. "How long do you think before the car is covered, too?"

Morgan did not let the words sink in. She would not let herself get bogged down in fear. If she thought about it too much, she would have to admit things were much, much worse than she'd thought. Instead, she went with her usual defense—cold, unflinchable logic.

"The angle of the car will work in our favor." Morgan felt more confident in her assertion with each word she spoke. "It won't get buried as quickly as it would if it was on flat ground. We have time."

"And the rental car company will report the car missing, so they'll be looking for us."

Morgan's stomach churned again, harder this time. "I was supposed to return it to Rochester Airport."

"What?"

"They didn't have any one-way rentals available. In fact, all they had was the one car, so I took it even though I was supposed to return it to the same place I rented it."

"Which means they won't suspect you were driving it back to Washington, DC," Shelby said with a groan. "And no one will be looking for me at all."

"The rental car company knows where I live, so they'll put two-and-two together. Plus, every cop in the state will get the alert. Someone will think to look along the route I would have taken home and this place isn't too far off the interstate. They'll find us." Fear was threatening to overwhelm Morgan, so she made her little speech as much to convince herself as Shelby.

Shelby looked skeptical, but it was clear she wanted to be optimistic, too. She shrugged, then stood and grabbed Morgan's empty bowl. "Well, I'm not going to worry too much about it. I'm going to sit in front of the fire with one of those mystery novels and a cup of tea. Want to join me?"

She looked so sweet and unconcerned, Morgan couldn't help but play along. She still didn't like the prospect of a delayed rescue, but they had plenty of food, and the prospect of reading a book in front of a fire was actually really lovely. She was sure, despite her belief the car wouldn't be completely buried, that they were in for a long weekend, but they were safe and warm. Why not enjoy the down time while they had it?

"I call dibs on the armchair," Morgan said.

❖

Shelby was stretched out on the couch, a cup of tea steaming on the coffee table, a book in her hand. If it wasn't for the too large sweatpants and the scratchy upholstery beneath her, she would be able to convince herself that she was enjoying a relaxing Saturday afternoon at home. Not that she'd had one of those in a long time. Most of her Saturdays were filled with catching up on emails and updating the spreadsheet she used to track her customer interactions. The closest she came to relaxing on a Saturday was treating herself to a glass of low-calorie Chardonnay with dinner, but she did it in yoga pants, so that was something.

The crackle of the fire, in fact, added an element of coziness she found distinctly lacking at home. She was most definitely not at home. This was not her butter-soft leather couch beneath her or the imported Kusmi tea she loved in her mug. This was a stranger's cabin in the middle of nowhere with only one bed and a grumpy bitch of a housemate while they waited to see if anyone gave two shits about two single women living in a city that made them anonymous. She didn't even have a cat to starve to death if she was never rescued from this depressing cabin.

Shelby closed her eyes and took three long, deep breaths. There. She'd had her moment. Her pity party, table for one. Now it was time to get over it. It was time for her to get a grip and she only knew one way to do that. It was time to remind herself who she was. At the last moment, she remembered that she wasn't at home alone, so she couldn't say the words out loud like usual. She spoke them to herself, slow and clear, inside her own head.

I am Shelby Lynn Howard, granddaughter of Evelyn May Reeves. My bloodline is full of strong, confident women. Except my spineless, thoughtless mother, but never mind. My bloodline is full of strong, confident women. I am the best of all of them by far. Granny Reeves fought to give me a chance. I won't waste that chance. I will make her proud. I will make myself proud. I am a woman to be feared by those who doubt me and loved by those who see my strength.

Shelby opened her eyes and found she was herself again. As always, her speech had done the trick. She'd been giving it to herself since her very first pity party on her twenty-second birthday, three days after Granny Reeves's funeral. It grounded her in the ultimate truths of her life. Sure, she hadn't found that person to see her strength yet. That much was obvious in the fact that there was no one who loved her enough to miss her. There never had been.

But she was going to change that. She was going to get out of this frozen hell and go home and stop working seventy-hour weeks. She was going to find some woman who was beautiful and smart and appreciated her and also laid her out at least twice a week. Okay, maybe just once a week if she had a big sale on the line. She couldn't afford to let sex make her too tired at work.

Shelby shook herself. No. No sale would get in the way of her getting what she wanted. She'd been too worried about sales and not worried enough about finding her person. No sale was worth feeling like this again. Like she had nothing and no one in the world who cared about her.

Shelby finally stopped pretending she was reading. She let out a sigh and let her head fall back on the couch. It actually felt nice—stretching her neck and shoulders that she hadn't realized she'd been scrunching up. Then she sighed again, this time pushing all the air out of her lungs, making her shoulders drop even further into comfort.

"You okay?"

Morgan's voice came out croaky, like she was half asleep in her chair. Looking up, Shelby saw that she was, in fact, looking more content and comfortable than she had any right to look given their circumstances. In fact, if Shelby hadn't known better, she might think that Morgan was enjoying all this down time. But that couldn't be right. Not after she was so on edge when they talked about their chances at rescue during breakfast.

Nevertheless, there she was, looking completely relaxed. Shelby didn't know anyone who could sit around for hours reading a book. What's more, she never would have expected this from Morgan, who had spent the entire week at the trade show walking around like the human embodiment of stress. The tension that usually knotted her shoulders had slipped away. The worry line that cut between her eyes had smoothed out.

Shelby watched her and wondered if this was what she normally looked like. If this was how she normally spent her Saturdays. Maybe the Morgan she'd met at the trade show hadn't been the real Morgan. Maybe this was the real Morgan and she wasn't usually so uptight and rude. Maybe she could be a fun person to hang around with on a Saturday afternoon. Doubtful, but wilder things had happened.

Apparently, Shelby silently stared at Morgan too long, because she raised an eyebrow and asked again, "You okay?"

"Uh, yeah. Just hungry." Shelby dropped her book on the floor and hopped to her feet. "Want to break into our potato chip supply?"

Shelby thought Morgan would scowl and make some comment about how they should be logical and ration their food. She was all set to argue when Morgan surprised her again.

"Sure. Especially if they're served with a glass of that terrible bourbon."

Shelby couldn't help but smile at the mischievous twinkle in Morgan's eye. "I think we can make that happen."

Rather than scrounging out of the bag and drinking straight from the bottle like they did last night, Shelby decided to do a proper service of their snack. She grabbed bowls for their chips and juice glasses for their bourbon. For some reason, she wanted to pretend like she was entertaining a friend back at her condo in Alexandria instead of being stranded with a stranger in the woods. It probably had a lot to do with her recent promise to have a personal life, but Shelby decided not to analyze it too much.

When she brought their snack back into the living room, Morgan took her bowl and glass with almost friendly grace. She raised the bourbon to her lips with a grimace that didn't seem to have anything to do with the quality of the alcohol.

"Are you okay?" Shelby asked.

"Just sore." Morgan rubbed the back of her neck and took another sip of bourbon. "This is a decent painkiller though. How about you? How's your shoulder?"

Shelby was pleasantly surprised, both by Morgan's interest and in her candor about her own pain. Morgan was obviously a guarded person, but she opened up to Shelby, who couldn't help but do the same.

"My shoulder is sore as hell, honestly, but I'll survive."

Morgan nodded, but when she would have gone back to quietly reading, Shelby decided to draw a little more information out of her unintentional roommate.

"Where do you live?" Shelby asked, relaxing back into the couch cushions. She was met by a blank stare. "You put my address into your GPS when we started this drive, but I assume you live somewhere in Northern Virginia."

"Why would you assume that?" Morgan asked, but the words didn't carry the bite of accusation Shelby was used to.

Shelby ticked off her evidence on her fingers, flicking off some cheese dust as she went. "We both work in the DC Metro, so it's either DC, Maryland, or Virginia. Only lobbyists and ex-presidents can afford to live in the District, so that's out. You aren't the best driver I've ever seen, but Maryland drivers are much worse. So you must live in Virginia."

"Considering I drove our rental car off the side of a mountain, that's saying something." Morgan punctuated the sentence by crunching a potato chip followed by a sip of bourbon. There was a self-deprecating twinkle in her eye that shocked Shelby so much she dropped her chip. Morgan Allen had a sense of humor, who knew?

"Only a hill. A Maryland driver would have driven us off the side of the hill, into a tree, through a burning building, and into the ocean. All without using a turn signal."

Morgan snorted a laugh around a mouthful of sour cream and onion. It was an adorable, albeit brief, moment that made Shelby's insides warm far more than they should have. She really needed a date. Or a friend. If all it took to find an obnoxious, rude woman like Morgan charming was being stuck in a cabin with her for twenty-four hours, Shelby was in serious need of companionship.

"Manassas," Morgan said.

"Hmm?" Shelby had been intent on her inner musings and the word didn't penetrate.

"I live in Manassas. Right outside downtown. Near the train station."

Morgan didn't quite meet Shelby's eye when she described her home. She shuffled around in her bowl, apparently looking for the perfect chip, but Shelby was too good at reading people to buy that.

Manassas was probably the farthest away from Washington, DC, you could get while still technically being in the suburbs. Whereas Shelby's neighborhood in Alexandria would be considered chic and maybe even hip, the same could not be said for Morgan's home. For as densely populated as it was, Manassas was shockingly rural and one of the few conservative areas in the deeply blue rim of the state. It was also one of the few places where houses were somewhat affordable.

Morgan was probably embarrassed to live there because the zip code alone was enough to telegraph her socioeconomic status. Shelby, who had spent most of her adult life poorer than Morgan could possibly imagine, couldn't care less about that. What she did care about was that Manassas, being deeply conservative, would not be a comfortable place for a single lesbian to live. While Morgan wasn't so butch she would be clocked as gay by everyone who walked down the street, something told Shelby she wasn't the kind of woman to stay in the closet even for her own safety.

They continued their pleasant if stilted small talk until the chips were gone and Morgan went back to reading her book, but not before Shelby gained a new level of respect for her. Morgan was infuriating and had a chip on her shoulder, but maybe she had a reason or two for that never-back-down attitude.

Chapter Ten

Morgan tried desperately to hold onto the soothing blanket of sleep. She knew she was asleep. She knew she was dreaming. She was warm and comfortable and there was an absolutely heavenly voice humming in the distance. The humming was what really told her she was asleep. The voice wasn't familiar, but she was so drawn to it. It was wonderful, like hearing a lullaby sung by a grandmother who died before she was born. It was gentle and clear and had that deep alto pitch she was so drawn to. She knew it was a voice crafted specifically for her by her subconscious to keep her locked into her perfect cocoon.

She wanted to stay in that cocoon. To slip back into the depths of sleep that cleared out all her thoughts and worries, following the dream voice. But her focus on the sound was drawing her further away from those depths. It was drawing her to wakefulness despite her desperate desire to rest.

Morgan came fully awake, and if she'd thought that voice was alluring, it was nothing compared to the delicious smells of food cooking on the stove. The same way she picked apart the voice in her dream, she picked apart the scents of dinner. Onions and garlic and the rich, heartiness of pasta boiling. But what really caught her attention was the unmistakable hiss of meat sizzling in a hot pan.

She finally peeled her eyes open, but the leadenness of sleep still lingered in Morgan's limbs. Her eyes came into focus and she watched Shelby flitting around the kitchen, going from one pan to another, her face wreathed in steam from the pasta pot, quietly singing the final notes of a song Morgan didn't recognize.

Morgan sat in her armchair—sprawled in it really—and let herself wake up slowly from her nap. This was her favorite part of a Saturday afternoon—the nap before dinner. It was self-indulgent probably, to give herself a lazy Saturday every weekend, but she had to do it to maintain her sanity. So much of her life these days was wrapped up in work. In the lab, everything was so simple. She went into work when her shift started, did the same testing on every sample that came through the door for ten hours, and then went home when the clock struck the correct time. Someone else took over the work and when she clocked out, she was done.

Then she took this huge leap to leave the lab and start this new career where it felt like the work was never done. There was always a quote to prepare for a potential new sale or a question to answer from her boss or a customer. There was competitor research and studying trends and diving deeper into the technological theory. She could stay up until midnight every night answering emails and still not be caught up. She had, in fact, done that more than once. She felt like she never clocked out. Except on Saturday afternoons, of course.

And it wasn't just the hours. She'd been born and raised in Richmond, Virginia. It was a city and it was growing, but it wasn't that big and it wasn't that expensive. Her new job, however, required her to move up to the Washington, DC, area, and that city was very big and very expensive. Her new role had come with a significant bump in pay and the potential for massive sales-based commissions, but she'd never paid so much for a place to live. Even with the big raise, her budget was shockingly tight and the margin between making it work and losing her townhouse was razor thin.

Morgan could feel the frozen edge of panic creeping into her blood. It happened so often when she thought about her finances that she was all too familiar with the feeling. Soon she would spiral into full-blown panic, and she didn't want that. She couldn't do that. Not here. Not with Shelby across the room and no way to pull herself out of that fear.

Before she could fall into the spiral, Shelby turned around and spotted her. A smile sprang onto Shelby's lips, and the warmth of it was so surprising given their recent tension that Morgan forgot all about the precarious nature of her professional life.

"Hey there, sleepyhead. Have a good nap?" Shelby's playful tone was so friendly it made Morgan laugh at herself.

"I did actually."

"I'm jealous. I never have been able to take naps. I always wake up grumpy after."

"If I hadn't taken a nap, I'd be so grumpy I wouldn't be fit to live with." When Shelby didn't respond with so much as a diminishing of her smile, Morgan said, "Not that I'm much fun to live with now."

"I expect to be rescued tomorrow. I can survive anything for a day." Shelby punctuated her joke with a wink that made Morgan's heart rate skip up for a few beats. She didn't want to analyze that, so she focused on forcing her lethargic limbs to push her up out of the chair. The rumble of her stomach helped. The whole cabin was now filled with those delicious, savory scents coming from the stove.

"You didn't have to cook dinner all alone," Morgan said.

"I'm glad I got the chance, actually. I love to cook, but it makes me nervous when someone is watching me. You sleeping through dinner prep probably saved me a finger."

"Okay, well, you have to let me cook tomorrow since you've made all our meals today."

"Sure, you can do that."

Shelby's mood was oddly light as she turned back to the stove and stirred one of the pans. It was the first time since they'd left the airport that Shelby had that joy she'd shown at the trade show. Morgan was happy to see it at first, but then she remembered the last time Shelby looked so carefree. It was at the banquet when Morgan was returning from the bathroom to their shared cocktail table. When Morgan overheard her telling Chad that she loved those type of events. A column wrapped in black and gold streamers had blocked Shelby's view of her, which was probably why she felt comfortable telling Chad the exact opposite thing she'd told Morgan moments before.

Of course, Shelby probably hadn't expected her to be back from the bathroom so quickly. She probably wouldn't have been if she'd actually gone to the bathroom, but she hadn't. She had simply needed to walk away. Seeing with her own eyes and hearing with her own ears the friendliness between Eric and Shelby had been something. Then there was the way Eric hadn't recognized her. That man had dropped a bomb into her life and he didn't remember her name. He had destroyed something deep inside her and he couldn't even recognize her. Anger and hatred had wrapped around her lungs and she'd seen stars. Walking away had been preferable to passing out in front of them all, so she had excused herself to catch her breath. The moment she was out of sight, she'd ducked behind a column and leaned against it to catch her breath. Fortunately, she hadn't been out of earshot for when Shelby had given herself away.

Just thinking about that moment had Morgan's face burning with embarrassment. She had been such an idiot. She'd gone to the banquet knowing exactly who Shelby was. Knowing that she was the kind of woman who said whatever it took to get ahead. Still, while they'd stood at that high-top table, sharing a drink and connecting over what Morgan had truly believed was a shared interest in documentaries and avoiding crowds, she'd forgotten. She'd had fun with Shelby. She'd had a moment where she thought…she didn't know what she'd thought was happening between them. Then she'd left the table for a moment and returned to find Shelby was a liar. Based on the conversations she'd had with some of their male colleagues, it was more than likely Shelby had been trying to trick Morgan into being a trade show hookup.

She'd felt like such a fool. She'd kept her distance the rest of the night, hard as it had been when Chad suggested they share a table, and Shelby had the nerve to look confused or maybe even hurt by that distance. Probably more like disappointed she'd wasted her time trying to butter her up. The most frustrating thing was Morgan had no idea whether Shelby had been lying to her or to Chad. But that was the thing with Shelby. She had so many faces there was no way to tell what the real one was.

The click of burners turning off caught Morgan's attention, pulling her out of her own thoughts. Shelby turned that radiant smile on her again and somehow Morgan couldn't stay mad at her.

"Dinner's ready," Shelby said.

"Smells great."

"Thanks, but you should temper your expectations. I didn't have a lot to work with. Just some canned goods and spices that look like they've been open a while."

Shelby grabbed a plate in each hand and carried them over to the table. Morgan followed, the enticing scents billowing in Shelby's wake making her mouth water. Despite Shelby's warnings, the meal looked amazing, with sizzling strips of meat nestled in around pasta and peas. Morgan dropped gratefully into her chair and it took all her willpower to wait for Shelby to sit before digging in.

It was worth the wait. Morgan twirled noodles around her fork and the sauce clung to it. She speared some meat and veggies and shoved the whole thing into her mouth before Shelby had even settled her napkin onto her lap. Morgan's eyes literally rolled back in her head as she chewed. The pasta was perfectly chewy and coated in a thick, deliciously creamy sauce that would have been over seasoned if there was even a single grain more of salt. As it was, the salt brought out the sweetness of the peas and the earthiness of the mushrooms. Strips of meat with a crispy crust gave the meal texture, and onion brought the whole thing together beautifully. If there had been cloves of roasted garlic instead of the powdered variety, she might have said this was one of the best pasta dishes she'd ever had.

"Oh my God, Shelby, this is incredible." Morgan groaned between bites.

"You're sweet." Shelby took her first bite. A smile spread over her lips as she chewed and the pride in her voice was evident.

"What exactly is in this?" Morgan asked as she speared another mushroom slice.

"Just regular old spaghetti noodles with onion soup mix, a can of peas and mushrooms, some spices, and crispy SPAM."

"I don't think I've ever actually had SPAM before."

"It gets a bad rap, but it's delicious if you sear it really well," Shelby said.

"I'm a believer."

Morgan's plate was nearly clean and she eyeballed the counter to see if there was more. Shelby saw the look and laughed, but hopped up out of her chair to grab the pan.

"There's no way you just came up with this looking in the pantry, right? If so, I have to really step up my cooking game," Morgan said.

Shelby split the rest of the pasta between their two plates. "No need to worry, it's not a new recipe. It's actually pretty close to one of my main staple recipes from my twenties. Except the mushrooms. I didn't usually have the luxury of the peas with mushroom slices mixed in."

"I'm surprised you didn't get fresh mushrooms. They aren't that hard to work with and you're obviously a great cook."

Morgan didn't miss the bright blush that lit Shelby's cheeks or the speed with which she turned away.

"It wasn't my choice actually." Shelby avoided her eyes until she sat down, but then she fixed Morgan with a challenging stare. "I was broke back then and got everything from the food bank. They almost never had fresh produce."

Shelby's stare didn't waver, but Morgan's did. Maybe it was because Shelby was so sophisticated bordering on pretentious, so it was hard to imagine her needing the food bank. Even when Morgan was struggling right after college, she'd never needed public assistance or charity food banks. In fact, while she had never been rich, she wasn't sure she'd ever known anyone who had needed that much help. Then again, there was such a stigma with poverty in the United States, she wasn't sure folks would have told her if they had. And yet Shelby, someone Morgan didn't think very highly of, had no problem admitting it.

"Well, your creativity is amazing. I can't believe you made this meal from that meager pantry," Morgan said, doing her best to cover her shock.

"I've made more with less."

Morgan must have passed the test, because Shelby shrugged and some of the rigidity went out of her shoulders. Still, Morgan felt a little self-conscious about her surprise. She didn't like to think of herself as judgmental, but maybe she had painted an unfair picture of Shelby in her first assessment. Besides, it was easy to forget how hard it was to be young and just starting out.

"I'm impressed you even ate vegetables when you were that young. The only time I ate anything green in college was when I went home to my parents' on the weekends," Morgan said.

To her surprise, Shelby seemed even more upset by that statement than when she talked about going to a food bank. She definitely avoided Morgan's eye and grabbed their empty plates before scurrying back into the kitchen. Obviously, Morgan wasn't winning any points with her attempt at small talk, but it never had been her strong suit.

"I'll get that." Morgan hurried after Shelby and planted herself in front of the sink. "You cooked. I'll clean. You go relax on the couch."

Shelby's discomfort had fled just as quickly as it had come. She tossed the dish towel Morgan's way. "I'll take you up on that one."

❖

Shelby wandered off in the general direction of the couch. The sound of water pounding against the metal sink joined the gentle crackle of the fire and the whistle of the wind through the trees outside. She focused on the water, desperate to distract herself from the mental funk she'd fallen into.

She should have known better than to cook one of her old recipes. In fact, she was shocked that she still remembered it. She'd spent so much time trying to forget those years. So long pretending there hadn't been a time in her life when she'd had to live off of food bank staples and wear donated clothes. What she wouldn't have given in those days for just one meal in a restaurant. Hell, she went to restaurants for most of her meals these days.

She should be more thankful. She shouldn't have let herself forget those times. She shouldn't let it hurt so bad to think about Morgan being able to go home for family meals when she was in college. Granny Reeves had been around for a while, and even after she died, Shelby had been lucky sometimes. Sometimes she'd had a bestie or a girlfriend who brought her home for the big holidays. Still, it was never quite the same. The way they smiled at their parents or teased their siblings. At the time, Shelby had been so jealous that she'd had to bite her cheek not to cry when she saw that stuff. She liked to pretend it didn't bother her anymore, but she couldn't fool herself like that. Some wounds never really healed, they just grew more and more layers of scar tissue.

That train of thought was certainly not going to pull her out of her melancholy mood. Shaking out her shoulders, she headed back over to the bookshelves to snoop. She'd already thoroughly examined the novels on offer, but there were a few shelves that didn't hold old *New York Times* bestsellers. Kneeling in front of the far shelf, she found stacks of slightly battered jigsaw puzzle boxes and some well-worn playing cards.

"Hey, roomie." Shelby held out a puzzle box displaying some dogs playing poker in one hand and a pack of playing cards in the other. "Which is more your style?"

Morgan was leaning against the counter, drying the last plate. She squinted in Shelby's direction, so focused she might've been choosing between two houses to buy. After a moment of intense scrutiny—or perhaps just disgust, it was dogs playing poker after all—she shrugged. "I'm game for either."

Now that was surprising. Morgan struck her as the kind of woman who had an opinion on everything and wasn't shy about sharing it. Maybe Shelby had read her wrong. Unlikely, but stranger things had happened. Whatever the reason for this strange behavior, Shelby wasn't the type to look a gift horse in the mouth. She tossed the playing cards on the coffee table and carried the puzzle over to their little dinette.

While Morgan put away the clean dishes, Shelby peeled the top off the puzzle box and dumped the pieces out on the table.

After stowing the box away in the corner, she sat down and started spreading out the pieces.

"Where's the top with the picture?" Morgan asked. "I didn't really get a good look from across the room." She sat across from Shelby.

"Oh, you don't get to see it. The mystery is half the fun."

"Wait. We're putting the puzzle together without the picture to reference?" Morgan's eyebrows knitted together as she frowned, and the expression was so predictable it was almost comical. She'd clearly gotten over whatever wild hair made her give Shelby the power to choose their activity.

"You're a big picture gal." Shelby laughed. "I should've seen that coming."

"What's that supposed to mean?"

"Just that you should trust the process. Maybe you'll find that you're so good at puzzles you don't need the reference picture."

Morgan opened her mouth like she wanted to argue, but clearly decided against it. She turned her attention to the pieces in front of her, flipping them over so forcefully they snapped when they hit the table. She grumbled a little under her breath as she worked, but she seemed to channel her frustration into solving the puzzle, just as Shelby had predicted. With some people, a little challenge was all they needed to fall right into her hands.

In fact, as they settled into the task, the two of them worked pretty well together. Shelby had a very organized method of solving puzzles, separating the side and corner pieces from the central ones so she could focus entirely on the border. Morgan was more chaotic, and spent her time grouping similar colored pieces together, whether they were middles or edges. That process meant she was easily distracted when she found new pieces with the same colors. She spent a lot of time putting those pieces together before getting frustrated and going back to previous groups.

While she worked on the puzzle, Shelby added this new information to what she already knew about Morgan. She was indeed a big picture person, but she was easily derailed. The hyperfocus would be wonderfully helpful in her sales work, but the tendency to be distracted and frustrated would certainly work against her. Their work always had a thousand things going on at once, and it was easy to accidentally drop things if you tried to hold too many at once. It required a lot of sorting and organizing tasks and staying the course. It had taken Shelby years to work out her method of doing that efficiently.

"This would be so much easier if I knew what this big brown blob was." Morgan tossed the offending piece back into the pile in the center.

Shelby smiled but wasn't going to let Morgan bully her into cheating. Instead, she sorted a few more pieces into their correct piles. Just the way she did with her work email. Considering how flustered Morgan was getting over a simple puzzle, Shelby could tell she didn't adapt to new, unexpected situations quickly. Which probably meant she hadn't worked out a method for organizing her work either. Shelby snuck a peek across the table. Should she offer to help Morgan with that? Morgan squinted at another puzzle piece and tossed it aside, this time with a little more force than last time. Nope. She should definitely not offer to help. Morgan would most likely not take it well.

"What's the matter?" Morgan waved her hand at Shelby's side of the table. "You aren't bored with puzzling already, are you?"

It wasn't until that moment Shelby realized she'd been so distracted by analyzing Morgan that she'd stopped working on their project.

"Just thinking about work." Shelby scooped up a handful of pieces and Morgan grunted. "I'm always thinking about work, you know, but it's hard not to get worried about how behind I am after the conference."

Morgan's scowl deepened and she stared at the window. It was too dark to see the snow, but last they'd checked, it was still coming down as hard as ever. Looking at the lines deepening in Morgan's face, Shelby chastised herself for bringing it up. It was just going to cause more tension between them. Being stuck out here together and already being something of professional rivals, no good would come of focusing on work.

Shelby forced herself to laugh and waved away the topic with a flippant wave of her wrist. "We shouldn't worry about that now. We've got enough to tackle with this mystery puzzle."

Morgan didn't really relax—her shoulders remained bunched together and the lines between her eyebrows were as deep as ever—but she did focus back on the puzzle and Shelby would just have to take that as a win.

Chapter Eleven

"I don't think I can keep my eyes open another minute." Shelby punctuated the remark with a wide yawn. "You're going to hassle me about wanting to sleep on the sofa again, aren't you?"

Morgan smiled, knowing she'd earned the mistrust. Then she steeled her nerves. "Actually, I am, but not for the reason you think."

"Oh?"

"That sofa. Well, truth is, it isn't a sofa, it's a torture device."

"Really? It's a very effective disguise." Shelby leaned her chin on her hand and gave Morgan a cheeky grin.

Morgan cleared her throat and felt heat rising in her cheeks. "It's too short, even for me. I barely slept last night."

"Oh no, I'm sorry."

She really did look it, which only made the heat rise higher in Morgan's cheeks. "I was wondering how you would feel about sharing the bed?"

"Of course."

There wasn't a moment of hesitation and that made Morgan feel like a Grade A jerk. Despite her dubious associates, it was clear Shelby was a thoughtful person. Once again, Morgan was faced with the possibility her initial impressions of Shelby had been off the mark. Sure, she was friends with dirtbags and sure she wasn't always genuine in her interactions, but she hadn't spared a moment to worry about her own discomfort in order to relieve Morgan's.

Not that Morgan was overly comfortable with the idea of sleeping next to Shelby. She'd spent half the day weighing losing sleep versus the potential dangers of sleeping in the same bed as Shelby. Especially after their awkward encounter that morning. In fact, every time Morgan thought about sleeping next to Shelby, all she could think of was the glistening, sumptuous curves of Shelby's naked body.

"We can line up pillows between us," Morgan said in a rush. "Maybe I should sleep on top of the covers. Bring the blanket from the couch or something. Or we could sleep head-to-foot. Whatever would make you more comfortable."

Shelby's laughter cut through her babbling and that did nothing to help the burning on her cheeks. "I'd rather not wake up with your big toe in my eye, thanks. And it's way too cold for you to sleep above the covers. I'm sure I can trust you to behave yourself. Unless it's me you don't trust?"

"I trust you." Honestly, the twinkle in Shelby's eye was making Morgan distinctly nervous.

"Great. Then let's go to bed. I'm exhausted." Without another word, Shelby headed back to the bedroom. Morgan was slower to follow, thinking it would give Shelby a chance to get ready for bed in private, but there was only so much puttering she could do in the living room. She grabbed the blanket from the sofa and brought it with her just in case Shelby changed her mind.

Considering that neither of them had their usual toiletries, they didn't linger in the bathroom. Morgan used her full bladder as an excuse to close the door between them long enough to catch her breath. While she was in there, she removed her bra and the flannel shirt. It wasn't too weird to sleep in a T-shirt and sweatpants, especially in a cold winter cabin.

Morgan prayed that Shelby would already be under the covers when she emerged, and her hopes were realized. Somehow that didn't make it less awkward for her to shuffle around to her side of the bed and crawl under the covers. Shelby didn't exactly watch her every movement, but she didn't look away either. Morgan focused on not focusing on the fact that Shelby slept on the right side of the bed and Morgan always slept on the left. Not that it mattered that they were compatible sleepers.

"Good night." Shelby switched off the bedside lamp.
"Good night," Morgan whispered into the darkness.

❖

Morgan woke up—or rather finally gave up trying to sleep—early the next morning. To her surprise, she'd fallen asleep after only a few minutes obsessing over Shelby's body heat beside her. Unfortunately, she was wide awake just two hours later, staring at the ceiling, a thousand worries chasing themselves through her head. As usual, nine hundred ninety-nine of those worries were about work. Worrying how many potential clients she'd lost because she couldn't respond to their emails. Wondering how many hours she'd have to spend next week making up for all this lost time.

She usually forced herself to stop work at seven every night during the week. It wasn't so much a decision she'd consciously made, but a biological imperative her body forced on her. She just crashed after so many hours working. Especially since she always treated Sunday as if it was just another workday. So she followed her body's demands to stop work each night because her quality of work suffered so much if she didn't.

This coming week, though, she'd just have to find a way to power through. She didn't have any other choice. Worse, the longer they were stuck out here, the more hours she would have to put in making up for it. She would have to suffer a little bit now or else she would never recover.

Slipping out of bed and tiptoeing out of the room, she wondered if that ship had already sailed. She'd missed Friday and now she wasn't going to be able to work Sunday, either. If they weren't rescued soon, would the mountain of past due work be insurmountable?

She closed the bedroom door silently behind her and crossed straight to the living room window. It was too dark to see outside and figure out if the snow had finally stopped. She'd have to go outside to really know. After checking the wood stash next to the low burning fire, she realized she'd have to go outside anyway. The last thing they needed was for the fire to go out.

Being as quiet as possible, Morgan pulled open the front door and slipped out onto the porch. The cold smacked her like a punch the moment she was outside. Her face immediately started to ache at the sharp slice of winter, and each breath burned her lungs.

Still, she could handle the cold since she was buoyed by the unmistakable fact that the snow had finally stopped. The pre-dawn was completely silent. Even the wind had stopped blowing. The only problem, as her stinging cheeks reminded her, was that it wasn't warm enough to melt any of that snow. In fact, the deep freeze might create a layer of ice on top of the snowpack, making travel even more treacherous.

Would their crashed car be visible from the road? And would anyone even use that winding backroad any time soon? It hadn't seemed like a well-used path. If it had been, there would certainly have been a guardrail at that dangerous curve to keep people from driving off it during a snowstorm. Of course, they wouldn't even have been on the road at all if Shelby hadn't distracted her with her damn music while she was driving.

Morgan closed her eyes and took a deep breath. Her hand slipped into her pocket and wrapped around the stone without conscious thought. After a moment, her heart rate slowed and some of her panic and anger receded. It wasn't fair to blame Shelby. She hadn't been driving. She hadn't insisted on ignoring the directions and turning onto that winding road. She probably wouldn't admit it to Shelby any time soon, but she could admit it to herself. The crash had been her fault. The only thing Morgan could do was try to fix it.

After grabbing a large armful of wood, Morgan went back inside. She stoked the fire before heading purposefully into the kitchen. She couldn't control the weather or the state of the roads, but she could make them a good breakfast. Of course, a good breakfast would be hard to achieve with the slim pickings in their pantry. Shelby had certainly been right about it being basic.

Morgan wasn't keen on living off cans of condensed soup and SPAM. They were going to have to do something about being rescued. There had to be some way to help themselves in this situation, right? Maybe they couldn't walk out of this forest on their own, but they could figure out a way to shorten the odds on help finding them.

While Morgan was making oatmeal, Shelby emerged from the bedroom. Her hair was tousled, but her eyes were remarkably clear for someone who hadn't had any coffee yet. Clearer even than Morgan's and she'd stepped into the icebox outside to help her wake up. The tousled hair was cute though. So was the soft smile and the way she hugged herself around the middle.

Morgan turned back to the stove and told herself to get a grip. She didn't like Shelby with her mystery puzzles and her shady sales practices. It didn't matter how cute her smile was first thing in the morning, Morgan could never respect a woman like that.

It wasn't until she'd served them both oatmeal and coffee that Morgan realized how quiet Shelby was being this morning. In fact, she hadn't actually said anything yet, and that was not like her. She didn't seem upset. Her eyes weren't puffy and she was eating just fine. So what was the deal?

"Are you okay?" Morgan finally asked.

Shelby lit up like a Christmas tree. "I'm great, thanks."

"Why are you being so quiet then?"

"Oh, well, it seemed like you were in your head this morning. I didn't want to interrupt." Shelby pulled up her knee and tucked it against her shoulder, then sat back and sipped her coffee. Her gaze didn't linger on Morgan and she didn't push. As much as Morgan wanted to be mad at her, she couldn't deny it was actually really nice that Shelby was giving her space. How strange.

"I was in my head. Thanks for giving me time there," Morgan said.

"You're welcome."

Something about the gentle, unassuming way Shelby accepted her thanks made Morgan feel like a real jerk. Or maybe it was the memory of how she had acted the night before. So they had different ways of solving puzzles. Why had she taken it as a challenge? Morgan sighed. This whole thing would be so much easier if Shelby didn't make her think so much. Especially about herself.

"I guess I'm thinking too much because I didn't sleep well," Morgan said.

"Shoot. Our plan to get you better sleep didn't work? Do I snore?"

"You don't know if you snore?" Morgan knew she wasn't focusing on the important part of the situation, but she couldn't help asking. She hadn't expected Shelby to blush like a schoolgirl.

"I guess I haven't had anyone in the position to tell me." She shot a shy glance at Morgan. "Not recently anyway."

Morgan tucked the interesting tidbit away for later. "Rest assured, you don't snore. I just woke up worrying about work."

"You're going to treat this like a vacation and stop worrying about work." Shelby's smile was disarming and somehow also no-nonsense. "No arguments."

"It's not like I—"

Shelby held up a single finger, stopping Morgan's speech dead. "No arguments."

"But I—"

"Nope."

"Why won't you let me speak?"

"You can speak," Shelby said. "You can say 'that sounds like a great idea. I'll relax all day and not think about work.' If we aren't rescued, of course."

"I'm planning on the rescue."

"And if there's no rescue?" Shelby asked.

Morgan sighed and held out her hand. Shelby shook it with a self-satisfied smirk. Morgan responded with a dramatic eye roll that made Shelby laugh. They both sat back, sipping their coffee. The silence that followed as they digested their breakfast was surprisingly comfortable. When was the last time she'd shared a cup of coffee and a quiet morning with someone? She couldn't remember. Certainly not her last girlfriend, and that had been ages ago when she was still living in Richmond. Her mother would never allow a silence to continue this long, even though her conversations were almost always one-sided. Of course, her mother knew better than to expect civil conversation from Morgan before eleven a.m.

"It's not just the bad sleep," Morgan said. "I'm not much of a morning person."

"You don't say."

Shelby winked at her and all sorts of warm things happened in Morgan's chest. Instead of dwelling on those warm feelings, she decided it was time to open up a little bit.

"I spent most of my career in the lab working evening shift. Two p.m. to eleven p.m. I never got used to waking up early, even when I moved to day shift."

"Oh, that's right. I forgot you mentioned you used to work in a lab." Shelby's eyes lit up with interest.

"Yeah. I went to a big hospital chain right out of college. I did pretty much everything when I started, but I really liked microbiology, so I specialized in that when a day shift position opened up."

"What made you leave the lab?"

It was an innocent question, but Morgan's heart twisted and she squeezed the stone in her pocket. Maybe opening up was a bad idea. Since it was too late, she gave the easier answer. It was still true, just not the whole truth.

"I really fell in love with the Pulsar DNA Expert. It's intuitive to operate and it really freed up so much of my time so I could focus on the more complex testing. I had lots of lab tech friends who struggled with being overworked. I just wanted to be a part of getting that instrument into more labs and making my colleagues' lives easier." The words all tumbled out before she could stop them, and then it was too late and she'd been talking too long. She looked up to see Shelby smiling at her, and her first instinct was to be annoyed. Shelby was laughing at her. She thought Morgan was naive and silly, but it didn't matter. Just because she didn't care about anything but money didn't mean Morgan had to feel that way.

"That's the perfect reason to get into sales." Shelby actually sounded genuine when she said it. "I'm so glad you were able to pursue your passion. So few people get to do something they really believe in."

That had been the last thing Morgan had expected her to say, and she felt herself flush from the compliment. Maybe Shelby wasn't as disingenuous as she appeared. Morgan smiled back at her, and it felt real. Not the tacked-on smile she had to use so often at work. It was nice and almost made her forget her worries from the morning.

Shelby hopped up and grabbed their empty bowls. "I call dibs on the reading chair."

❖

At lunchtime on Sunday, Shelby read the last page of her chosen novel. It was fine. The male protagonist, who had never held a gun before, had killed the last terrorist even though at least ten seasoned federal agents had failed to do so. He had gone home with the woman who was so far above him on the hotness and coolness scale that they weren't even breathing the same air. The president had shown up in his backyard to thank him for his service to the country. It was all so predictable and ridiculous, but she had enjoyed every cheesy second of it.

Mostly Shelby had enjoyed the book because it was the first time in a long time she had actually finished reading a book. It might have been the first time since that literature class she'd taken in college, she couldn't quite remember. She always had good intentions. She would pick something up from the local bookstore around the corner from her condo—usually around Christmas time when she had a few guaranteed days off work—and she would start reading. But she never finished the books before it was time to go back to work. Something would distract her, and the book would sit on her nightstand, half finished, for a few months until it joined the collection of abandoned books on her bookshelf.

In this cabin, however, there were no distractions. There wasn't that one more email. Her phone wasn't ringing at all hours. It wasn't closing in on budget time for the government, when they would release cash to the labs who would then have to snap up an instrument quick before some dispute in Congress took the money away again. Here there was only her, a roaring fire, cheap bourbon, and an endless supply of Earl Grey tea bags. And Morgan.

As though she could hear her thoughts, Morgan looked up from her position splayed out across the tiny couch. She waved toward Shelby's closed book with her own and asked, "Finished?"

"Yep."

"How was it?"

"Fine I guess. Heavy on the testosterone, but most books are, right?" Shelby shrugged.

"Not the ones I read, but it's not like we have a ton of options here."

"What do you normally read?"

Morgan pushed herself up so her neck wasn't at such an awkward angle. "I still like a good procedural and a romance every now and then, but only ones with queer women."

"That would be amazing. This book would've been five hundred percent better if the dashing hero was a dyke." Her mental image of the hero shifted with surprising ease to a butch lesbian. She would give anything to have read that book over the last two days. "Next time we get stranded, we should break into a lesbian bookworm's cabin."

Shelby held her breath, waiting for Morgan to clam up and grumble. She was so easily offended that any offhand comment could send her into a tailspin. She didn't scowl at Shelby, though. There was a moment of hesitation, but it was followed by a charming, almost self-deprecating smile that sat well on her sharp features.

"I'll keep that in mind next time," Morgan said.

It seemed foolhardy to push her luck, so Shelby got up and made them both a cup of tea. While she waited for the water to boil, she stared out the little kitchen window, hoping every moment to see a park ranger striding purposefully through the trees toward them. Heck, she'd even be grateful if it was a cop, here to arrest them for breaking and entering. After all, there would be a working phone at the local jail.

The kettle whistling drew her attention and she busied herself with the process of making tea. Two mugs in hand, Shelby returned to the couch. Morgan seemed happy enough to toss her book aside to sip her tea even though she was nearly finished.

"I'm surprised you haven't read any sapphic books." Morgan blew the steam from the rim of her mug. "It's so cool to see people like me in the books I read."

"Honestly, I don't read that much."

"Really? As quick as you read that one, I figured you loved to read."

"I do love reading, I just don't get a lot of time. Work, you know?"

Morgan grunted as her reply, which might've been because she was drinking tea or might've been because she wanted to avoid talking about work.

"Maybe it's because I'm reading books about boys, though. Do you read a lot?"

"Not as much as I used to." Morgan was quiet so long Shelby thought she was done talking for the day, but she finally said, "I used to read during my lunch break at the hospital. We had our own breakroom in the lab so it was usually empty and I could focus."

"What's a lunch break?"

Shelby couldn't but help laugh and Morgan joined her. "Yeah, I haven't had one since I moved up here."

The mood was souring again, and Shelby didn't want that. Morgan was cold and sometimes rude, but there seemed to be an interesting person underneath all that. If she could pull Morgan out of her shell, maybe they could find a way to get along. She remembered the way Morgan came to life when she talked about wanting to help other lab techs with better instruments. Maybe that was the way in.

"Tell me what it's like in the lab. What do lab techs do?" Shelby asked.

"You're in labs all the time, aren't you? You don't know what we do?" Morgan's eyebrows had come together again, and Shelby couldn't tell if she was being defensive or if she was offended.

"I usually only get to talk to the lab directors," Shelby said. Morgan scowled even deeper at that. "If I'm lucky, I meet the head of the microbiology department since that's the group that uses our instrument. But there are other departments in the lab and I don't know anything about them. I'm curious is all."

For a moment, she thought Morgan wouldn't answer. After all, she'd been standoffish since they'd met, but Shelby had hoped her obvious excitement about her work and her affection for her old colleagues would win out, and they did.

"You know lab techs do all the scientific testing on the blood and urine samples doctors collect?" Morgan asked.

Shelby nodded in encouragement. "I'm squeamish about blood, but I know that's what labs work with. You don't have to do that, do you?" Shelby asked.

"Sometimes. All lab techs can draw blood, but we're—they're usually needed to run the tests, so nurses or phlebotomists draw the blood."

Morgan was definitely starting to warm up. This was where Shelby shined. Her ability to draw people out of their shells by showing interest in their interests. Most of the time she used that skill to improve her sales chances. It was nice to use it now without ulterior motives.

"But if I had a blood-drawing emergency, you could step in, right?"

Morgan smiled and even blushed a little which was honestly really cute. "I could but you probably wouldn't want me to. I've never been a big fan of needles, no matter what side of them I was on."

"Morgan Allen, afraid of needles?" Shelby pretended to be shocked and she laid it on pretty thick.

"My one vulnerability."

Morgan was smiling now, and her voice carried a hint of laughter. It looked good on her. Humor looked good on her. She had carried this air of superiority since Shelby had met her. It occurred to her that it might have been bravado. Acting the part of the confident, too-cool-for-school loner as a defense mechanism. The realization made Shelby all the more interested in getting to know the real Morgan.

"Lab techs are essential in the medical field." Morgan's tone was serious again. "Over eighty percent of diagnoses involve at least one laboratory test. We save lives."

"But no one knows. As far as most people know, doctors and nurses are the only ones working in hospitals. Meanwhile y'all are doing this important work."

"Exactly." Morgan sat up now and her eyes had that fire of pride in them.

As Shelby suspected, this was the way to get to know the real Morgan. It wasn't even flattery. Just interest in work that was clearly important to her. Truth be told, Shelby knew most of what Morgan had said already. When she first started at Ashworth, she sold centrifuges and similar generic lab equipment, so she knew the basics about how labs functioned. She'd only moved into the specialized equipment at the start of COVID. Still, it never hurt to let people explain their passions. There was always something new to be learned. And today Shelby had learned that Morgan was proud of her field of study and cared deeply about the work she'd done. She'd also learned that getting to know Morgan was worth fighting through the prickly exterior.

Chapter Twelve

Morgan's sleep wasn't much better Sunday night than it had been the previous two. It helped that she wasn't trying to sleep with her knees practically tucked under her chin. The couch was so short she'd never been able to truly get comfortable, but it also smelled like musty old cabin furniture. The bed, however, carried the lingering aroma of lavender and some other, indescribable scent that clung to Shelby. Morgan couldn't quite figure out how Shelby managed to smell so good when they were stuck in an old man's cabin that probably hadn't been aired out since the first Clinton administration.

Then there was the unmistakable warmth of another body in the bed. Shelby had the annoying habit of falling asleep the moment her head hit the pillow. There was the benefit of her not staying up all night, chattering away in the dark like the other players on teenage Morgan's traveling softball team. The disadvantage was the feel of her there, her breath slow and even and making Morgan feel safe and terrified at the same time. She only told herself it was an accident when she shifted enough on the bed that her pinky finger rubbed against Shelby's arm. Then there was an almost overwhelming urge to reach out further. To pull Shelby's body toward her, to run her hand along the plane of her stomach, to wrap her tightly against her body and fall asleep with Shelby curled against her. Morgan had to clench her teeth and fight the urge. She had to squeeze her eyes shut and tell herself not to move. Eventually, the urge passed, but only because she fell into a deep sleep.

Unfortunately, that sleep had included some dreams about Shelby that she did not want to admit having, even to herself. Not when she woke up, her body dangerously close to Shelby's, and not while she was sitting at the little cafe table, so close that their elbows were almost touching as they worked on that silly puzzle.

Despite frequent breaks to fret over not being rescued yet, they were almost finished with the puzzle. Now that it was so close to completion, Morgan could see it was a ridiculous scene of dogs playing poker. Honestly, if she'd known this was the image they were working on from the start, she might have decided against the puzzle altogether. It was silly and not her style at all. She was glad she'd gone ahead with it, though. She'd had a surprisingly good time watching the scene materialize in front of her as they constructed the puzzle. She probably wouldn't have enjoyed herself half as much if she'd known the goal from the start. She admitted—to herself only, of course—that Shelby's method of solving puzzles actually made it more fun.

"I miss real food." Shelby settled a large piece into place that revealed the basset hound in the foreground had a full house. "I know it's only been three days, but I'm already getting sick of canned food and oatmeal."

They'd eaten the last of their gas station sandwiches for lunch the day before. Even though the bread had gone both soggy and stale, there was at least lettuce on them. Now they were down to the contents of the pantry and half a bag of pork rinds. As far as Morgan was concerned, the pork rinds were worse than canned peas, so she couldn't help but agree with Shelby.

"Me too."

"What's your favorite food?" Shelby asked.

"Italian."

Shelby set another piece into place and then turned away from the puzzle. She settled her chin onto the heel of her hand and squinted over at Morgan. It would've felt like interrogation a couple days ago, but Morgan had come to see that Shelby got this weirdly intense focus when she asked other people about themselves. It was like an alien scientist studying humans for the first time, but somehow it wasn't as unsettling as it should have been.

"Too generic," Shelby said. "What's the specific meal you love more than any other? Your favorite food memory."

"Food memory?"

"You know that meal that you'll never forget the taste of or how it made you feel."

"I don't know that I have one." Now Morgan was starting to squirm. Not because Shelby was making her uncomfortable, but because she suddenly wondered if she'd ever had a meal she would remember like that. Was she supposed to? Did other people have those memories and she was the only one who didn't? "What about you? Do you have one?"

"Sarah's Empanadas."

"Beg pardon?"

"Sarah's Empanadas." Shelby's face took on a faraway expression like she was talking about an ex-lover. "It's in Raleigh, North Carolina, and it's absolutely divine. You wouldn't think so to drive up to it. It's in this little strip mall in the middle of nowhere and it's got cheap particle board tables and those plastic cafeteria chairs."

That dreamy look didn't mix with the description Shelby gave. If Morgan had been forced to guess, she would think Shelby's favorite restaurant would be one of those steak places where all the prices were listed as "market" or a French place that served snails and foie gras. Of course, that image of Shelby had been formed before she knew how poor she'd been in her twenties. Maybe plastic cafeteria chairs made a little more sense now.

"They have all these wonderful, unexpected flavors of empanadas. Like Cuban sandwich and shrimp and grits. And you can get them frozen to go, too." Shelby tapped her fist on the table like she'd made up her mind. "When we get out of here, first thing I'm doing is driving down to Raleigh with a big cooler and getting a dozen of each flavor to fill my freezer."

The conviction was adorable, especially considering she was talking about strip mall frozen empanadas. Morgan laughed and said, "I can't believe you're already thinking about getting back into a car after what we've been through."

"I'm a jump right back onto the horse after you fall off kind of gal." Shelby's eyes locked on her, and Morgan's breath caught. Her eyes flashed like sapphires catching the sunset and her lips curved up tantalizingly slowly. It should be illegal to have that sort of sexy, captivating confidence. "You'd understand if you'd had Sarah's Empanadas." Shelby's voice was low, almost sultry, almost like she was flirting, which was ridiculous. Shelby didn't have any more interest in Morgan than Morgan had in her.

Still, Morgan couldn't help test how far Shelby would take this. "I'll have to give them a try." Morgan matched Shelby's tone.

"Maybe I should invite you over to give you a taste."

Morgan's blood thundered in her ears. Had Shelby really said that? Had she meant it the way she made it sound? Because it definitely sounded suggestive.

"I'm surprised you would want to spend more time with me after this," Morgan said.

"Actually, I'm enjoying our time together very much." Shelby's lips curled up at the corners and there was a hint of color in her cheeks that hadn't been there before. "Are you enjoying it?"

Morgan's stomach did a funny little lurch, and it was possible her hands were sweating in her lap. What was going on here? Shelby couldn't really be enjoying this, could she? For a moment Morgan was sure it wasn't possible, but then she realized she was, in fact, enjoying herself. Flirting aside, she was having a great time reading and relaxing and she was definitely happy she wasn't here alone, but it wasn't just not being alone. It was being here with Shelby. Especially flirty Shelby.

She shouldn't enjoy that. There was no way Shelby really wanted her. And her own physical reactions didn't mean anything. She was stuck alone with nothing to do with an objectively gorgeous woman. Of course, her mind went to places it shouldn't. Boredom led to lust for a lot of people, and that was all this was. Without the cabin fever element, Shelby would never think twice about her and her own stomach would be thoroughly un-butterflied.

The question had hung between them too long unanswered, but Morgan didn't trust her voice. She nodded and Shelby's smile turned from seductive to wide and friendly in a heartbeat.

"Glad to hear it," Shelby said.

Shelby turned her attention back to the puzzle and Morgan finally released her breath. Her body settled down and she congratulated herself on correctly reading the situation. It was just a teasing exchange, nothing she needed to further analyze.

"I'm more of a cat person than a dog person," Shelby said. "But I wouldn't mind a dog who could win me some cash in a poker game."

Morgan laughed unsteadily, but she was starting to get herself under control. "My luck I'd adopt the Labrador who's all in on a pair of sixes."

"You do have pretty rotten luck."

"My mom always said better bad luck than none at all."

"My grandmother said that, too," Shelby said. "But I think she'd sing a different tune if the family dog blew her paycheck on poker games."

They joked and chatted as the sun slowly sank outside, and Morgan welcomed the distraction from her body's confusing reactions to Shelby.

❖

On Tuesday morning, Morgan started pacing the cabin as soon as they finished breakfast. Shelby washed the dishes and inventoried the pantry just so she could distract herself from Morgan's frenetic energy.

Unfortunately, the dishes were clean long before Morgan's anxiety waned. In fact, as the morning wore on, it seemed like her energy only got more frantic. By ten o'clock, the pacing was setting Shelby's teeth on edge. When Morgan marched into the kitchen for the fifth time to pull the curtain aside and look out into the woods, Shelby'd had enough.

"Will you please relax?" Shelby slapped her book on the coffee table to emphasize the demand.

"Relax?" Morgan's voice went to falsetto, sending another spike of annoyance through Shelby's nerves. "How am I supposed to relax when we've been stuck here for four days?"

"It hasn't been four full days."

"Fine. Three and a half. Does that make you feel better?"

"I would feel better if you relax," Shelby said. She knew it was a bad idea to tell anyone, particularly someone who was stressed, to relax, but she couldn't help it. Her fretting wasn't helping. In fact, it was making the whole situation ten times worse.

"I would feel better if I could get out of here, so I guess we'll both be disappointed." Morgan stormed out onto the deck, slamming the front door behind her.

"I guess I deserve that," Shelby said to the empty living room.

But honestly, it was just too annoying for Morgan to freak out like this. Sure, the situation was bad and probably getting worse with each day they were trapped, but panicking wasn't going to help them. They had to remain calm or they'd do something stupid and that could lead to a real disaster. They had a roof over their head, a heat source, and food. Things could be a lot worse.

To Shelby's annoyance, the creak of the porch floorboards proved that Morgan hadn't stopped her pacing, she'd just taken it outside. Shelby knew she was looking for someone to rescue them, as though her presence on the porch would somehow make that more likely. As though they had any power in this situation at all.

Now Shelby was freaking out just as bad as Morgan, so she hopped up off the couch and went into the kitchen. Preparing food had always done wonders in calming her down, and today was no different. The moment she set about making them a snack of peanuts, raisins, and oyster crackers, her nerves settled. She was able to stop focusing on the sounds of Morgan futzing around outside as she turned her attention to boiling water for tea.

Morgan came back into the cabin. "I don't hear or see anything."

Shelby bit back her sarcastic comment and continued making their snack. Soon she could hear Morgan settling more firewood into the rack by the hearth. She'd almost thought Morgan had taken the hint, but then Morgan continued, her voice still unnaturally high.

"I'm worried the car is buried in the snow. I think I should go uncover it and maybe walk down the road a bit to see if I can find help."

An icy hand of fear gripped Shelby's heart. There were so many ways that could go terribly wrong it was laughable to even consider it.

"That's a really bad idea, Morgan."

"You have a better idea?" Morgan glared at her across the counter.

"Yes, we stay inside where we're safe until rescue comes."

"But if they can't see the car, it will never come."

Now she was just being ridiculous. "The snow will melt eventually and they know we're missing by now. We just have to be patient."

"For how long?" Morgan was shouting now, setting Shelby's teeth right back on edge.

"For as long as it takes." Shelby tried not to shout, but Morgan was being so difficult it was hard to contain her anger. "Your coat isn't thick enough to be outside that long and you don't have the right shoes."

"There's a pair of rain boots in the utility room."

"They're way too big for you. It wouldn't be safe to climb the hill at the crash site in those." Shelby took a deep breath, but it wasn't helping. She tried to be calm. "Be reasonable, please."

"How is it reasonable to just sit here all fucking winter, waiting for people who don't know we're here?"

"You're just being impatient. Calm down before you make everything worse."

The silence that followed those words was deafening. She could actually see Morgan puffing up with anger. If she was honest, Shelby knew why Morgan was angry and even agreed it was a rude and dismissive thing to say, but she was well past caring what Morgan thought right now.

"Stop telling me to relax," Morgan said in frighteningly even tones.

Shelby came so close to pointing out that she'd told her to calm down this time, not relax, but was able to stop herself at the last moment. It might have been the wisest decision she'd ever made in her life, but it wasn't the start of a trend. Shelby couldn't seem to stop herself from saying things that would make it worse. "Well, your attitude isn't very helpful."

"You're the one with the attitude. You've been snippy with me all day."

"That's because you've been like this all day and I can't deal with your anxious energy."

"God forbid Shelby Lynn Howard has to deal with anything other than herself," Morgan said.

"You see, this is what I'm talking about. You're just so bullheaded and you don't listen to anyone else's opinions. It's not the sort of attitude people like and that's what's holding you back at work."

As soon as the words were out of her mouth, Shelby wished she could take them back. Sure, she'd thought things like that about people before, but she would never throw it in their face. If she was generous and friendly with the person, she might find a kind way to steer them toward the conclusion on their own so they could adjust, but she was neither of those things with Morgan. Rather than being helpful, her words could only be hurtful.

After a long moment of staring daggers at Shelby, Morgan said, "That was way out of line."

"I shouldn't have said it like that."

"You shouldn't have said it at all. You don't know me and you never will."

Shelby had been all set to concede the point and apologize, but the acid in Morgan's voice didn't sit well. Instead of backing off, she slammed her fists onto her hips and doubled down. "Of course, I know you. You make everything so obvious and I'm very good at reading people. That's why I'm so successful in sales."

"You're successful in sales because you lie and put on a facade. You succeed by pretending to be someone you're not. Is there a single person in your life who knows the real you? Is there a real you or just a chameleon who does whatever she has to do to make a buck?"

Morgan had yelled the reply, but that wasn't what made Shelby's ears ring and her heart race. She had never, in her whole life, put on a facade. She knew for damn sure because she had achingly personal knowledge of the damage done when people tried to save face. How dare Morgan stand there and pretend like her greatest strength was a weakness? Not only a weakness but a despicable, horrible action. Maybe Shelby had started this by getting too personal, but Morgan had taken it way over the line.

"Caring about other people and their feelings enough to get to know them is not putting on a facade. How dare you?"

"How dare I?" Morgan's face was red and her teeth were bared. Her anger had turned her wild and Shelby was glad she was showing her true colors for once. "I'm not the one who shows every person she meets a different face. You want to talk about my faults, why don't you look at your own?"

"Oh, I'm well aware of my faults, but you refuse to see yours and I know why," Shelby said.

"Oh please, enlighten me. Since you know so much about me."

"You're sabotaging yourself."

That clearly caught Morgan off guard, she'd already opened her mouth to yell back, but the words she spoke next were obviously not what she had intended to say. "I'm what?"

"You're sabotaging yourself." Shelby felt such a savage self-righteousness. This fight had been a long time coming. "You're not letting yourself succeed. You're giving yourself an escape route because what you really want is to go back to the lab where you make less money but you feel safe."

"Safe? Are you serious?"

"The lab is protected. You can sit in your little breakroom and read your little books and let the doctors and nurses have the hard conversations. In the lab you never have to make yourself vulnerable and have uncomfortable conversations like you do in sales. You want back there so bad you'd be willing to tank your own career for a little safety."

"Uncomfortable conversations? You think that's what this is about? You have no idea why I got into sales." Morgan's eyes were wild and she whipped her hand out of her pocket, her fist gripped tight, and waved her fist at Shelby. "You want to know how safe it is in the lab? Let me tell you about my friend Gail."

Anger still burned hot in Shelby's chest, but the non sequitur threw her. She didn't say a word, but just blinked at Morgan and waited.

"Gail loved the lab. She loved science and solving mysteries. Most of all she loved people. She loved the other techs and the way she could mentor us all, but she loved the patients more. Even though she rarely met any of them, she remembered their names. Every tube of blood that came through our doors was a chance for her to save someone's life."

The last words came out on a choked sob and Morgan opened her clenched fist. Shelby could just see the stone nestled in the center of her palm, but the pale pink faded into the color of her skin, and she held it less like a stone and more like an egg whose shell might crack at any moment.

"When COVID hit, Gail was in her element. She would tell us how the rest of the world would know what lab techs did once the first tests came out." Morgan sat down hard in the dining room chair, her eyes fixed on the stone in her palm and tears building walls around her eyelids. "Our hospital scrambled to buy an instrument that had a COVID test, but inventory was decimated. We didn't know what we were going to do, and then your buddy Eric showed up."

There was a burning hatred in Morgan's eyes when she glared at Shelby, and it turned her blood to ice.

"He was so good at those—what did you call them—uncomfortable conversations? Even wearing a mask, Gail and I knew he was grinning like the Cheshire Cat. And he made promises. Oh, the promises he made. We thought they were too good to be true, but not our boss. No, Hazel ate it up and the next thing we knew, there it was in the lab."

Shelby's brain buzzed. She knew all too well how slick Eric was and he never let honesty get in his way. It wasn't just the disgusting sexual advances he'd made to her that made Shelby hate him. Telnet's COVID instrument was a piece of junk and everyone knew it. When their test was recalled Eric and Joshua were the least surprised.

"The minute we started using it, Gail and I knew something was off. Our positive results were too low. Lower than everyone else in the state. Eric was there all the time. Checking in. Bringing free food and Telnet swag. Every time we tried to bring it up, he just congratulated us on being the safest hospital in the area. Hazel was thrilled because the majority of the patients weren't in the isolation unit, so she could send lab techs to draw blood from the rest of the hospital.

"They cut staff almost immediately. They canceled so many surgeries and it was a for-profit hospital. They couldn't lose money by having us all around. But Gail's husband was on disability and her kids came home from college. She couldn't afford to have her hours cut, so she picked up shifts drawing blood in the wards."

Shelby tried to remember back to those early days of COVID, but it felt like a lifetime ago. She already worked from home, so she didn't get the novelty of quarantine. She'd watched *Tiger King* and worried she'd run out of toilet paper, but that was it. The fear, though. She remembered the fear. Before there were vaccines. When the world ran out of ventilators. It had been scary for her at home. How must it have been for someone who went to a hospital every day and saw all that?

"She wore her mask and sang 'Happy Birthday' when she washed her hands and she was so careful. She didn't want to get her husband sick. That's what I remember most. Her fear of getting her husband sick. That and these stones she got us." Morgan held it up and Shelby could see the word etched into its face. Strength. "She said we were important, so we had to be strong. She looked each of us in the eye and told us we could do this. We could be strong. She started coughing the next day."

That's when Morgan started to cry. Like really cry. One minute, she was speaking almost calmly considering how they'd been shouting at each other, the next moment, she was sobbing. Her whole body rocked with her tears and she clutched her hair with claw-like fingers. Then she was shouting again and Shelby's heart clenched in fear and pity.

"We got tested every day and hers were negative so she said she had walking pneumonia and kept working. Around that time your buddy Eric stopped coming in to visit. We had a skeleton staff so Gail kept working since she was negative. Picking up double shifts and she kept getting worse because she wasn't resting. On the fifth day of negative tests, Gail could barely stand. I had a friend from school at another hospital who had a Pulsar. We went after work and of course she was positive. She'd always been positive, but Eric's miracle machine sucked."

Morgan wasn't crying anymore and she wasn't angry. She was empty. So deflated it was terrible to witness, but she wasn't done with her story.

"I started researching and found out about hundreds of notifications of false negatives on the Telnet. The FDA was in the process of pulling it. I took everything to Hazel and she called Eric with me right there in her office. He said there were 'challenges' but they were being targeted. It was all crap. We ordered a Pulsar, but it was going to take a month to get it in. Gail was already on a ventilator by then. Her husband and kids never saw her again, but we did. The techs all went up to visit her, even after she was unconscious and couldn't see us through the window."

Morgan hopped up and started pacing again, the manic energy back and worse because it was mixed with those wild tears. Shelby started to worry about her then. She was spiraling and Shelby had no idea how to bring her back down.

"If we'd had the Pulsar, those patients would have been in isolation. If I'd done my research before we'd bought the machine. If I could have out-talked fucking Eric Ferguson. Gail would never have gone into those rooms. Maybe Gail would still be here. Safe in the lab? It's not fucking safe in the lab. We die and no one even knows who we are. I can't go back. I can't fail them. I can't fail Gail."

Morgan was almost hyperventilating, her breathing ragged and way too fast. Shelby's heart raced with fear for Morgan. She was so deep into her emotions Shelby worried she might not easily find her way out.

"Hey, Morgan, look—"

"No. Don't. I can't."

She whipped around, charging off down the hall toward the back of the cabin. Shelby couldn't move. Couldn't follow. She was so shocked and frightened and her heart broke for Morgan. She couldn't imagine what that had been like. Shelby hadn't known anyone who died of COVID, especially in those early, terrifying days. What Morgan had gone through would have been unbelievably traumatic, and she was carrying too much on her shoulders.

Morgan came back down the hall, shoving her arms through a second flannel shirt, the huge rain boots in her hands.

"Morgan, you can't—"

"Stop telling me what I can't do." Morgan said, her voice a low growl. "I'm not going to let fear keep me from getting rescued."

In a heartbeat, she had shoved her feet into the boots and charged out the front door with her coat over her arm. She ignored Shelby shouting at her to wait and think. She was too far gone for that. The panic rising in Shelby made her want to chase after, but how could she? Morgan had the only pair of boots, and she was terrified what would happen if they both left the cabin. What if the fire went out and they couldn't restart it when they got back? What if they couldn't even find the cabin again after they left?

No, Shelby couldn't follow. All she could do was stand by the window and watch Morgan disappear into the snowy distance.

Chapter Thirteen

Morgan found herself standing in front of the crashed rental car far sooner than she thought she would. Truth be told, she didn't remember much of the journey. She knew it was probably not the best idea to come out here while she was angry. In fact, she knew it was foolish and reckless and dangerously impulsive, but she didn't really care.

She needed to get out of that cabin. She needed to get away from her grief and her fear and the way Shelby's stare had gone from furious to pitying.

Besides, now that she was here, she'd known it was the right choice. The rental car was completely buried in snow on the side that faced the road. If she hadn't known it was around this general area, she would have looked right over it, thinking it was just part of the slope down from the road. No one driving by would have seen it. Part of Morgan wondered if anyone had already been past. Had they already missed their best chance at rescue? Her panic attack had withered in the face of the biting wind and frozen ground, but the sight of the buried car was enough to throw her right back into it.

Morgan crossed the last few yards at a full sprint and attacked the loosely packed snow blanketing the hood. She'd barely gotten down to the bright blue paint before she had to stop and cradle her wet, freezing fingers against her body. She forced herself to take a step back and think. There was no chance she could clear off the car without gloves. More than that, it was pointless to clear off the hood, which couldn't be seen from the road.

"Calm down before you make everything worse." Morgan spat the words through clenched teeth.

Of all the horrible things Shelby had said, that was the one that stung the most. Morgan knew she was being ridiculous, but to say she was making everything worse was a low blow. Well, she'd show Shelby. She would clear off the car and they would be rescued and it wouldn't be because Shelby was hiding in the cabin, too afraid to so much as lift a finger to help them. Morgan would be the hero. Morgan wouldn't stand by and watch someone die. Not again. Morgan would finally do something right.

Of course, that would require her being able to clear off the car, which wouldn't happen with bare hands. Morgan was pretty sure she had a pair of gloves in her suitcase. If not, she would wrap her hands in socks if she had to. Anything to help. Anything to be useful when people needed her.

The driver's side had been the opposite side of the wind, so it only had a shallow dusting of snow. Morgan pulled her coat sleeve down to cover her hand so she could clear off the handle, but she still had to blow warmth back into her fingers when she was done. There was a tense moment when it seemed like the door might've been frozen shut, but with a little persuasion, it finally opened.

Morgan's elation over getting the door open was short-lived. She was shocked by the state of the car's interior. Intellectually she had known they'd been lucky. Car accidents were scary when it was a fender bender in slow moving traffic. Running off the side of a snowy road and crashing down an embankment was a different story altogether.

Since she'd been rattled and knocked unconscious by the crash, Morgan hadn't taken the time to look around the car. Now that she was taking stock, she wondered how they'd managed to walk away unscathed. The deflated airbags hung from the steering wheel and dashboard like tattered clothing. A fine layer of white powder that she assumed had come from the air bags coated every surface, with only a few bare patches where their bodies had been. Telephone charging cords, napkins from their gas station haul, and a crumpled coffee cup lay in strange places at stranger angles. The windshield was a spiderweb of cracked glass, and something had knocked the rearview mirror askew. In short, it looked like a car crash in there and the view was deeply unsettling.

Morgan swallowed down the lump of fear in her throat and averted her eyes from the mess. It took her longer than she would have liked to find the lever to pop the trunk. The trunk popping open sprayed a fine mist of powdery snow into the air. Far worse than disturbing the snow, the force of the trunk opening disturbed the car. With a loud crunch, the car shifted position, sliding a few inches down the slope. It settled again almost immediately, but Morgan couldn't say the same for her nerves. She hadn't realized until that moment how precarious the vehicle's position was. Maybe Shelby had been right and coming here had been a bad idea. She definitely did not want to be close to the car if it moved again, so she determined to get the snow off as soon as possible and get back to the cabin.

Scrambling up the bank, Morgan slipped a few times as her feet slid around in the too-large boots. Instinct made her reach out more than once to balance herself against the car, but she thought better of it. In the end, she had to scramble part of the way on hands and knees, which only made her clothes and skin wetter and colder.

When she got to the top of the hill, she was faced with an even greater problem. Despite being able to see her suitcase wedged into the trunk, the angle of the car where it had tipped over the roadside made it nearly impossible for her to reach it. She could grab it easily if she leaned most of her body weight on the back bumper, but she didn't dare do that after the car's previous shift of position. It was simply too dangerous. No matter how much she stared at the bag, however, she couldn't come up with a way to grab it.

Morgan shuffled forward a few steps, awkwardly searching for the drop-off with her massive rain boots. She leaned over at the waist, pushing her butt high into the air in an attempt to grab the bag. She was almost there. Her fingertips were inches away from the handle. Scooting forward another couple steps, she reached again. This time her fingers closed around the padded fabric handle at the top of her suitcase.

Taking a long breath of triumph, Morgan steeled herself. She couldn't lose focus now. Not when she was so close. She tightened her grip on the suitcase handle and tried to pull. Unfortunately, her body was so awkwardly positioned and so overextended that she didn't have the leverage to yank the suitcase out of the trunk.

Knowing the moment before victory was often the most precarious, Morgan was more careful than ever scooting first one foot, then the other forward. Shockingly, she found there was still undeniably solid ground beneath her feet. After bending her knees and adjusting her grip on the bag, Morgan gave an almighty yank to dislodge the suitcase from the trunk.

That's when everything went wrong. Morgan heard the snow beneath her left boot crunch and break away. Then she felt it slide out from under her. The fall felt like it took half a second and an hour all at once the way everything slowed down and sped up. Her right foot flew out from underneath her as her momentum carried her body down. Multiple impacts sent brief bursts of pain throughout her limbs. First her calf smashing into the bumper, then her ribs hitting the curve of the slope, then one arm against the side panel.

The one that hurt the most—the one that mattered—was the searing, stabbing pain when her left foot caught on the back tire while the rest of her body continued tumbling down the hill. Her body jerked to a halt and she heard a pop followed by a blinding flash of pain from her ankle. But the pain didn't stop. She was hanging halfway down the hill, her body weight pulling on her trapped ankle and with each second that passed, the pain magnified and magnified until it was almost unbearable.

Morgan let out a primal scream like no noise she'd ever made before. She refused to look at her leg, but she knew the trapped ankle was twisting it at an unnatural angle. She had to free her foot to make the pain stop, but no matter how she scrambled and jerked and rolled, she couldn't get it to come free. All she could do was change the character of both her pain and her scream.

Just at the moment she thought things couldn't get any worse, the car shifted again. All her flailing was making it slide down the hill of snow. She thought she'd been frightened before, but nothing compared to the absolute terror that gripped her as the car slipped another inch, the back side tilting toward her. She was literally pulling the car down on herself and, if she didn't get out of here, she would be crushed beneath it at any moment.

She lost all track of time and thought. Pulling frantically at her leg and screaming with each new burst of pain, all she managed to do was get her foot wedged deeper under the tire. That and she managed to make the car slide sideways toward her another few inches.

Where was everyone? Where was Shelby? Surely someone had heard her screaming? Someone would come and help, wouldn't they?

Snow trickled down the back of Morgan's neck and the shocking cold finally snapped her out of it. She forced herself to stop screaming and grit her teeth through the pain. Holding herself still, she was able to take a deep breath and think. She was like a fox caught in a hunting trap. The more she struggled, the tighter it clamped around her leg. If she wasn't calm, she might do something stupid like chew her own leg off.

After a few deep breaths, she was able to think straight. She needed to get her body weight off her foot because that pressure was keeping it trapped under the tire. Her path to freedom was clear, but it would hurt. She knew that. It would hurt and it might not work.

Morgan took another slow breath and then allowed herself to cry. She slipped deep into her fear and her pain and let herself feel every inch of it. She let herself cry for her bad luck and her stupidity and her humiliation. She let herself feel all of it now so she wouldn't have to feel it later, and it felt really good to let herself be sad and angry without anyone watching or judging. Then she closed all that emotion and self-pity in a box and snapped the lid on tight.

Dragging herself up to a sitting position didn't hurt as much as she thought it would. Her fingers were so numb with cold now that she didn't even feel it when she wedged them against the snow under her butt. She took three quick breaths, then a slow breath, then she pushed herself up on her hands and kicked her trapped leg up the hill. It popped free easily and she rolled the rest of the way down the hill until she was at the bottom with her face planted in the snow.

Lying face down in the snow seemed like a good idea, so she stayed there for a moment. Her ankle was still blindingly painful, and she didn't think she could walk on it all the way back to the cabin. She knew for certain that she couldn't stay here. There was snow inside her coat and all over her face and hands. Everything down to her underwear was wet and cold and getting colder by the minute.

Morgan knew she couldn't make it back to the cabin. Even if her ankle wasn't broken it was injured enough to make walking that far out of the question. She also knew she couldn't lie here in the snow or even climb into the car. Both options would lead to her freezing to death, alone in the middle of nowhere. She couldn't go and she couldn't stay, so what was the point? It was hopeless.

She'd almost decided to just lie there until hypothermia made the decision for her, but then a voice spoke up in her head. Normally, the voice in her head was Gail, telling her she was strong. Gail was easy to argue with because she was so obviously wrong. But the voice that popped into her head this time wasn't Gail's.

You're sabotaging yourself. You're looking for an escape route.

The sound of Shelby's voice in her head made her blood run hot with anger. Shelby acting like she knew her. Shelby possibly being right. That's what upset her so much, though, wasn't it? The possibility that Shelby had read her correctly. That she was frozen in place in her professional life because she was already convinced she'd fail and so she was afraid to try. After all, that was Morgan's instinct right now—to not even try. To lie there in the snow and slip into oblivion rather than face the possibility of trying to get back to the cabin and failing.

Well, fuck that. She wasn't going to just lie here and take it. She wasn't going to prove Shelby right. She was going to march back into that cabin and show her that Morgan Allen was not the kind of woman to lie down and take it. She was going to live just to spite Shelby.

It was easier than she thought, pushing herself up onto her hands and knees. Once she was there, it was easy enough to crawl over to the hood of the car and pull herself up until she was standing on her uninjured foot, her busted ankle hanging limply beneath her. She decided the best way to deal with the inevitable pain was to hurry through it.

She made it three steps before she fell. She clenched her teeth rather than screaming until the pain subsided. The second time she made it five steps. This time she did scream and her body begged her to give up. To lie down in the snow. After all, she had tried now. That should be enough.

"I won't let her be right about me," Morgan said.

The only way she could prove she was right was to make it back to the cabin and tell Shelby. If she couldn't walk, she could crawl. So she set out on hands and knees. Every time she put one hand in front of the other, she told herself it would be worth it to laugh in Shelby's face.

By the time she made it to the tree line, she knew she wouldn't be laughing in anyone's face. Her hands were now unbearably cold and wet. Ice was cutting into her palms and her foot was absolute agony. Her ankle had swollen so much it was pressing against her shoe, which pressed against the inside of the oversized boot.

Morgan rolled onto her butt and yanked the boot off her injured foot. The sight of her swollen ankle was shocking and she forced her numb fingers to untie the shoe and toss it aside. The release of pressure was immediately soothing, but it didn't take long for her to recognize her mistake. Her ankle was far too swollen to get the shoe back on and it was already starting to freeze in the chilly air. If she put the boot back on without the shoe, it would fill with snow and her toes could get frostbite.

Hopelessness washed over Morgan. She'd done it again. She'd made everything worse. Tears poured out of her as she scanned her surroundings. Now she was too far from the road to use the limited shelter of the car and she couldn't trek back through calf-deep snow with no protection for her foot.

How did she manage to keep doing this? No matter what she tried, she fucked it up. She was a failure in every sense of the word. Just like with her sales job and her dating life and her friendships and her family. She fucked everything up. She tried and all she ended up with was a townhouse she could never afford without the job she was a complete failure at. She made everything worse. She was halfway between her past and her future with no hope in either direction.

She let herself fall back into the snow, her arms stretched out to the side and tears running down her face. She stared at the sky full of insubstantial pale cloud and trees draped in blankets of snow. She lay there, staring at nothing, until the chill seeped into her bones and her eyes fogged over. All she could feel was the crushing weight of life's expectations on her lungs, the throb of her broken ankle, and the small, familiar weight of a stupid pink quartz stone in her pocket.

The last of her tears slipped into the corner of Morgan's mouth, then she pushed herself to her feet and hobbled off in the direction of the cabin, the boot on her injured foot quickly filling up with snow as she struggled.

Chapter Fourteen

Shelby stared out through the cabin window, watching the bright, clear daylight turn to the orange-salmon glow of evening. It would be dark soon and Morgan wasn't back. Shelby wrapped her arms tightly around herself and paced across the living room, then back to look out the window. On her third trip around the room, it registered that this was exactly what Morgan had done earlier that had so annoyed Shelby. It didn't make her stop though. Nothing would make her stop this anxious, almost frenetic pacing except Morgan walking back through that door.

Thinking back on their fight that morning, Shelby couldn't quite piece together how it had all happened. Especially since they had passed much of the previous day by flirting. She had thawed—albeit slowly, but thawed nonetheless—to Morgan in the last few days. She was even starting to think she might like Morgan. Like her more than she had liked anyone in a long time. Then Morgan had woken up nervous, jittery, and worried and Shelby hadn't been sensitive to that. Not just insensitive. She'd been a Grade A bitch with all the bells and whistles. She had practically pushed Morgan out that door and now she was the one who was nervous, jittery, and worried.

The bottom line was Morgan couldn't stay outside all night. Shelby had taken a trip out to the porch earlier for an armload of firewood and it had been frigid. Well below freezing and that was before the sun had gone down. Surely Morgan was chilled to the bone by now. Even if she was still mad at Shelby all these hours later, she couldn't possibly think it was a good idea to stay out all night in this much snow. She'd freeze out there all alone.

Suddenly, a new fear struck Shelby. What if she wasn't alone? What if she had gone to the road and had been rescued, but was so pissed at Shelby that she hadn't sent help back to the cabin? She could easily say she was the only one in the car. After all, it was only her name on the rental. She could simply tell a rescuer that she had been alone when the car crashed and leave without another thought.

Morgan wouldn't do that, would she? Sure, Shelby had been pushy and unkind that morning, but it was stress, not an unforgivable sin. Wasn't it? A voice popped into Shelby's head unbidden to remind her that other people had abandoned Shelby for far lesser sins. She squeezed her eyes shut, trying to block out the nagging voice and the fear. Morgan would come back. No matter how much of a bitch Shelby had been, Morgan wasn't that kind of person. She wasn't like Shelby's family. She was mad, but she wasn't cruel. Right?

Shelby thought back to the story Morgan had told. She was sure there was more to it, but what she did know made Shelby deflate like a two-day-old birthday balloon. Morgan wasn't out there mad. She was terrified. Terrified they'd never be rescued. Terrified she was failing at work. Terrified what that professional failure would do to her, financially and emotionally. Terrified of failing a ghost.

She should never have let Morgan go out there when she was so upset. She should have chased after her and dragged her back into the cabin. Maybe not physically—Shelby wasn't nearly strong enough to toss Morgan over her shoulder and carry her back—but she could have talked Morgan out of it. Shelby was good at talking. She was good at connecting with people.

But would Morgan have listened? After all, she thought Shelby was a two-faced liar. Morgan's voice echoed in her mind.

Is there anyone in your life who knows the real you? Is there a real you?

Even thinking the words made her cheeks burn so hot it felt like little needles pricking her face. It wasn't anger this time, though. It was shame. Was there anyone in her life she was truly honest with?

How long had it been since she'd trusted another person enough to be vulnerable with them? Maybe some of her girlfriends back when she was too young to be truly jaded, but certainly not for a very long time. She hadn't really thought about it that way before.

She's always thought she was so clever for adapting her sales style to her client, but was Morgan right? Was she doing more than adapting her sales pitch? Was she adapting her whole personality? She had to admit it wasn't just when she was making sales that she adapted to the people around her. Most of the women she picked up at Riveter's and the other lesbian bars she visited back home in DC didn't see the real her. They saw exactly what they wanted to see so she could seal the deal. Shelby cringed at the thought. It sounded really bad when she put it that way.

But she wasn't always like that. Sure, she needed to play a part when she was looking for a hookup, but that was a reasonable defense mechanism, right? And she didn't always avoid making honest connections with people. She'd been connecting with Morgan these last few days. She'd connected more—been more honest about herself and her past—with Morgan than she had been with anyone in years. Of course, that sort of proved Morgan's point and also gave her more ability to see through Shelby to the truth.

"Whatever." Shelby ran her hands through her hair and slammed a full kettle on the stove, intending to make herself a cup of tea to relax. "That's not important now."

While she waited for the water to boil, she marched back over to the window. Pressing her face to the glass, Shelby scanned the visible horizon. She'd become intimately familiar with that horizon in the last several hours, which was why she immediately spotted the distant dark shape that hadn't been there before. It was right at the edge of what she could see, and the darker it got, the harder it was to make out.

When the dark spot on the horizon moved, Shelby jumped. It had to be Morgan. It just had to be. The dark spot was alive and moving, but it was far too low to the ground. Why would Morgan be lying in the snow? She watched the far-off spot for a long time, waiting for it to get closer so she could be sure it was Morgan and not a bear. But it wasn't moving anymore. It wasn't getting any closer, it was just lying there in the snow.

"Not it, you idiot. Morgan. That's Morgan lying in the snow." Saying it out loud made the pieces click into place. She must be hurt. That's why she'd been gone so long. She hadn't abandoned Shelby by being rescued. Something had happened out there and she couldn't make it back to the cabin on her own.

"Fuck," Shelby shouted to the empty cabin. She bolted for the door, not bothering to stop and get her coat. If Morgan was hurt, she didn't have time to waste. She could have been lying in the snow for hours, just now able to drag herself close enough to be seen. She was probably halfway to hypothermia at least.

The snow was ankle deep even this close to the cabin and it slowed Shelby down. The cold bit into her arms and cheeks and snow filled her ankle boots by her third step, but she struggled on, never taking her eyes off Morgan's crumpled form. Fear seeped in as persistently as the snow, but she set it aside. All her focus was fixed on Morgan.

Shelby collapsed onto her knees at Morgan's side, and for a moment her fear got the better of her. Morgan was lying face down in the snow and she had one of her shoes in her hand. Before she took the time to wonder why Morgan had taken her shoe off, she saw how deathly white Morgan's hand was. She wasn't wearing a glove and it looked just about frozen.

When Shelby shook her, Morgan stirred and tried to push herself up. Her relief that Morgan was conscious was short-lived. She was mumbling incoherently and kept fumbling in her attempts to get to her hands and knees. Then there was the shivering. Her whole body shook like a leaf in a hurricane. Hypothermia was definitely setting in.

"Come on, we've got to get inside," Shelby said.

Morgan mumbled a reply, but Shelby didn't bother trying to decipher it. Instead, she dragged Morgan's arm over her shoulder and tried to haul her to her feet. They were almost standing when Morgan screamed in pain and fell back to her knees, dragging Shelby with her.

"Well, that explains the missing shoe." Shelby brushed snow out of Morgan's hair. "But I'm sorry, we don't have time for an injury."

The sun was setting so fast, and the temperature was dropping along with the light. They had to get back to the cabin and get Morgan warm. In the lengthening shadows Shelby could see a long trail of disturbed snow leading out of the woods. Morgan must have dragged herself a long way. Even as she followed the trail with her eyes, the darkness swallowed it. The only reason she could still see the cabin was the light spilling through the open door.

Shelby grabbed Morgan's chin and forced her unfocused gaze to lock on her. "Look, I need you to work with me. I'm going to help you walk, but I can't carry you. I know it's going to hurt and I'm sorry, but you've got to do it, okay?"

Morgan was shivering so badly she couldn't really maintain eye contact, but she must have heard. When Shelby wrapped her arm around Morgan again, she worked to stand up. It wasn't easy and they moved so slowly Shelby wanted to scream in frustration, but eventually they climbed the few stairs up to the porch and into the cabin.

When Shelby released her to close the cabin door, Morgan remained standing, but she was shivering so badly she looked like she was having a seizure. More than that, she looked a real mess. Every piece of her clothing was drenched and covered in melting snow. She held all her weight on her right foot, her left toe tapping against the floor as she shook. If Shelby waited too long, she would fall down and she doubted Morgan would be able to get back up.

Moving with renewed purpose despite the exhaustion of their trip, Shelby threw more wood on the glowing coals in the fireplace. The logs lit immediately, roaring to life and bathing the room in heat. It wouldn't be enough though, not with how wet and cold Morgan was. She could never warm up while wearing clothes that were at least fifty percent melted snow.

Morgan didn't protest as Shelby peeled off her coat and two shirts. When Shelby told her to sit on the rug in front of the fire, she practically crumbled. Shelby sent boots and socks and jeans flying in her haste. She forced herself to be clinical when she reached to pull off Morgan's underwear and it wasn't difficult since her skin was deathly, frighteningly pale. Morgan, however, came to life when she realized what Shelby was doing. She tried to swat Shelby's hands away.

"I have to take them off. They're soaking wet. Your bra, too," Shelby said.

Morgan probably wanted to continue struggling, but she was clearly too cold to have much fight in her. She did, however, curl into a fetal position once she was naked, but whether that was modesty or hypothermia, it was impossible to tell.

Shelby grabbed a thin blanket off the couch and tossed it over Morgan. She tried to rub some warmth into her limbs, but it didn't seem to be helping. Morgan was shivering worse than ever and it didn't help that Shelby's shirt was wet, too. Now that she was inside, she could feel the chill herself.

As she was unbuttoning her soaked flannel shirt, Shelby finally identified the harsh whistling she'd heard since returning to the cabin. The kettle on the stove must've boiled while she was helping Morgan and her mug, tea bag already waiting at the bottom, was next to it equally forgotten. She tossed her flannel aside as she entered the kitchen. She needed to get Morgan warm and some hot, sweet tea seemed just the ticket.

"Sit up and drink this, okay?" Shelby asked gently.

When Morgan didn't respond, Shelby dropped down next to her and pulled her into a sitting position. The way Morgan moved, like a complacent if tense rag doll, did not inspire confidence. Neither did the bone-deep chill of her skin when Shelby touched her. The fire and blanket weren't helping, and though she did get Morgan to drink some of the tea, it wasn't enough. Not that Shelby was that surprised. Even with the wet flannel off, she was still too cold herself and she'd only been in the snow for a few minutes.

"In for a penny, in for a pound." Shelby kicked off her shoes.

After she'd stripped down to bra and panties, Shelby climbed under the blanket with Morgan. She hissed in shock when her bare skin touched Morgan's. She'd never felt anything like it before. How was Morgan even alive when she was this cold? As she pressed the length of her body against Morgan and tried again to rub warmth into her skin, she realized how close she'd come to losing her. If she'd waited five more minutes to go to the window it might've been too dark to see her. If Morgan had collapsed just five feet farther from the cabin, she wouldn't have been visible. She had come shockingly close to dying out there.

Scenes played unbidden in Shelby's mind. Finding Morgan's body after it was too late. Never finding her at all and having to explain everything to her family. And if that had happened, Morgan would never know how sorry Shelby was for her earlier outburst. Tears pooled in Shelby's eyes and she squeezed them shut, burrowing her face into Morgan's neck. She hardly knew this woman at all, but she was so afraid of losing her she could hardly breathe.

As Morgan's body warmed, her shivering lessened. After a little while, a soft, contented sigh brushed against Shelby's collarbone. Morgan snuggled in closer. Her eyes were shut, but she nuzzled into Shelby's neck. She was whispering something that might have been a name, and the movement made her lips slide against Shelby's neck in a way that sent a pleasant shiver through her body.

Just when Shelby thought Morgan had fallen asleep, her hand started to move. It was subtle at first, a fumbling swipe of fingertips across Shelby's side. She thought maybe Morgan was subconsciously mimicking her own movements as she tried to warm her up, but Morgan's touch lingered on Shelby's hip. When Morgan's touch moved up her ribs, Shelby had to bite her lip to keep from groaning.

There was something decidedly intimate in the caress and Shelby knew she should shut it down. She should stop Morgan. After all, she was definitely too out of it to know what she was doing. But Shelby couldn't bring herself to stop her. She wasn't touching anywhere risqué yet and it had been so damn long since Shelby had been touched by a naked woman. What would it hurt to let Morgan stroke her side?

Morgan pushed her chin up higher and the press of her lips against Shelby's neck was far more like a kiss now. Her touch was more sure, her thumb stroking across the point of Shelby's hip. God, it felt good. Morgan's breast pressed between Shelby's, her nipple hard against her skin. Her thigh pressed against Shelby's, soft and firm even if her skin was still frigid. Shelby let her eyes flutter shut, hoping that Morgan's hand and leg and lips didn't wander too far. If they did Shelby would have to stop her and she didn't want this to stop. She didn't want to end the tingling under her skin and the quickening of her breath.

Just when things were getting interesting, Morgan groaned and pulled her body away a fraction of an inch. Her shivering actually seemed worse now, and it made her words almost indecipherable.

"Cold. So cold," she stuttered.

"I know." Shelby rubbed her palm harder against Morgan's skin. "I know. We'll get you warm."

"Please. Too cold."

Morgan was right. She was too cold. Far too cold and nothing was working. Shelby looked around the cabin, desperate to find a solution. First aid for hypothermia wasn't something she'd thought to learn about growing up in North Carolina. She looked over at the mug of tea, half drunk and abandoned on the brick hearth with coils of steam rising from the surface of the liquid. It could help, but Morgan needed more. She needed to be warmed from the inside and the outside. Shelby's mind caught on the tea and whirled through a million disjointed thoughts. For some reason, it landed on her tea back home. The delicious Kusmi Earl Grey. Sometimes she treated herself to an indulgent Sunday morning with a cup of milky tea and a bubble bath.

"Bath!"

Morgan jumped at her outburst and Shelby slipped out from under the blanket. Morgan made an adorable whimper at the loss of her body heat, but Shelby couldn't focus on that now. In fact, she thought as she sprinted to the tiny bathroom at the back of the cabin, it would be best for her to not think any positive thoughts about Morgan right now.

Water roared from the tub faucet, turning from ice cold to steaming hot quicker than Shelby thought possible. Once she had the stopper down and the tub started to fill, she hurried back to the living room, bracing herself mentally for what she was about to do. This bathroom seemed destined to be the scene of many an awkward naked encounter between them. But unlike their first morning when Morgan had walked in on her fresh out of the shower, Shelby wasn't the one who had to worry about her modesty.

"Morgan, I need you to stand up, okay?"

Morgan's eyes were unfocused and full of confusion, but they stayed fixed on Shelby even as she shivered.

"We need to get you in a hot bath." Shelby forced herself not to think about Morgan naked, but they had been so intimate just a moment ago, it wasn't easy. "Just to warm you up."

Morgan's eyes sharpened slightly at the mention of warmth, and she was much more helpful in moving for herself this time. Shelby did her best to keep Morgan from putting weight on her injured leg as they shuffled down the hall, but she wasn't sure Morgan could really feel the pain through the cold. Lowering her to the edge of the tub wasn't hard either, but she lost her balance and splashed down hard into the water. Shelby was soaked from head to foot, but at least it was warm water this time. Morgan didn't seem overly perturbed either. She sank into the warm water with another sigh of contentment. She didn't even protest when Shelby held her up to make sure her chin didn't slip under.

Morgan soaked for a long moment with her eyes closed, but the shivering stopped almost immediately. Her injured ankle was an angry red against the shocking white of Morgan's skin. Shelby lifted the foot out of the water and propped it on a folded towel to keep it elevated. One arm was also out of the water, and Shelby lifted it to place it in the water, but she noticed a bruise forming on Morgan's forearm. In fact, as she studied Morgan's body under the water, she saw a few injuries.

The most obvious was the one from the seat belt crossing her chest. It was yellowing now, but still looked painful. Morgan hadn't complained about it, but she was a stubborn woman. It probably didn't feel great. Fresher bruises were showing themselves on Morgan's calf above the swollen ankle and, worse than the rest, an angry red patch on the ribs of her right side. Shelby reached under the water to touch the spot and Morgan hissed the moment her fingertips made contact.

"Hurts," Morgan said without opening her eyes.

"Hurts how much? Can you take a deep breath? Any sharp pains?"

Morgan's response was a mumble, but it sounded like a negative mumble. Shelby pressed a little at the spot and didn't feel any shifting bones. Just a bruise then, not a broken rib. Still, it must've been a nasty fall that caused all this. Scanning the rest of Morgan's visible flesh, she didn't see any other bruises or blood.

Satisfied that Morgan wouldn't die on her just yet, Shelby sat back on the tile floor. She told herself to look away from Morgan's body—that this was not the time or appropriate moment to ogle—but she couldn't help herself. Morgan was soft in all the places Shelby liked her women soft and lightly muscled everywhere else. It was a remarkable body. One that had felt extraordinarily nice against her own.

She'd thought about Morgan's body, of course. Hell, they'd been sharing a bed for the past three nights and Shelby had fallen asleep and woken up all too aware of the warm presence beside her. Her dreams had been full of tantalizing fantasies and she had halfway hoped to wake up one morning with Morgan spooning her in her sleep. To her disappointment, they had both been perfectly appropriate while unconscious. But now, with Morgan's naked body laid out before her eyes, she couldn't help but take it all in. After all, Morgan had gotten an eyeful of her their first morning. Wasn't she allowed a little peek?

Morgan stirred, turning slightly in the bath, her eyes still firmly shut. Shelby was grateful for the movement, though. It reminded her to stop being a creep. Shelby decided to give her another few minutes in there to warm up before wrestling her to bed, but she took the precaution of wedging herself against the wall between the sink and the tub. Sitting there, she couldn't see more than Morgan's feet, and that was definitely the most appropriate view for right then.

Chapter Fifteen

The first thing Morgan noticed when she woke up was the throbbing in her ankle. The intensity of the ache took her breath away and she very nearly gasped out loud. She took a few deep breaths, willing herself to relax, knowing that would lessen the pain. Sure enough, the throb eventually settled into something a bit more bearable.

With the pain sorted, she became aware of a naked thigh between hers, pressed lightly against her center. Then she noticed the silky swell of a breast cupped in her hand. That sent the throb from her ankle zinging directly to her core.

Morgan's eyes flashed open, taking in her surroundings with brutal swiftness. She was lying on her side, face to face with a sleeping Shelby. It was Shelby's thigh pressed against her core and Shelby's breast in her hand. If it hadn't been for the insistent and growing desire pulsing through her, Morgan wouldn't have believed her eyes.

Her mind was a complete blank and not just because it was clouded with lust. She had no memory of the previous night. How did she get here? Had she and Shelby had sex? Their positions told a pretty clear story, but wouldn't she know if she'd spent the night getting intimate with her least favorite colleague? She didn't have the stale taste of alcohol on her tongue, so this compromising position wasn't the result of their stock of bourbon. But what the hell had happened?

The last thing she remembered was struggling through the snow on her hands and knees because she couldn't walk on her busted ankle. The cold had seeped so deep into her that she could barely move, but she'd seen the lights from the cabin. They were coming closer and closer and she kept telling herself to keep going. Gail kept telling her she was strong and she had to keep going. She'd been talking to Gail. She'd been apologizing for letting her down. She'd promised to keep going and the cabin lights got closer and brighter.

Morgan was still struggling with her brain, trying to force it to remember, when Shelby snuffled and shifted in her sleep. She leaned forward and the movement pressed her thigh hard against Morgan. A jolt of pleasure shot through her and her eyes rolled back.

That was the moment Morgan realized she was completely naked. Shelby's thigh was pressing hard into Morgan's clit and she was one more sleepy adjustment away from an orgasm. Morgan's shock made her jerk backward, away from the enticing thigh and lacy bra-clad breast. Unfortunately, the movement put weight against her injured ankle and the shift from blinding pleasure to blinding pain made her cry out.

Morgan's yell of pain woke Shelby, who scrambled away in the opposite direction, popping to her feet beside the bed. The duvet pulled off Shelby and Morgan couldn't decide if she was relieved or disappointed to see that Shelby wasn't naked. Not that the lace bra the same blue as her eyes and simple cotton bikini-cut panties left much to the imagination, but they did seem to indicate they hadn't had sex last night.

Several quiet moments passed before Morgan realized she was spending a little too much time tracing the lines of Shelby's underwear with her gaze. Apparently, Shelby hadn't noticed the inspection, though.

"What the hell is going on?" Morgan asked, her voice scratchy and her throat painfully dry.

"Don't worry, you're okay now." Shelby propped her hands on her hips, making no effort to cover up her body as a look of concern washed over her face. "You are okay, right? Are you in pain?"

Morgan had a hard time thinking straight while her clit was still throbbing, but Shelby didn't seem affected by their intimate position. She seemed far more concerned about Morgan's well-being, which was probably natural.

"My ankle hurts."

Shelby reached down and grabbed a blanket from the top of the pile of blankets and sheets. After she wrapped the blanket around herself like a bath towel, she circled to Morgan's side of the bed, reaching for her ankle. Morgan pulled her foot away, ignoring the slice of pain the movement caused, and tucked the covers more securely around herself.

"Do you remember anything from last night?" Shelby asked.

"Not how I got back here."

"What do you remember? What happened to your foot?"

Morgan grimaced in pain just thinking about it. A chill went through her whole body and she pulled the covers tighter around herself. She knew she wasn't really as cold as she'd been last night, but the memory was far too vivid to dispel right now.

"I found the car and it was covered in snow. Completely buried." Morgan couldn't help a little smirk at that. She'd been rude, impulsive, and stupid yesterday, but she'd also been right. That didn't make her ankle hurt any less, though. She described trying to get the suitcase out of the trunk and losing her balance. Shelby winced along with her as she explained getting her foot caught under the tire and the popping sound she'd heard. And the pain. She couldn't adequately describe the pain, of course, but Shelby could see how swollen and bruised it was.

"It hurt and the swelling was making it hard to walk, so I took my shoe off to relieve the pressure." Morgan waited for Shelby to call her an idiot for that, but she didn't. "Which was a bad idea cause then I couldn't get it back on and the rain boots filled up with snow."

"And you still didn't have gloves," Shelby said.

"Right. Which was a problem because I had to crawl on my hands and knees because of my ankle."

"Which is how you got so cold." Shelby nodded and sat on the edge of the bed, reaching again for Morgan's ankle. When she pulled it away again, Shelby snapped at her. "Stop being stubborn. You're hurt and we need to do something about it."

"What if it's broken?"

"It's not," Shelby said flatly.

"How can you possibly know?"

"Two reasons. First, you heard a pop, not a crack. Second, you wouldn't be able to walk at all with a break and it would most likely be numb, not painful."

Arguing seemed pointless since Morgan didn't know if that was true, but she didn't think Shelby would lie about it. She nodded to Shelby and didn't move as she lifted her ankle. Shelby's touch was incredibly gentle. She settled Morgan's ankle in her lap and pressed on the flesh, but not enough to hurt. In fact, it was sort of sexy the way she was touching Morgan and the intensity with which she focused on the examination.

"I know it doesn't look great, but you're going to be just fine. I'm going to go look for a bandage. Don't move."

Shelby sprang to her feet, the blanket still wrapped around her body like an oversized towel, and marched out of the bedroom without another word. Honestly, Morgan was glad she had a moment alone to settle her hormones. The intimate way they'd woken up mixed with Shelby's confidence during the examination was really fucking with Morgan's head. This was the second time she'd seen Shelby naked and her body definitely didn't want that to stop, no matter how much her brain screamed that she hated this woman.

To distract herself, Morgan took a look at her ankle. Shelby had been generous. It wasn't just not great, it looked terrible. Her ankle bones were completely hidden beneath incredible swelling. The flesh was stretched so tight it looked like it might split at any moment and it was bruised to a sickly purple. The bruising went all the way down her foot, ending in toes that were red. Morgan wiggled them and they all moved. She thought she remembered that they wouldn't move if her foot was broken, but she had no idea if that was true.

When Shelby returned, she was fully dressed in the previous day's clothes and Morgan's brain reminded her body that was a good thing. Her body still disagreed, but Morgan did her best to ignore that. Instead, she focused on how Shelby was carrying a wide elastic bandage that looked relatively new.

"I'll wrap your ankle and we should elevate it and put ice on it today and tomorrow," Shelby said.

Morgan had stopped anticipating a rescue at any moment, and now it was pretty clear Shelby felt the same way. As optimistic as they both wanted to be, last night's adventure had taken a toll. Shelby sat down and, just as gently as before, transferred Morgan's foot into her lap.

"You still haven't told me how I got back here and, um, why we were both naked," Morgan said.

"I wasn't naked. Not completely." Shelby winked.

As she wrapped Morgan's ankle, Shelby told the story of pacing around the cabin and looking out the window all day. She kept her eyes on her work, so Morgan didn't have to see any sign of annoyance. Shelby also didn't see the guilt Morgan felt for worrying her so much. When Shelby got to the part where she spotted her face-down in the snow and ran out of the cabin without even putting her coat on, Morgan's heart lurched.

She hadn't really thought Shelby would be that worried. Angry, sure. Annoyed, definitely. But she hadn't expected worry. Worry seemed to indicate a level of, if not affection, at least the base humanity of concern for another person. Morgan was sure she would have been anxious if their roles had been reversed, but she didn't know she would put herself in so much danger for her rival.

"When we got back here you were too cold. Even when I got you out of your clothes and had you in front of the fire under a blanket, you weren't warming up so I got under there with you to help you warm up. Eventually I got you into a hot bath and that seemed to work. You're not the easiest person to move around when you're out of it, you know. Once I got you into bed, I was too exhausted to get dressed."

Shelby secured the bandage and sat back to examine her work. It felt so much better to have the ankle wrapped. It wasn't so tight that it hurt the way her shoe did, but it felt stable.

"Thanks," Morgan said quietly. "For the wrapping but also for the…you know."

"For the naked bed time?" Shelby teased her with a grin.

"For helping me not get hypothermia."

"You're welcome." Shelby's cheeks pinked ever so slightly and Morgan's brain told her heart not to thud that hard.

"I should get dressed," Morgan said to keep herself from saying anything else stupid.

"Of course. Let me help."

"No, it's okay." She didn't want Shelby to think she was being stubborn again. "You've done so much. I can handle it."

Morgan struggled to her feet, gripping the blanket tight around herself, and tested putting weight on her foot. It wasn't fun, but she managed to stay upright. Shelby looked like she might argue for a moment, but she wisely chose to let it go. Maybe they were both learning to pick their battles?

"I'll make some breakfast. I'm sure you're starving," Shelby said.

Morgan's stomach growled in answer. She hadn't eaten since breakfast the previous day and quite a lot had happened since.

After Shelby exited, Morgan took two steps toward the closet, but her body clearly wasn't ready for that and her ankle protested loudly. She was sweating from the exertion and pain, and she had to take a few moments to sit on the bed and catch her breath. The whole time she wondered how on earth she had made it back to the cabin the night before.

More even than her shock at her solo journey, she was floored by the realization that Shelby had come out to help her through the last leg. If Shelby hadn't seen her, she would surely have frozen to death overnight. Just sitting here in the bedroom, as far as possible from the fireplace, was a little chilly. Outside had been frigid in a way Morgan had never experienced living her whole life in Virginia. They got snow maybe once a year and it was usually more of a nuisance than anything else. Every five years or so they would get a bad storm, but it was always in January or February, when she was already used to the cold. This cold and this snow were both something else entirely and it was only November. Shelby had been right, she was not prepared for that journey yesterday and she had nearly paid a very high price.

But Shelby had risked herself to save Morgan's life. Even after Morgan had said cruel things to her and acted like a complete brat, Shelby hadn't hesitated. The person Morgan had created in her head—the lying, two-faced villain—was as far as possible from the person Shelby had proven herself to be.

From now on, Morgan would do better. She would be a kinder, more thoughtful person. She would give Shelby a chance. She would give her the benefit of the doubt. She might even take a moment to think back over the insights Shelby had made into her character and decide if maybe there was some merit to them.

No matter what happened from here on out, Morgan would try to be better.

❖

Once the bedroom door clicked shut, Shelby finally allowed the story of Morgan's injury and the memory of collecting her from the snow really settle in. Last night and this morning she'd been in fix-it mode. Her entire focus had been on making sure Morgan was alive and then assessing and treating her injury. She hadn't allowed emotions to get in the way.

Experience, however, had taught her that she needed to get into the messy emotional part sooner rather than later, so she dropped into it now. Morgan's description had been so vivid, she felt like she had seen it herself. Morgan hanging helplessly by a severely sprained ankle and the cold creeping in. Hell, her ankle looked like it had been run over by a steamroller, so goodness knew how she hadn't broken it. More, though, Shelby had worried about frostbite, what with the exposed toes and fingers. It had been a miracle that she'd come away from the experience alive and in one piece.

A fork clattered to the tile floor at Shelby's feet. She'd been using it to turn over the planks of SPAM she'd been frying. Now her hands were shaking so bad she couldn't hold it anymore. The pan sizzling on the stove faded away as her heartbeat thudded in her ears and her ragged breathing threatened to overwhelm her. All the what-ifs and almost-weres flew through her brain. All the many places she might have found Morgan's frozen corpse. The possibility of the car sliding down the hill and crushing her slowly. Wild animals tracking her down. Human life had never felt so fragile as it did for Shelby in this moment and she had to grip the countertop, struggling to catch her breath.

She took long, careful breaths, blowing out the panicked fear of Morgan dying of exposure and breathing in the truth of the now. The intensity of emotion shocked her. After all, she barely knew Morgan and she didn't like her most of the time. Heck, the last time they had a real conversation, Morgan had been nasty to her.

Shelby forced herself to look out the little window over the sink and count her breaths. Was she really surprised Morgan had been nasty to her yesterday? It had been unkind of Shelby to start psychoanalyzing Morgan without the context of her fear of failure. The weight she carried from her friend's death. COVID had been hard for everyone, but medical professionals had a unique burden. Particularly folks like lab techs, whose existence and sacrifice had been ignored by society at large during the pandemic. Even as everyday people learned terms like PCR test, they only acknowledged the sacrifice of nurses and doctors, neither of whom actually performed those tests.

Of course, Morgan had been snippy and standoffish. She had been living in a constant state of anxiety for two years and had no one to share it with. She'd admitted on their first day in the cabin that she didn't have any close friends or family that would miss her. So she probably hadn't had anyone to talk to about her anxieties. There hadn't been anyone to talk her off a ledge when she was spiraling or hold her when she cried.

That made it even more meaningful that she'd held Morgan last night to help her pull through. At least that's what she told herself. Shelby couldn't deny, however, how amazing it had been just to hold Morgan while they were both naked. Or mostly naked in Shelby's case. She'd woken up several times throughout the night to find their bodies entwined closer and closer together. She'd told herself she should get up and maybe move to the couch. Morgan had long since been warm.

But Shelby hadn't gotten up. Morgan felt too good in her arms and it had been far too long since anyone had felt that good in her arms. Her hook-ups of late didn't spend the night and she was okay with that. Or at least she'd thought she was okay with it until last night. She'd almost forgotten what it felt like to have a woman's arm around her waist, holding her close while she slept. The weight of Morgan's arm, completely relaxed, had a gravity it was hard for Shelby to break out of even now.

The bedroom door whipped open, snapping Shelby out of her thoughts. She could feel how hot her cheeks were and turned quickly back to the stove. The water for the oatmeal was boiling and the meat was just on the edge of burnt. Another minute or two of fantasizing about last night and she would have ruined their breakfast.

While Morgan shuffled slowly over to the dining table, Shelby forced herself to focus on completing their meal. She was stirring raisins into the oatmeal when Morgan coughed and cleared her throat. Shelby looked over at her, but she avoided eye contact and her cheeks were an adorable pink. Maybe her mind had been in some of the same places Shelby's had been?

Shelby took her time plating their meal and carrying everything over. She'd expected Morgan would dig right in because she was eying her breakfast like a yard dog who'd been presented with a medium rare ribeye, but she didn't. She waited until Shelby had poured them both coffee and sat down. Even then, she didn't so much as pick up her spoon.

Morgan finally looked into her eyes. "Thank you for saving my life."

The way Morgan's ice-blue eyes shone and the soft timbre of her voice made Shelby's mouth go dangerously dry. She swallowed with difficulty and forced a flippant smile.

"Oh, you know, you were practically on the porch when I found you. I didn't do much."

"You did everything. You kept a level head for one thing." Morgan finally looked away and that gave Shelby a chance to finally breathe. "I know it was foolish for me to run out alone and try to clear the car. You were right. I shouldn't have gone."

For a headstrong—okay, stubborn—woman like Morgan, the admission had to be one step short of devastating. Shelby could laugh this off, too, and relieve the tension, but that wasn't fair. Not when Morgan put herself out there. The least Shelby could do was meet her halfway.

"My rudeness certainly helped push you out the door. It was my fault, too, and I'm sorry."

"No. Not at all." A crease formed between Morgan's eyebrows, highlighting the sincerity in her words. "Please don't blame yourself. I was rude first and, well, look, you were right about me."

"No, I wasn't right about you," Shelby said. Morgan didn't look likely to accept that. "I know what it's like living with fear. Living with regret. Knowing that any moment could be a disaster. One mistake and you could end up living in your car. So yeah, I know a thing or two about choosing between duck and cover or cut and run. I've been there, too."

"You have?"

The disbelief in Morgan's voice almost made Shelby laugh, but it was too serious a moment for that. Not to mention Morgan was clearly intrigued and she wasn't sure she was ready to tell the whole story.

"Living like that is hard and it's impossible to be your best self during that. So please allow yourself some grace," Shelby said.

"It still doesn't excuse my rudeness," Morgan said. She was clearly swallowing down a million questions.

"I'll accept your apology if you accept mine." Now it was Shelby's turn to avoid eye contact. "You might've been a little bit right about me, too. I've spent so much of my life being what everyone else wants that I don't spend a lot of time being genuine."

"I don't think that's true. Even when you say what other people want to hear, you can't help but be you."

"That's sweet." Shelby laughed and fiddled with her spoon. "Actually, these last few days are the first time I've been my genuine self in a long time. You already hated me so I guess you gave me enough space to be authentic. It didn't matter who I pretended to be."

Shelby felt so foolish for it, but she looked up at Morgan, desperately hoping to see something like forgiveness in her expression. What she saw was so achingly genuine, so perfectly open, that it made her hope for something she knew she would never have.

"I don't hate you. Not at all."

"I'm happy to hear it."

Shelby looked into her eyes for a little too long, but Morgan didn't look away. For possibly the first time since they'd met, Morgan didn't look away. Shelby let herself get lost in that look, wondering which of them would be the first to break it. A flicker of interest lit inside her when Morgan wasn't the first. Nor did she look like she had any intention of looking away any time soon. But something had been nagging at her for almost a day now and she had to say something about it before it ate her alive.

"Not to bring up a sore subject," Shelby said. Morgan tensed slightly. "You said something yesterday I really want to correct. You said 'your buddy Eric.'"

Morgan cleared her throat and looked away. "Yeah, I shouldn't have said that. It's not your fault. What he did."

"He's not my buddy. Not by a long shot." Morgan's eyes shot back to her. "He made a pass at me the first time we met. When I turned him down and told him I was gay… Let's just say his response was enough for me to talk to his manager."

"Really?" Morgan's eyebrows shot up. "But you were chatting with him at the conference. Talking about mutual friends."

"He pushes himself into my space to try to get under my skin and I don't like confrontation so I don't make a scene."

Even as the words came out of Shelby's mouth, they soured on her tongue. If that wasn't more evidence of her saving face rather than being authentic, she didn't know what was. Morgan didn't call her out on it, though. Instead, she was kind.

"Thank you for telling me. I'm sorry I made the assumption."

"You had every reason to believe he was my friend," Shelby said. "But he most certainly is not. Even if he had been, he wouldn't be now. Eric has a hell of a lot to answer for in the way he treated your hospital. I'm so sorry about your friend. It sounds like she was a lovely woman."

"Thank you." Morgan whispered the words and looked away, but there was a bittersweet smile on her lips.

Shelby gave her a moment to let the sharpest pang of emotion dissipate before reaching over and squeezing Morgan's hand. Morgan looked at her then and the emotion of her stare made all sorts of things happen in Shelby's chest. The look wasn't unlike the one Morgan had given her in the bathroom that first morning—full of unexpected depth and an intensity like nothing Shelby had ever seen.

"Eat your breakfast before it gets cold," Shelby said.

She was delighted to see that pink color come back into Morgan's cheeks in the moment before she turned her attention to her food. Shelby watched her eat, giving herself a few moments before she started on her own breakfast. She had to wait for the butterflies in her stomach to dissipate before she could swallow a mouthful.

Chapter Sixteen

Morgan tried to read, but she kept getting distracted. She was lying on the couch, her foot propped on a pillow on the arm of the couch. Shelby was curled up like a contented cat in the armchair, lazily turning a page. Since they'd both finished their first books, Shelby insisted they switch and read the book the other had finished.

"We can talk about them after," she'd said. "Like a book club for two."

Morgan had realized halfway through chapter two that Shelby was implying they'd be stuck in the cabin long enough to finish two books. They'd already finished one puzzle and were planning to start a second one after lunch. Neither of these two things made Morgan anxious about how long they'd been stuck here or how much longer they would be stuck. On the contrary, she was looking forward to spending more time with Shelby.

When discussing starting the new puzzle, Shelby had offered to let them solve it Morgan's way, using the picture on the box top as a guide and taking a methodical approach to completing it. Morgan had refused. She found she liked Shelby's approach. She liked the way Shelby made her take the task, and maybe even herself, less seriously. She wanted Morgan to have fun. Was there anyone else in Morgan's life who wanted her to have fun?

Morgan's mother had grown up poor and had worked in a factory outside their small town her whole career. She wanted Morgan to go to college and make something of herself. Everything Morgan did had to have a purpose. Something to improve her financial position so she'd never be reduced to working in a telephone factory.

She didn't play sports in high school; she joined the debate club. She didn't play in the band or act in the plays or sing in chorus. All of her time was focused on her homework or extracurricular activities that would look good on a college application. By the time Morgan discovered that being a lab tech wasn't all that intellectually different from working in a telephone factory, she had too many bills to pay to make a switch. Not to mention she would never have the courage to tell her mom how dull the work was. Not when her mom had worked so hard to send Morgan to college.

"You're not reading." Shelby's voice made Morgan jump, and the movement jarred her tender ankle. "Is your foot okay? It might be time for another round of ice if it hurts."

"No, I'm fine. Just taking a break."

"Want some more aspirin?" Shelby asked.

They hadn't found any painkillers in the house, but Shelby had a partial bottle in her purse. The bottle only had seven more pills, however, and she wanted to save them for nighttime in case the pain kept her awake. When Morgan shook her head, Shelby turned back to her book. Suddenly, Morgan wanted nothing more than to hear more of Shelby's voice.

"Can I ask you a personal question?" Morgan asked before she lost her nerve.

Most people got nervous when they were asked that question. They tensed up and either refused to answer or agreed with such obvious reluctance it put the asker off. Shelby did neither of those things. In fact, she smiled and set her book aside as though there was nothing more she wanted than to be asked a personal question by someone she barely knew.

"Sure, ask me anything," Shelby said.

Morgan thought hard about what she wanted to ask. The revelation about her true relationship with Eric made her realize she knew essentially nothing about Shelby, and anything she thought she knew she had assumed. Was it really so surprising that she would try to be civil with him? After all, what would she gain by being antagonistic? Morgan had known men like him at just about every job she'd ever had. She guessed most women in America had been put in the same position Shelby had been in at the banquet. It was time to stop making assumptions and get to know her.

"You obviously know your way around canned goods and you mentioned earlier about knowing what it's like to be on the edge of homelessness."

Shelby deflated a little at Morgan's words, and she wondered if this had been such a good idea after all. But she didn't refuse to answer.

"I'm from a pretty wealthy family. Well, wealthy by North Carolina standards, which wouldn't get you much more than a cup of coffee and a ride on the subway in New York," Shelby said.

Morgan struggled to sit up a little straighter on the couch while Shelby picked at the corner of her book.

"They were very prominent in our little town. Good, God-fearing folk who sinned regularly and judged all their neighbors for their sins. They were politicians and community leaders." Shelby curled her lip. "It was North Carolina, so you can guess what kind of politicians they were."

"They're pretty conservative I take it?"

"They fly Confederate flags and rail against homos and illegals. All the worst aspects of southern life personified."

"It couldn't have been easy to come out to them," Morgan said.

"It was not." She leaned forward and tossed her book on the coffee table in an obvious attempt to buy time before she told the rest. "I had secret girlfriends in high school, but then I went to college and my parents started pushing for me to get married to one of the boys at the country club."

"I take it you didn't like him much."

"They didn't have anyone in particular in mind. Anyone with pastel polo shirts, loafers with no socks, and a gun rack in his truck would do," Shelby said.

"Sounds like just your type," Morgan said in an effort to lighten the mood. Shelby stuck out her tongue at Morgan, but she smiled after so the ploy worked.

"I lost a lot of important relationships because the women I dated didn't want to stay in the closet. One day I realized I didn't either. I went home and told my mother I was a lesbian."

Shelby was quiet for a long time. She stared into the fire, but it was pretty clear she didn't see the ashes piling up or the flames lazily licking the logs. Eventually, Morgan couldn't stand the suspense.

"What happened?"

"She slapped me so hard she split my lip and told me never to say such a thing again."

Shelby said the words so matter-of-factly it took a while for their meaning to sink in. Morgan's heart clenched at what Shelby had gone through. Her own mother was single-minded and perhaps a little cold, but she had been supportive when Morgan came out. And she'd never raised a hand against her.

"She told me to think about what the neighbors would think if they heard that. She told me to shut up and pick a husband before people started to talk."

The very thought of it made Morgan's heart clench. What would it feel like to find out your mother cared less about her child's happiness than the neighbors' opinions?

"I almost did what my mother said, you know? I'd never been slapped before and certainly not by my docile mother. But the snarl on her face when she hit me." Shelby's words trailed off and it took her a long time before she spoke again. This time she looked over at Morgan and her jaw was set in determination. "I realized I would turn into that woman if I married some man and pretended for the rest of my life. I would be one of those women at the country club who play one round of half-hearted tennis in the morning and then spend the rest of the day drunk and mean."

Morgan was so compelled by the story and the woman who told it. She was half in the cabin with her and half in that country club as a teenager, seeing all her mother's friends for the first time. As awful as that slap from her mother had been, part of her was clearly happy it woke her up so she could see the world around her for the first time.

"How many of those women are just miserable?" Shelby asked. "How many had been forced to toe the family line? And for what? If I'd done what my mother asked and become someone else, what would I gain? A lifetime of bitter martinis and a loveless marriage? No thank you."

"I can't believe how brave you were at such a young age," Morgan said.

"Oh, I don't know if it was bravery or the stupidity of youth. Either way, that wasn't the hard part."

"What could be harder than your mother hitting you?" Morgan asked.

"My mother telling me she would cut me off. No money, no tuition, no apartment, no family. I'd lose everything if I didn't marry one of the boys from the country club."

"Jesus." Morgan's voice was barely above a whisper.

"Oh, trust me, she brought him up, too. Lots of talk about how I'd burn in hell."

"And you still did it? Even though you lost everything."

"Not exactly everything. My grandmother didn't abandon me so easily." Shelby turned the ring on her right finger that had left the healing cut on her forehead. "She gave me a car and I had a partial scholarship. I knew I could get a job and make my own way, so I left."

"I still say that's brave. And you're here now, incredibly successful, so it couldn't have gone too bad."

Shelby's laugh was musical and bitter at the same time. "Bad enough that I looked up one of the guys I played golf with three months later."

"What? Really?"

"All I found was his obituary. He'd smashed his four-wheeler into a tree after drinking a handle of cheap vodka the summer after our senior year. I took it as a sign."

"That's dark," Morgan said.

"So was my apartment when I couldn't pay the light bill again."

Shelby's sad smile told her she wasn't quite so callous as she was pretending to be, but Morgan was intimately familiar with coping mechanisms, so she let it slide.

"My grandmother died very soon after and I was well and truly alone. I'd never had a job before and it wasn't easy. I got two part-time jobs that worked around my class schedule and I was still scraping by. One of the jobs was at a cafe and I ate a lot of stuff other people would've thrown away. It wasn't enough, though, so I had to use the local food bank."

"You were able to keep your apartment?"

"Oh no. I couldn't afford it. Plus the high school friend I shared it with didn't want to sleep down the hall from a lesbian," Shelby said.

"She didn't already know?"

"I was very discreet." Shelby's wink was far too distracting. "I shared a two-bedroom apartment with three other girls in a crummy building with a creepy landlord. My grades tanked and I lost all my friends."

"Because you came out?"

"No, because everyone wants to spend their college years partying, but I didn't have the time or the money so they lost my number."

"Wow, you had terrible friends," Morgan said.

"Everyone's terrible at twenty years old."

Morgan didn't really agree, but she could see the shadow of old pain there. She thought back on her own college years. The endless parties and full refrigerator. Her mother worked hard to ensure Morgan's college experience wasn't like Shelby's. She should have been more appreciative at the time.

"A year after my family cut me off, my brother showed up at one of my jobs to ask if I'd come to my senses yet," Shelby said.

"He didn't."

"He sure did."

"How did that go?" Morgan asked.

"Not how he expected." Shelby laughed. "He thought I'd take one look at his fancy clothes, big shiny watch, and new BMW and come crawling back."

"He didn't know you well at all. What did you do instead?"

"I yelled for him to go fuck himself at the top of my lungs."

"Oh shit! Really?"

"Yep."

"I'm almost afraid to ask how he responded to that," Morgan said.

"He told me he always knew I was a fuck up and he was happy I'd done it. Our parents doubled his allowance when I left." Shelby swallowed hard and balled her fists in her lap. "He told me our father said I would die destitute in a gutter somewhere and they wouldn't claim my body because I was a disgrace."

Morgan's eyes filled with tears. The thought of a parent saying that about their child. Of a sibling passing that along. What kind of sick, heartless people would act like that?

"He told me he would marry well and give them the grandchildren they wanted so he could inherit everything." Shelby finished in a flat monotone.

It took a long time for the gumminess to clear from Morgan's throat enough for her to answer. She had the feeling Shelby didn't want her pity, and Morgan had never respected anyone more.

"That must've been hard to hear," Morgan said.

"It was." A sense of calm descended over her and she sat back in the armchair, her legs curled up to her chest. She said, "I realize now I've been laser-focused on being the best ever since that moment. I work seven days a week, fourteen hours a day, and have no personal life to speak of. All because I wanted to prove them wrong. It isn't healthy and I'm not going to do it anymore."

"That's great." Even as Morgan said it, she worried that she wasn't working enough hours. If Shelby worked that hard to be successful, maybe she should add a few hours to her day. Before she could get lost down that rabbit hole, she said to both Shelby and herself, "The real revenge isn't being rich like them, it's being happy like they aren't."

Shelby's eyes landed on her and they were far too shiny. Morgan's arms itched to reach out and pull Shelby into a hug. To tell her she wasn't that person her parents said she was. To show her she was special. But that was the real problem. Her body was still too keyed up from their intimate embrace this morning and she couldn't trust herself to not do more than hug Shelby.

Morgan cleared her throat noisily. "So what happened with your brother?"

Shelby went back to that cheeky, wistful smile. "I told him that, unlike him, I wasn't willing to be our parents' whore."

"Oh fuck," Morgan said before she could stop herself.

"Yeah." Shelby laughed, and it was magical. "I might've gone a step too far with that one. He stormed out and I got fired, but it was worth it."

Morgan roared with laughter and it felt so good to cut loose with someone. If someone had told her a week ago that she would be laughing with Shelby Lynn Howard like this, she would have told them to get their head examined.

"You are a woman with surprising depths," Morgan said.

"You have no idea."

❖

Shelby was focused on her puzzling. Or her new version of focused, which meant she had just found two puzzle pieces that might have the same color on them and so she'd abandoned the edge pieces she'd been working on for a half hour to try to fit them together. She was turning one of the pieces a different direction and realized she'd already tried that combination when she heard a soft noise from across the table.

Looking up, she saw Morgan asleep in her chair. Her chin had drooped down onto her chest and her long eyelashes swept across her cheeks. Her breathing was deep with the barest hint of a whistle at the end. She looked so peaceful.

In fact, Shelby realized that Morgan had looked peaceful all day, despite her harrowing experience and injury the day before. None of the usual tension coiling in every muscle. None of the doubt in her thousand-yard stare. She almost looked like a woman on vacation.

If she was honest, Shelby felt like a woman on vacation, too. She sat back, watching Morgan dozing in her chair, and let her mind wander to all the ways this could have been a lovely, relaxing week.

Neither of them really seemed the type to vacation in a secluded cabin, but perhaps the unexpectedness would make it all the more fun. What might it have looked like?

Instead of stopping at a gas station for pork rinds, they'd have gone to a nice grocery store for cheeses and baguettes. Maybe some nice steaks and an expensive bottle of wine or two. And of course, they'd hang onto the car so they could go pick up more supplies whenever they wanted.

Shelby let her head fall back and closed her eyes. She'd definitely be wearing a little black dress instead of a stranger's oversized sweats. Maybe some sexy lingerie to go with it? What would Morgan like? Black lace bra and matching thong? What would Shelby wear if she'd packed for fun rather than practicality? How wonderful it would've been to be here with Morgan by choice. Maybe she could even have convinced Morgan to get naked with her of her own volition. Wouldn't that have been something. Shelby could bet that ever-present tension would go away for good if she could give Morgan a few toe-curling orgasms. The thought made her body temperature soar and she had to bite her lip to keep from groaning at the very thought.

Easing her eyes open, Shelby gazed over at Morgan, still peacefully napping in her chair. Despite some of the lingering looks they'd shared recently and the apologies and bonding, Morgan didn't seem interested in Shelby at all. The thought sent an unexpected wave of disappointment through her. Did she really want Morgan to be interested? It would certainly complicate things. They were professional competitors and in totally different places in life. And though Shelby usually stuck to the briefest of relationships—a few hours at most—she had an inkling that she wouldn't be able to hook up with Morgan without catching feelings. In fact, she might already have caught them.

She wasn't entirely sure why, other than the fact that Morgan was the first person in a long time to call her on her shit. Morgan had challenged her, but also worked to understand her. Sure, when they met she had all the charm of a cornered cottonmouth, but Shelby found it refreshing when someone could admit their first impression had been wrong. Morgan might not have said it in so many words, but she clearly showed it. Shelby could admit that she'd been wrong, too, and maybe even a little culpable in the wrong impression.

Morgan's shoulders twitched and her head rolled on her neck. A crease of discomfort appeared between her eyebrows and she smacked her mouth sleepily. Each new, adorable movement made Shelby's heart pound a little harder in her chest. So much for the question mark at whether she'd caught feelings. When had she ever been so drawn to the adorable things another woman did? That was so domestic and Shelby had never been domestic. Of course she knew why. It had everything to do with her family and the way they ruined the idea of connections for her. Still, she was sitting here, her body still tingling at the thought of Morgan in her underwear and her heart thudding over her blinking herself awake. What was this woman doing to her?

Morgan's sleepy eyes settled on Shelby and she smiled sheepishly. "I guess it's past my bedtime."

It took everything in her to tear her gaze away, but Shelby finally forced herself to look at the window. To her surprise, it was pitch black outside even though it felt like they'd just finished their dinner of condensed soup. She checked her watch next and her jaw dropped.

"When did it get so late?" Shelby asked.

Morgan shrugged and yawned, which of course made Shelby yawn right along with her.

"I don't usually fall asleep at the table. I'm guessing it's the bourbon you forced me to drink."

"That was medicinal. For your ankle," Shelby said.

"And the glass you had for yourself?"

"Medicinal. To deal with your crankiness when your ankle started hurting."

Morgan gave a soft laugh and held Shelby's gaze. God, there was a smolder there Shelby couldn't quite get enough of. If only she could convince Morgan to give the two of them a chance. They'd probably never make it. No one had ever stuck with Shelby long. But it would be so good while it lasted.

"I should probably lie down before I fall down." Morgan pushed herself up, not quite putting weight on her wrapped foot.

"Come on, I'll help you to bed."

"I can sleep on the couch," Morgan said. She was clearly still uncomfortable about the way they'd woken up that morning.

"Oh no. We're not having this argument again." Shelby made sure there was the proper amount of steel in her voice. "You need a good night's sleep on a mattress and I'm not taking no for an answer."

She could see Morgan swallow hard and knew she'd made her point. She moved around the table, positioning herself beside Morgan, who backed away awkwardly.

"Okay, but you don't have to help me down the hall or anything."

The way she avoided putting weight on her injured foot and the overall unsteadiness of her posture took all the strength out of the argument. Part of Shelby wanted to let her try to walk down the hall without assistance, but then she'd just have to pick her up off the floor when she fell. It was just bravado anyway. Morgan didn't like to need help from anyone and Shelby was fine playing along by being insistent.

Shelby made a show of rolling her eyes and grabbing Morgan's arm to wrap around her shoulders. As she expected, Morgan didn't protest too much. She slipped her arm around Morgan's waist to steady her as they moved together. What really caught her notice was the way Morgan's breath hitched when Shelby's thumb grazed across her side. She did her best to hide her smile, but she couldn't stop the thought that maybe she could convince Morgan to give them a chance after all.

Chapter Seventeen

Thursday morning Morgan took a shower for the first time since her accident. She still couldn't put much weight on her left foot and it throbbed and ached being unwrapped for this long, but she didn't care about that. All she cared about was the simple, intoxicating joy of cleaning her body. It wasn't just washing off the multiple layers of dried sweat, grime, and woodsmoke. It was the down-to-the-bones warmth only a steaming hot shower could provide. No amount of layered blankets could match it.

As she shampooed her hair for the second time, Morgan's only wish was that she could scrub her brain as easily as she scrubbed her body. She could dislodge bits of bark and pine needles from her hair, but thoughts of Shelby were stuck much more stubbornly. The way she held Morgan with such strength and gentleness as they walked down the hall to the bedroom last night. There had been a moment, when Morgan turned on her pillow to say good night, that she got lost in Shelby's sapphire eyes. Maybe it was her imagination how long they stared into each other's eyes, but Morgan had to clench her hands into fists to keep from reaching across the mattress.

Even though she'd managed to avoid that disaster, she'd lain awake long into the night, listening to an owl hooting in the distance and thinking about those eyes. The color reminded her of waves on a moonlit beach. Morgan had fallen asleep to a fantasy of the two of them on a sundrenched, deserted beach. Both of them in bikinis, their skin warm from an afternoon lying in the sun, reading books that they chose rather than what some stranger had on his shelves. Walking back to their room as the sun set across a lazily lapping ocean.

Fantasy Shelby was sleepy from a lazy afternoon, her long lashes drooping not quite low enough to shield her sparkling eyes, blue as the water behind them. She laid her head on Morgan's shoulder while her thumb rubbed up and down her side. They took a shower together to wash off the sunscreen.

Morgan's injured foot took a little too much weight, sending a sharp stab of pain zinging up her leg. The pain was enough to snap her out of the dream just in time to realize her hand had been drifting down her abdomen, just thinking about last night's fantasy. She slammed the palm against the shower wall, trying to steady both her body and her raging hormones. The last thing she needed was to get caught masturbating in the shower.

After catching her breath and washing the last of the soap from her body, Morgan carefully stepped out of the shower and sat on the toilet to dry off. She was particularly careful drying her ankle, which still looked terrible. The swelling had gone down a little, but not much, and she wondered if there was maybe something broken in there despite Shelby's assurances. She'd sprained her ankle before, but it had never taken this long to improve. There wasn't much she could do about it, though, so she just wrapped it again and hoped another day of ice and elevation would help.

No matter how hard she tried, she couldn't keep her treacherous mind from returning to her fantasy. Eventually, she just let it happen. What was the harm, after all, of a few lustful thoughts while she brushed her hair. She decided, however, to keep her thoughts less risqué now that the sounds of the shower couldn't cover any efforts to relieve the ache between her thighs.

Instead of returning to the fantasy shower, she wondered what it would be like to spend a long weekend with Shelby. Would they read the same books on the beach like they were here? If they did, they could talk about them on the long flight home from their beach paradise. What would that be like? Morgan had only ever spent time like that with her family. She hadn't spent a long, lazy weekend with any previous girlfriends, just for the pleasure of sharing space with them.

Why was it so easy to imagine it with Shelby when it hadn't been with any of the women she'd actually dated? Maybe because of that unnamable something in Shelby's eyes last night. The hint that, had Morgan reached out, she would have instantly reached back. Somehow Morgan felt like Shelby would want more than one night. Was that even possible for them? Wouldn't a bitterness seep into their relationship? Hell, it had seeped in already and they weren't even friends. Morgan was self-aware enough to know she would be the one to ruin a potential relationship with her professional jealousy. They'd barely even had a conversation about work because Morgan knew she would react poorly. How could they date and not talk about their work?

"Why are you even thinking about this?" Morgan said to her reflection in the foggy mirror. "Shelby doesn't want anything to happen and neither do you. You're just going stir-crazy and you're horny because you're bored. Don't do something stupid."

She stared into her own eyes for a long time after she said the words, trying to determine if they'd sunk in. After a few minutes, she realized she wasn't looking at herself anymore. She was picturing Shelby in a bikini again. Thoroughly annoyed with herself, Morgan wrapped her towel tightly around herself and retreated to the bedroom to get dressed.

The process of putting on clothes with an ankle that ached was enough to drive all the lust out of Morgan's body. She was sweating and grinding her teeth by the time she got to the kitchen, but Shelby didn't give her a hard time. In fact, there was a tightness to her eyes and lips that made it clear she hadn't slept well. Morgan fretted that Shelby had felt the moment between them and it had made her uncomfortable, disturbing her sleep. She chastised herself even more. When Shelby didn't sleep well, she wasn't the bubbly, bitingly funny roommate Morgan had come to enjoy so much. Morgan should control herself better.

While Shelby showered and got dressed, Morgan made breakfast. She wasn't half the cook Shelby was with her full range of motion, and hopping around on one foot meant the oatmeal was watery and the coffee was scorched. When Morgan playfully alluded to her poor performance, Shelby finally perked up with a little teasing.

"You're lucky I'm not a coffee connoisseur," Shelby said. "But I appreciate you cooking for me in your state, no matter what the results."

Morgan sat back with her coffee and adjusted the bag of melting snow icing her ankle. Now was as good a time as any to find out if she and Shelby could even make a friendship work. She would only know if she could talk about work with Shelby by trying.

"Are you a big coffee drinker usually?" Morgan asked.

"Oh yeah. I drink coffee all day. Basically until I switch to wine."

"I was never much of a coffee drinker in the lab, but now I'm either in the car driving all over town or staring at a computer screen all day. Coffee's the only thing that keeps me awake."

"Oh yeah, you learn really quick where the gas stations with the best bathrooms are in this job," Shelby said.

"I've got that covered in Northern Virginia, but my sales area goes all the way out to West Virginia and down to North Carolina." Morgan fortified herself with another sip of coffee. "How big is your area? Are you on the road a lot?"

If she thought she could slip in the question subtly to open the conversation, she was sadly mistaken. Shelby gave her a long, searching look before quirking up one corner of her mouth. "Are you sure this conversation is a good idea?"

The answer was most certainly no. Not only because Morgan wasn't sure she could talk to Shelby about work without getting jealous, but also because that teasing, flirty glint was back in Shelby's eyes, making Morgan's heart rate pick up.

"If we're going to be friends, we have to be able to talk about work, right?" Morgan asked.

"Are we going to be friends?" It should be illegal to put that much innuendo into a single word.

"I want to try," Morgan said a little breathlessly.

Shelby's smile seemed to spread wider than the prospect of making a new friend warranted. Maybe she understood what Morgan was doing. Maybe she liked to tease. Either way, that smile made a shiver of anticipation spread from the tips of her swollen toes all the way to Morgan's scalp.

"We have larger territories than you for sure. I cover Pennsylvania down to South Carolina and a little sliver of Tennessee, but I don't go there much," Shelby said.

"Wow, that's a huge territory. How do you manage all that?"

"It's a lot of miles, but not many customers, so we're spread pretty thin."

"What do you mean not many customers? You're killing it out there. I've lost at least three contracts to you in the last quarter alone."

Shelby's laugh was hollow, bordering on bitter. "I'm barely keeping my head above water. And don't worry, you'll have those customers back in a year or two at the most."

Morgan leaned forward, all thought of jealousy evaporating in her confusion. "What do you mean? Why would I get them back?"

"Oh, come on, you know why." When Morgan didn't respond, Shelby said, "Because your instrument is so much better than ours. It's not a ticking time bomb like Telnet, but it can't hold a candle to yours when it comes to ease of use. I can get people to buy mine, but anyone who's worked with the Pulsar will be disappointed and probably a little mad they switched. They'll ditch us the minute their contract runs out."

"What?" Morgan's mind was spinning and she felt like she couldn't get her bearings.

"Don't act so surprised. You know your instrument is better than mine."

"Well, yeah, but I didn't know you knew that."

Shelby threw her head back and laughed. It was a sweet, glorious noise and her neck stretched enticingly. Morgan couldn't help but enjoy the way Shelby could just let loose like that, even when she was admitting to being with an inferior company. For someone so successful, she didn't seem to have any competitiveness in her.

"Look, I'm not shy. I know I'm an amazing salesperson." Shelby grinned bewitchingly. "I could sell anything and I chose to sell instruments that could help fight COVID. But Pulsar wasn't hiring, so I ended up staying with Ashworth. It isn't the perfect job, but I love what I do."

"You moved to instrument sales because of COVID?" A buzzing in Morgan's brain made it hard to slot all the different words together.

"Yes and no. I was already working for Ashworth, but when COVID started I wanted to help. We brought out our test a few months after Pulsar, so I made the lateral move."

"So you gave up your client base to start over just because of the pandemic?"

"You aren't the only one with a conscience. Does it surprise you that I wanted to be part of the solution?"

"No." Morgan knew she'd answered too quickly by Shelby's skeptical eyebrow lift, so she pivoted before she called it out. "What did you do before?"

"Pharmaceutical sales. I started right out of college."

"There's a lot of money in that," Morgan said.

"Especially for a pretty blonde with big blue eyes and a Southern accent." Shelby rolled her eyes and her cheeks flushed a pretty pink. "I was an idiot but I'd also spent the better part of three years starving. I batted my eyelashes and smiled, and every paycheck was bigger than the last."

Morgan wanted to be angry, but after hearing about Shelby getting kicked out of her home, she had a little more compassion. She guessed the money wasn't half as addictive as the admiration. It was probably life-saving for Shelby at the time.

"It must've been a big step down in pay. It's pretty incredible you made that move," Morgan said.

"Don't go singing my praises just yet. The opioid crisis was what made me realize I had to make a change. I wasn't half as pushy as some of my colleagues, but the whole industry encouraged overprescribing narcotics. I'd been part of the problem."

"But you're part of the solution now and that's a big deal."

"Are you shocked that I have a moral compass?" Shelby stood and reached over to grab Morgan's empty coffee cup. "There's more to me than just my sex appeal, you know?"

As she headed off into the kitchen to clean up, Morgan couldn't help being impressed. There certainly was more to Shelby than her sex appeal, and the more Morgan learned about her heart, the more appealing she became.

❖

Shelby stepped out onto the porch, registering dimly that the cold wasn't nearly so sharp today as it had been earlier in the week. While she loaded her arms with firewood, she wondered whether the snow would melt enough for them to walk out of there soon. Morgan's ankle wasn't in great shape, but in another day or so she'd be able to make a trek to the road. Today marked the sixth day stuck in the middle of nowhere, so whether Morgan was ready or not, they'd have to make a move soon.

As she reached for the doorknob, Shelby froze. She whipped her head around to stare off into the trees, certain she'd heard something in the distance. She held perfectly still, waiting to hear it again. She couldn't say what she thought it was, but she didn't hear it again, so it must've been snow falling from a tree or an animal making a racket. Or more likely, it was just wishful thinking. Her stir-crazy mind trying to convince her rescue was on the way.

Shelby made quick work of tending the fire, laying new wood crosswise on the glowing coals and leaning in close to blow gently until new flames burst up to consume the new logs. Through the crackle of flames and the heady woodsmoke, she felt eyes on her.

Turning her head, she noticed Morgan wasn't reading her book anymore. In fact, her attention was focused rather intently on Shelby leaning over the hearth.

"Are you checking out my butt?" Shelby put a teasing lilt into the words and arched her back just a little extra for the perfect angle.

"What? No. Sorry. Lost in my thoughts. Staring into space. I didn't mean to stare."

Shelby laughed at the blazing red on Morgan's cheeks and the flustered way she blurted out her excuses. She couldn't help but notice, however, that Morgan's eyes went back to her butt every few seconds, even as she struggled to sit up straighter on the couch.

"Are you saying I don't have a cute butt?"

Shelby turned, putting on an exaggerated pout and crossing her arms to look sad. It did the trick. Morgan's mouth dropped open and she made a few noncommittal noises, clearly struggling with whether to agree or disagree. It was absolutely adorable and more than a little sexy to see how hard she struggled to be honorable and chivalrous and all that sweet lesbian stuff.

After a few moments of torture, however, Shelby decided to let her off the hook. She dropped the pout and patted Morgan on the shoulder on her way to the kitchen. While washing the soot and bark off her hands, she noticed the nearly empty bottle of bourbon on the counter. They'd had a couple of drinks for fun since arriving, but most of it had gone to pain relief once their pathetic supply of aspirin had been exhausted. With a shrug she grabbed the bottle and a couple of glasses to take back to the couch.

Shelby handed over a small glass of whiskey but waited to catch Morgan's eye before releasing it. She whispered, "For the record, I don't mind you checking out my butt."

Shelby poured herself a slightly larger glass and then dropped onto the other side of the couch. Morgan's legs were stretched out and she tried to move them to make more room, but Shelby grabbed them and guided them onto her lap instead. Morgan held her breath as Shelby unwrapped the bandage, but when she exposed bare skin and used her fingertips to check for tenderness, Morgan tipped her glass back.

"How does it feel?"

Morgan's face was still twisted into a slight grimace from downing her drink, and there was a rasp to her voice. "Better."

Shelby paused to sip her whiskey and catch Morgan's eye, then went back to examining her ankle. It was less swollen today, but the bruising was still a deep, angry purple and it was obviously difficult for her to put weight on it. Shelby was convinced there was no break, but she guessed the sprain was worse than she'd originally suspected. Still, there wasn't anything to be done that they weren't already doing.

When she'd wrapped the ankle back up, Morgan looked like she might take her feet away, so Shelby settled her hands on top of her shins to keep them in place.

"Tomorrow's Friday. We'll have been here a week," Shelby said.

"Time flies." Morgan leaned forward to grab the whiskey bottle and refill both their glasses.

"Have you ever done happy hour in the city?"

"I'm not really the happy hour kind of girl," Morgan said.

"You're more the dance until midnight in a dark nightclub kind, huh?"

"Yeah, right." Morgan snorted into her glass and her smile was as intoxicating as the cheap whiskey.

"What do you normally do to unwind?"

"I thought you'd figured out by now," Morgan said. "I don't really unwind."

"Surely you do something other than work."

Shelby was already feeling a little tipsy, but she refilled their glasses anyway. Each sip made her fall a little deeper into Morgan's eyes. They were such a pale blue it was like looking into the morning sky. The moment just before the sun rose enough to shoot golds and oranges through the clouds and the light was only just bright enough to chase away the darkness without bringing color.

"I do laundry," Morgan said. The liquor shined in her eyes.

"That sounds thrilling."

They laughed together and Shelby found her thumb drawing circles on the bare patch of skin above Morgan's ankle.

"What about you?" Morgan asked. Her voice sounded lower than Shelby remembered it. Not quite husky but close enough to intrigue. "Do you do anything other than work?"

Shelby waggled her eyebrows. "Laundry."

Morgan laughed again and Shelby knew in that moment they would go to bed together. Her skin burned for it. She wanted to be touched. To be tasted. To discover all the sensitive spots on Morgan's arms and legs and back. Their bodies entwined together. Tasting her breath and her tongue and all her most intimate flesh. Shelby loved the dance, but she loved the chase just as much and she was very patient. She trailed her fingertips lightly across Morgan's calf until she felt the slightest shudder across her skin.

"I like the weight of your legs in my lap," Shelby said. "It's nice."

"I like the way you're rubbing your thumb over my skin."

There was a sparkle in Morgan's eye that surprised her. She'd expected Morgan to blush or stammer. She hadn't expected her to be so forthright. Shelby leaned forward to set her whiskey glass on the coffee table, but also used the movement as an excuse to scoot closer. Again, she was surprised when Morgan did the same. They were so close together now that Morgan's legs weren't in Shelby's lap anymore. They were wrapped around her waist.

"Were you serious when you said you wanted me to check out your butt?" Morgan asked quietly, her eyes locked onto Shelby's.

"Oh, I was serious. Actually, I want you to check out a lot more than that."

Shelby leaned forward again, pushing into Morgan's space. Morgan didn't lean away. Their lips were inches apart now. She could feel Morgan's breath, tinged now with the oak and peat of the whiskey, on her cheek.

Morgan reached out, running her thumb along Shelby's cheek, then across her lips. The touch was featherlight and teasing and it made Shelby's body explode with hunger. It took every ounce of her self-control to keep from leaning in and tasting Morgan's lips. She wanted nothing more than to push her onto her back and see just how rickety this old couch was. As much as she wanted Morgan in that moment, she could see them shaking the thing to matchsticks with the intensity of their passion.

"Can I kiss you?" Morgan whispered.

"Oh God yes." Shelby knew it sounded like begging. Hell, it was begging. She wanted that kiss like she wanted oxygen and warmth and blood in her veins. Her body shook with need, and she had to fight not to claim Morgan's mouth.

Instead, she waited and God, was that the right decision. Morgan leaned in slowly, teasingly. She held Shelby's eyes until the last moment, when there was nothing but a sliver of daylight and the thick tension of their shared need between their lips. And then her eyelashes fluttered shut and her hand came up to cup Shelby's cheek. Her palm was cool against Shelby's blazing skin and the shock made her gasp just as their lips met.

Shelby would've guessed that Morgan would kiss exactly like this. Sweet and gentle, polite even. Shelby didn't want polite. She wanted the hunger she had seen in Morgan's eyes that first day in the cabin when she'd walked into the bathroom to see Shelby naked. She wanted the fire she showed in their screaming argument and the brazenness she'd shown by walking all that way through the snow while freezing to death. She wanted the primal side of Morgan to come out, but she was patient. They had all the time in the world and only one bed.

"Were you trying to get me drunk on purpose?" Morgan whispered as she pulled back.

"I wasn't going for drunk exactly." Shelby found it hard to form words. To form thoughts. Morgan's gentle kiss had stirred something deep inside her. "Just tipsy enough to make you brave."

When Morgan was silent, Shelby opened her eyes. There was something unreadable in the set of Morgan's jaw and the smolder in her eyes.

"Was that wrong?" Shelby asked. Disappointment and dread threatened to break through the thrill coursing through her veins. "We don't have to do anything you don't want to do."

Morgan's arm flashed out and wrapped around her waist, pulling Shelby as close as they could get on the tiny couch.

"You didn't have to waste the bourbon." Morgan breathed against her lips. "I've wanted to kiss you for a long time."

"Then kiss me again."

The request lit something inside Morgan. Her arm tightened, dragging Shelby into her lap, and the second kiss was anything but polite. The hunger Shelby had wanted flared between them. Morgan's lips were insistent and her tongue plunged past Shelby's defenses. Shelby had wanted fire and there was no denying the heat between them. The more their mouths danced together, the more Shelby wanted. All the passion that had been missing from Shelby's life recently flooded through. More than she had ever possessed, in fact. She was quickly becoming drunk on the feel of Morgan's lips.

Their make out session got heavy so quickly, Shelby barely registered it happening. Her hands ached to touch and she let them roam over Morgan's body with reckless abandon. Zippers and buttons flew and once she even heard the rip of fabric, but Shelby couldn't bring herself to care. It felt like her whole focus had been on wanting Morgan for days and now her dreams were coming to life before her eyes. She couldn't have stopped herself if she wanted to and she certainly didn't want to.

Time flowed and blurred and before she knew what was happening, Shelby found herself on her back on the couch, Morgan kissing down her neck and her shirt bunched up beneath her chest. Some patch of deliciously bare Morgan skin was pressed against her belly, and it seemed to be heading south in a hurry. Despite the ache in her body, Shelby allowed a moment of mental clarity to burst through.

"Are we going too fast?" Shelby panted and the words slurred on her tongue. "I don't want to mess anything up by going too fast."

"We won't mess it up." Morgan continued to kiss down her chest. "I won't. I promise."

The promise felt as flimsy as tissue paper in a snowstorm, but Shelby couldn't bring herself to care. All she could care about right now was the searing heat of Morgan's mouth making a path down her body and the throb in her core. She'd spent her whole life watching other people cut loose and be wild while she worked and went to bed alone. Fuck it. She would be wild this time. She would get what she wanted no matter the consequences.

"Then let's take this back to the bedroom."

Chapter Eighteen

Morgan was surprised how clear-headed she was, given the bourbon and the making out, as she walked down the hall to the bedroom. The dull ache of her ankle on every other step couldn't even break through her certainty. Shelby had taken her hand to help her off the couch and hadn't let go. Morgan trailed a half-step behind her as they crossed their little cabin, and the feel of Shelby's warm fingers between hers was her anchor.

If she was honest with herself, Morgan had known this had always been inevitable. Like the tug of an invisible hook behind her belly button, leading her down the path that ended in her naked body tangled with Shelby's. From the way her heart thudded at Shelby's grateful smile in the airport to waking up with Shelby's thigh pressed between her legs, there had been a path laid out before them. Neither of them could have veered off it had they wanted to, and Morgan had never wanted to change course.

She wanted Shelby. Wanted to feel her skin and hear her cry out. Wanted to taste her and watch her fall apart. Morgan couldn't remember ever wanting anything or anyone more. She wasn't sure when that desire had formed, but it was so deeply rooted in her now that it had become her heartbeat.

The bedroom door was open, the mattress that dominated the room neatly covered with sheets and duvet. Shelby led Morgan to the foot of the bed and turned to her. The fire in Morgan's veins told her to scoop her up, toss her across the bed, and devour her body and soul, but Shelby was avoiding her eye. There was a hesitancy wavering around her like a heat haze and Morgan forced herself to be patient.

"It's, um, been a long time for me," Shelby said, her voice small. "A really long time, actually."

Of all the possible ways this could go, Morgan never in a million years guessed Shelby would be the shy one. But then again, she knew exactly how Shelby felt and she loved the opportunity to take the lead.

Cupping Shelby's cheek, Morgan raised her face until she was staring into those eyes the royal blue of a deep ocean. "I'm in the same boat. Why don't we just see where things lead? No pressure."

When Shelby nodded and smiled in an almost grateful way, Morgan felt her own body relax. She'd always been nervous going to bed with a new partner for the first time, but there was something extra intimidating about Shelby. There was a weight to this moment. It felt more important than ever that she get it right, but she was starting to realize how much she ruined things by weighing them down with expectations. She didn't want to do that today. Her heart couldn't take it.

Still cupping Shelby's cheek, Morgan leaned in slowly, taking her time, giving Shelby the chance to meet her halfway. Shelby's lips were silk and candle wax and her tongue still carried the hint of smoke and sugar from the liquor. The longer they kissed, the more both their hesitancies burned away. Soon Shelby's hands cradled Morgan's hips, holding her close. Their bodies pressed together and there was no longer a question where things would lead. Their mutual need was so evident in their touch it was hard to believe they hadn't spoken the words out loud.

"Will you lie down?" Morgan whispered against Shelby's neck.

Morgan watched with something bordering on awe as Shelby crawled onto the bed and pulled herself up to the pillows. She was entranced by the contours of Shelby's body. They had all seemed sharp lines before, but now her softness was on full display and Morgan wondered how she could possibly have missed it.

"Is this okay?" Shelby asked when Morgan didn't join her.

"More than okay." Morgan finally tore her eyes away from the curve of her hip. "You are stunning."

Rather than make a joke or dismiss the words, Shelby soaked them in. Her smile grew and her shoulders fell back, showing off the delicious curve of her neck. Morgan's mouth watered at the sight before her, and she couldn't hold back any longer. She climbed onto the bed, fitting her hips between as Shelby opened her legs to accept her.

Not content to focus her kisses on those tantalizing lips for long, Morgan pulled up the hem of Shelby's shirt. Her stomach was smooth and pale and begging to be licked. Morgan leaned over and pressed a kiss on the patch of skin just beside Shelby's belly button. Shelby's gasp was almost inaudible but got louder when Morgan shifted a few inches lower. Her lips brushed against Shelby's waistband and they groaned in unison.

Making it her mission to kiss every inch of newly visible skin, Morgan made her way slowly across the plane of Shelby's stomach. She ran her hands up underneath Shelby's shirt, delighting in the feel of heat and silky smoothness. Soon Shelby's fingers were raking through Morgan's hair, keeping her close. She lost all sense of time and place while she lavished attention on all that incredible flesh.

When Shelby arched beneath her, Morgan looked up, trying to catch sight of her face. Instead, she saw the peaks of her hardened nipples through the thin fabric of Shelby's shirt. Morgan ached to touch those nipples. To find out whether she liked a hard pinch or a soft caress. Perhaps discover whether she preferred tongue or teeth. Her whole body throbbed with the need to touch, to caress, to please. Her mind buzzed with possibilities and she slid her hands up over Shelby's ribs.

Just as Morgan's fingertips grazed the underside of Shelby's breasts, hands shot out and gripped her wrists.

"Wait," Shelby said, her voice thick but sharp.

"Sorry. Is this too fast?"

Morgan tried to pull her hands away, but Shelby held them and shushed her. The buzzing in Morgan's ears picked up as her face heated with embarrassment. She had been the one to say they should just see where things led, but then she had gone too far too fast. Shelby sat up, Morgan's wrists still held fast in her hands.

"Do you hear that?" Shelby asked.

All Morgan could hear was the thudding of her own blood in her ears and the buzz of embarrassment across her nerves. But was that her nerves? Why did it sound so loud and why was it getting louder by the second.

"Snow mobiles," Shelby said. She finally released Morgan's hands and scrambled off the bed.

Morgan tried desperately to make her lust-soaked brain understand the words and the sounds, but she couldn't quite figure it all out. She climbed carefully off the bed to stare down the hall. Shelby had covered the distance from the bed to the front door in a matter of seconds, stopping there to yank down the hem of her shirt before throwing open the door.

Around Shelby's shoulder, Morgan could just see a pair of snow mobiles pulling up in front of the porch. The noise made sense only when the two men killed the engines and climbed off the machines. They looked like cops or park rangers or some mix of the two. Morgan's brain still couldn't quite piece together what was going on. As she limped down the hall, she heard Shelby speaking rapid-fire sentences to the men.

Vaguely, Morgan registered that Shelby was telling them about her trip to the car to clean off the snow and her injury. She was nearly to the living room when the rangers explained that they had followed the trail of disturbed snow. While she lowered herself to the couch, she heard Shelby tell them about her ankle. One of the men came over to examine her foot. He was less gentle than Shelby had been and a stab of pain radiated up her leg when he yanked back her jeans. Shelby barked at him to be careful, but he didn't apologize.

"It's a good thing you went out there," the ranger next to Shelby said. "We never would have found you all the way back here. People have been searching for you for days. It's been all over the news."

"She needs a doctor. Can you get her to a doctor?" Shelby said the words without looking at Morgan. She tried to catch Shelby's eye, to ground herself back in the moment, but she was too busy asking the ranger how far it was to a hospital.

"Nelson, go call for an ambulance to meet us at Dark Horse Saloon."

The ranger who'd been manhandling her ankle hopped up and ran outside. Morgan assumed Shelby would look at her now, try to make some connection, but she didn't. She kept her attention on the ranger in front of her.

"I'm so glad you found us. I'm sure my plants will all be dead when I get home, but better late than never."

The ranger laughed along with Shelby, but the world had finally seemed to come into focus for Morgan. They were being rescued. After six days stuck out here with all the pain and uncertainty and cold, they were going home. It had started to feel like a vacation in the last couple of days, but it hadn't been. They had been trapped and these men had freed them. She took a heartbeat to begrudge them their terrible timing, but at least they were going home.

As the real world flooded back in, so did the panic. So much time lost. So many unread emails and missed appointments. All those customers she could have had. Were they all lost opportunities now? How could she possibly make up for all these days?

Morgan scrambled to reach into her pocket. She had to lie back awkwardly with her leg outstretched to fit her hand into the bunched denim. When she expected her fingers to wrap around smooth stone and engraved letters, they found nothing. Her mind whirled and her breathing picked up until she was practically gasping. Where was Gail's stone? Was it in her other pocket? She slapped around at her clothes but didn't feel it anywhere. Which pocket had she put it in this morning? Had it fallen out on the bed? Or maybe on the couch when she and Shelby had been making out?

Dropping to her knees on the old carpet, Morgan flung aside cushions and blankets and pillows. There was no flash of opaque pink. No cold solidity. No strength. Soon she was gasping. Hyperventilating? She stopped and slammed her eyes closed. She thought back to this morning. To the shower and then struggling to get dressed with her bandaged ankle. She couldn't remember moving the stone over from the jeans she'd worn the previous day. In fact, she couldn't remember touching it in her pocket the previous day at all. Things had been so calm. So laid-back. She hadn't needed Gail's strength. Her reminder of which path to choose.

"Morgan?"

Shelby's voice was a faraway distraction. When had she touched the stone last? If not that day and not the day before, it must have been two days ago. That had been the day of her accident. She'd grabbed it once. She remembered being in the snow, hands and knees frozen and clothes soaked through. She'd been shivering and she'd felt like giving up, but she grabbed the stone and Gail had told her to keep going. Had she put it back in her pocket or had she crawled with it bunched in her fist? She wouldn't have done that, would she? Even if she'd been hypothermic and disoriented, she'd have remembered to be careful with Gail's gift.

"Morgan?" Shelby's hands were warm and solid on her shoulders and Morgan turned to look at her. "What's wrong?"

She could feel her eyes darting around the room. Both men were outside, but she could see them standing on the porch by the door. One of them kept looking over at her like she'd lost her mind. Maybe she had.

"I lost it."

"What did you lose, Morgan?"

Shelby was repeating her name. Morgan knew she was doing it to make her calm down. To make her remember herself. But how could she remember herself without Gail there?

"Gail's stone." She whispered so the men wouldn't hear her. "It's not in my pocket. I think I lost it in the snow."

For a moment, Morgan tensed herself for a fight. She assumed Shelby would make fun of her or tell her it was just some silly rock. She should have known better. That woman she'd thought Shelby had been wasn't real.

"I know it's scary to not have it," Shelby said, her voice gentle as a kiss. "But maybe that's a good thing. Maybe this is your chance to live for yourself, not for her."

Morgan's heart pounded so hard she thought it might break through her ribs and a sob half-caught in her throat before bursting past her lips. Shelby tucked her face against her neck, but tears didn't come. Thoughts didn't come.

Shelby's words played over and over in her mind like a skipping record until the rangers stepped back inside and told them it was time to go.

Chapter Nineteen

Shelby barely managed the energy to shut the door to her condo behind her when she finally walked in. Her home felt shockingly cold and empty after the blazing fire and cramped living space of the hunting cabin. All the lights were off and the afternoon sunlight streaming through the living room windows was the diffuse, empty light of early winter. It did nothing to make the white walls and pale blond hardwood feel lived in. Her gaze drifted across paintings she didn't remember buying and off again without sparking any emotion.

Shelby dropped the plastic bag emblazoned with "Patient Belongings" onto the tiled entryway floor. She doubted she would ever wear the clothes again, but it was too much work to walk to the kitchen to toss the bag into the garbage can. Her battered suitcase, waterlogged on one side from melted snow and dented on the other from the crash impact, clattered down next to the hospital bag. She took the time to carry her laptop bag to her office. That piece of luggage fared better than the rest since she'd taken it with her to the cabin.

Her office was equally as sterile as her living room, and she ignored the few generic decorations and thoroughly dehydrated potted fern. Once she'd plugged in her laptop, she dropped her shattered iPhone on the desk beside it. For a split second she considered going to the Apple Store to replace it, but she wasn't interested in that kind of hustle and bustle after the week she'd had.

All she wanted was a meal full of fresh vegetables and to sit in a bubble bath with the largest glass of low-calorie Chardonnay she'd ever poured. Hell, she might skip the glass and drink straight from the bottle. After the bath she would crawl into her own bed, dressed in her own pajamas. Hopefully the wine would help her forget how lonely the bed would feel without Morgan sleeping beside her.

Her energy fully gave out at the very thought and she dropped into her office chair. It spun a few degrees from the impact and it was fun, so she spun another few degrees, this time on purpose. Dropping her head back, she watched the ceiling spin above her. She let her mind go blank and it was nice for a few minutes, but she knew the thought would come sooner or later. When it did, she spoke out loud just to fill the awful quiet of the empty condo.

"I wonder what Morgan's having for dinner."

Shelby was relatively sure she wasn't going out for a meal. Even in the best of times, Morgan wasn't much for socializing and her ankle was probably still very painful. After leaving the cabin, they'd gone straight to the hospital, but it was only a routine checkup for Shelby before her release. Morgan had to stay longer for x-rays and orthopedic consult on her ankle.

In fact, Morgan had been in with a specialist when Shelby had been released. She'd wanted to stay and check in, but the local police officer who was tasked with driving her home wanted to get on the road. Shelby couldn't blame him too much. It was going to be several hours of driving and he was eager to get it over with.

Besides, what could she say to Morgan anyway? "Want to come back to my place and finish what we started?" She was relatively sure Morgan's answer would be no. They both had to get back to real life. Not to mention the emotional and physical whiplash Morgan had gone through out there. They both needed to check in with their real lives and no doubt Morgan needed time to decompress.

"Not to mention she'll want a break from you," Shelby said into the dead air.

Suddenly, Shelby was in desperate need to move. She was headed for the door when she remembered she was wearing hospital scrubs and she hadn't washed her hair in two days. She probably looked like a mix between Bigfoot and a Chupacabra. But her stomach was growling and that seemed like an easier problem to solve.

That's how she found herself, stretched out on the kitchen floor, staring at the ceiling, eating dry roasted peanuts and wondering if Morgan would ever call her again. Of course she needed a break after their harrowing adventure, but would that break ever end? Morgan wasn't exactly the type to show up on her doorstep with a bouquet of flowers. Was she even interested in relationships? Of all the things they had discussed while forced together for six days, they hadn't discussed their love lives. That couldn't be a coincidence.

"Stop doing this to yourself." Shelby took a long breath and began her mantra. "I am Shelby Lynn Howard, granddaughter of Evelyn May Reeves. My bloodline is full of strong, confident women. I am the best of all of them by far. Granny Reeves fought to give me a chance. I won't waste that chance. I will make her proud. I will make myself proud. I am a woman to be feared by those who doubt me and loved by those who see my strength. All I have to do is wait for Morgan to remember my strength and realize that she is madly in love with me."

Just as Shelby shook off her pity party, a series of persistent chimes sounded from her office. She guessed her laptop had enough juice to start up by now and all the work she'd missed for the last week was announcing itself. Since she couldn't do more than obsess over the chances of Morgan calling her this decade, she peeled herself off the floor to trudge back to her office. After a few steps she spun on her heels and grabbed the peanuts.

As she suspected, Shelby had dozens of messages piled up in both her email and her Teams app. Most of the early ones were annoyed, but the later ones had a note of concern. Her coworkers especially seemed shocked by her silence, and she was pretty sure the first news reports about her disappearance dropped on Wednesday based on the way those messages sounded more like obituaries than attempts to communicate. The cynical side of her noted that the concern was tempered. No one had attempted to call her until Thursday. Before that, they were professionally disengaged. But then of course she'd known that no one in her life really cared if she lived or died.

To stop the intrusive thoughts, she tried to focus on something else. In her desperation for distraction, her gaze fell on the art print over her desk. It was a sepia-toned photograph of a wooden dock, stretching out into a lake with an unfocused, tree-studded background. The print was enormous, taking up most of the wall in its brushed nickel frame. It was pretty. Probably meant to inspire folks who grew up in the woods or on a lake. Shelby had done neither. She chose it because it was pretty enough and she needed something for the space. Moreover, there was nothing in her life that she would want to remember, so she bought things that were pretty and generic. She slept with women who were pretty and generic. She made herself pretty and generic.

The peanuts soured in her mouth and she screwed the cap back on the jar and turned her attention back to her coworkers' pretty and generic messages. It probably wasn't that they didn't care. It was more that they didn't know her. Maybe she should change that. Scanning the senders in her Teams chats, she spotted quite a few names of people she really liked and even respected.

As she scanned the names, one of them popped up to the top of the list as a new message arrived. It was a member of her sales team who lived nearby. The message was simple—just how very relieved she was that Shelby had been rescued and back home safe—but it meant the world in that moment. Without a second thought, Shelby responded, thanking her for the note and reassuring her that she really was fine.

She assumed that would be the end of it. Jessica would send through a happy reaction to Shelby's message and the conversation would end. Instead, they sent a couple more messages back and forth, each one more genuine than the last. Then a message came through that made Shelby's jaw drop open and her hands slip from the keyboard.

Sounds like a wild story. You'll have to tell me all about it sometime, Jessica said.

Shelby stared at the screen, a terrifying and exhilarating idea taking up all her mental capacity. In the past, she would have avoided that conversation and keep everything surface. She'd want to be sure Jessica didn't see her sweat. It would have been easy to dismiss it with a joke or give a vague agreement that they should meet up sometime. But now she didn't want to keep it surface. She didn't want to dismiss the idea. She had formed a connection with Morgan that had made her feel good and seen. She craved another connection like that.

Okay, not one exactly like her connection with Morgan. The memory of Morgan's mouth on her skin was a searing heat settled into her core and she had no desire to feel that with anyone else right now. But the friendship part would be nice to replicate.

I'd love to tell you the story and I am desperate for a salad and a glass of wine. Want to meet up and hear all the details?

Shelby was expecting to wait with bated breath for an uncomfortably long time, but Jessica agreed right away. Shelby sat there, staring at the newest message in which Jessica recommended they meet at Alagash in an hour, and found tears had collected in her eyes. Was it really that easy? Why hadn't she done this years ago? Maybe she could have already corrected all the character flaws Morgan had pointed out before they met.

Before she could get too carried away with what-ifs, Shelby forced herself to go take a shower and make herself presentable. She might be on her way to making a new friend.

❖

The crutches made it hard for Morgan to get through her front door. It had been even harder to use them to climb onto the stoop of her rented townhouse and she was already dreading the trip to the third floor for a shower and change of clothes. She'd had to ask the nurse to teach her how to use the crutches, and the training session had been laughably brief.

After using the crutch to bang her door shut, she bent over to drop her computer bag in the entryway. She hadn't even attempted to bring in her suitcase, asking the officer who escorted her home to drop it in the garage. The suitcase had been mangled during the wreck and then she'd left the trunk open when she'd fallen and melting snow had gotten in. The suitcase was soaked through and she was pretty sure she'd have to trash everything. All of her nicest work clothes were inside and it would cost her a big chunk of money to replace them all.

As she slowly lowered herself onto the couch, she marveled at how little she worried about the long-term ramifications of dipping so heavily into her emergency fund. A week ago, she'd be freaking out, worried she'd run short on her bills. This evening, however, all her usual worries about failure weren't flooding in. Maybe it was because her damn ankle was throbbing so bad she couldn't care about the cost of a shopping trip. Maybe it was because Shelby believed she could succeed and that made her want to believe it, too.

Looking around her familiar surroundings, Morgan found herself relieved to be home. She was comfortable here. She had her bearings. Well, she was relieved, but not exactly happy to be home. It would be nice to have someone to greet her when she walked in the door. The place felt empty and colder than usual without someone else. She'd gotten used to having someone there when she woke up in the morning. A smiling face to say good night.

Honestly, she would do anything to have Shelby walk through that door. Relaxing alone in her living room didn't feel quite as good as it had before. Not that it was the most comfortable living room in the world, she thought as she adjusted her ankle brace on the coffee table. An ottoman would have been infinitely more comfortable, but she didn't have one. In fact, furniture was sparse in the entire house. She'd always told herself she was being practical. After all, why did a single woman need both a couch and an armchair?

But it wasn't practicality. She saw that now. Shelby had seen it right away. She hadn't bought a lot of furniture because it would be a hassle to move it all back to Richmond. Because she had assumed, even as she was signing a lease and filling a U-Haul, that she would fail. Maybe she hadn't allowed herself those exact thoughts, but she had made the choice to skimp on furniture because in the back of her mind she was already planning which pieces she would sell and which she would haul back home when she didn't make it in this new job.

Shelby had mentioned to their rescuers how worried she was that her house plants would die while she was gone for an extra week. Morgan didn't have any such fears. There were no plants here. There were no pictures on the walls. It was depressing how little effort she'd put into making her house feel like a home. Even the hospital room she'd just come from had more cheer than this place. After her talk with Shelby, she understood she'd done it on purpose.

"Not anymore," she said to herself.

She would commit to this life. She would commit to this job. And not because of lingering guilt over her friend's death. She'd used Gail and her stone as a crutch for too long. Now it was time to try. She still might fail, but at least she would give herself a chance to succeed.

As soon as her ankle was better, she would make a trip to IKEA. Sure, it wasn't the best furniture in the world, but it would be both an economical choice and a commitment to herself. Plus, it was the closest furniture store to her townhouse.

Morgan's doorbell rang and she had a burst of hope that it was Shelby dropping by to see her. She knew it probably wasn't. After all, they barely knew each other and surely Shelby needed a little time alone after their week together, but she still struggled to her feet with more gusto than an unexpected visitor normally inspired.

"Well, look what the cat dragged in." Chad was standing outside her door, holding a foil-wrapped baking dish.

"Chad?"

"Of course, it is. Don't tell me you've forgotten what I look like already? Or did you bang up your head in addition to your foot?"

Morgan's mentor had always been a boisterous, jovial guy, but she didn't expect his overflowing energy to show up on her doorstep the moment she arrived home. And yet here he was at the threshold of her townhouse even though she was pretty sure she hadn't given him the address.

"Aren't you supposed to be in Niagara Falls?" Morgan asked.

"Turned it into a long weekend when you went MIA."

He marched across her living room toward the open kitchen as though he lived there. Despite the bland way he made the announcement, the sentiment touched Morgan deeply. She'd been so convinced she didn't have anyone in her life who would miss her, but Chad had cut his vacation short to be there when she was found. Maybe that was just the kind of guy he was, she wasn't really sure.

Chad busied himself in the kitchen, searching cabinets for dishes and preheating the oven, while Morgan followed slowly. He was dressed down in jeans and a sweatshirt for a college she was pretty sure he hadn't attended. Did he have a kid in college? She'd never asked him anything about his life.

"The wife made some chicken rigatoni thing. She said it would be funny because it's a dish from somewhere near Rochester, but it's really just something easy she thought you could reheat this weekend while you get back on your feet," Chad said.

Everything happened so fast, Morgan wasn't quite sure when she lost control of the situation. Before she knew it, Chad was shuffling her over to the couch and propping her foot up with a pillow underneath. Then he went about tidying up while keeping a near constant monologue running about what had happened at work while she was lost. She didn't hear all of it, since he kept talking while he went up to her second-floor office to plug in her work computer and phone, but she honestly didn't care all that much about their boss's handwringing. She was just so touched and a little confused by how much Chad seemed to care. After the computer and phone, he retrieved her suitcase from the garage and took it up to her laundry room.

She was even more shocked when he settled down next to her on the couch with a tray carrying two steaming bowls of chicken riggies and two mismatched teacups. He let her eat, not even requiring her to ooh and ahh over his wife's cooking, before settling back with his mug of tea.

"So, tell me all about it," Chad said.

"What do you mean?"

"Oh, don't be coy. You must have a great story to tell."

She wasn't sure it was a great story, but she was frankly shocked he wanted to hear it. She tried to remember if she'd ever had anyone sit on her couch with her for a chat over a mug of decaf Earl Grey. It didn't take much thought. She wasn't the type. Or at least she hadn't been.

"I took your advice and reserved a rental car the moment they started delaying flights," Morgan said.

It was the right opener, for sure. Chad beamed with pride and let her tell the story. Well, right up until the part when she explained offering Shelby a ride.

Chad sat forward so far it reminded her of some of the older lab techs she worked with who timed their lunch breaks to coincide with their soap operas. "I was wondering how you got stuck out there with Shelby Lynn Howard. I thought for sure you hated her. It must've felt like a lifetime in that cabin."

Morgan's heart clenched at the words. He wasn't wrong, of course, but a lot had happened since the trade show.

"It wasn't that bad. We talked a lot and got to know each other." Morgan left out how close they'd gotten to knowing each other in the biblical sense.

"That surprises me even more. I've never known Shelby to open up and show her real personality to anyone." Chad sipped his tea nonchalantly while Morgan's head spun. Apparently, her shock amused him, because he smiled. "You didn't think I fell for her act, did you?"

"No offense meant. I just thought everyone did. She didn't even really seem to realize what she was doing," Morgan said.

"It's tough for women in this field. The men who run these labs either hit on you or dismiss you. Women who run labs get there by being competitive with other women. Both treat all salespeople like meal tickets without having any real intention of buying anything. It's a tough job, everyone puts up walls of one kind or another."

The old helplessness settled over her with his words. She'd thought it got easier. She'd thought it was just hard for her because she was new. If Chad still struggled to thrive, what chance did she have?

"I'm surprised you would think I'd be good at this job if that's how it is," Morgan said quietly.

She'd expected him to give her a fatherly lecture that boiled down to telling her to buck up and grow thicker skin. She hadn't expected him to laugh hysterically.

"What're you talking about?" he asked when he'd settled down. "You're the toughest person I know. Add that to how much you love these instruments and the way you know them inside out? Heck, I came into your lab to talk about my instrument and you knew more than I did. You think most lab techs do that sort of research and have those sort of questions? You're one in a million and don't you forget it. Shoot, you'll be outselling us all once you get your feet under you."

It felt good to hear, but she wasn't quite ready to take his word as gospel yet. "Shouldn't I already have my feet under me?"

"In two years? You're kidding."

"Not really. I expected to be settled by now," Morgan said.

"Let me tell you a little story." Chad set his tea down on the coffee table and leaned back, staring at the ceiling like he was remembering a tale from a hundred years ago. "I got started here at Pulsar back in ninety-three. I was a cocky kid and I did real well early on. I was convinced I'd be running this place within a year. Thought I'd do so well I'd buy out the business. Nothing was in my way."

"Well, yeah, you're top of the leader board nearly every month."

"That's now. Back then, well, let's just say that early success didn't stick. It comes in waves, you know. Some months you're on top, some you're all the way at the bottom. I didn't know that back then."

Morgan couldn't argue the point. After all, she'd done very well right out of the gate, mostly because Chad had handed over some of his ready-to-close sales. Things didn't start to go downhill until she was on her own.

"I'd sit in my office and cry," Chad said.

"You cried?"

"I've never been so scared in all my life. Thought I was going to lose everything. The car. The house. No way my wife would stay with a loser like me. She was going places and I was fighting just to keep my head above water."

Morgan tried hard not to fall into that very same feeling every single day. Right up until she crashed a rental car into a snow-covered ditch. "How'd you pull yourself out of it?"

"I didn't." He laughed fondly and tucked his hands behind his head. "My wife found me one day and told me I was being a dumbass."

"She what?" Morgan choked on her laughter.

"In a very nice, loving way, of course. Still, I'd pissed her off. She reminded me that her contributions to our household weren't meaningless. That we were a team and she was making good money, so we'd be fine until I figured it out. Those were her exact words. We'll be fine until you figure it out. Well, after that I didn't have a choice but to figure it out. Not with a beautiful, brilliant woman who believed in me."

"It helps to have someone in your corner."

Maybe it was the wistfulness in her voice or the way she stared off into the distance when she said it, but there was a knowing twinkle in Chad's eye after that.

"I'll be in your corner until you find your own beautiful, brilliant woman to support you and kick your butt in equal measure."

"Thanks." Morgan felt the heat creep up her cheeks.

Chapter Twenty

"The Ashworth ID-Flow 1500 is able to test fifteen samples simultaneously for more efficient hands-on time with reliable, easy to read results." Shelby was just getting into her usual sales presentation. She'd set up a demonstration instrument in a hospital lab's break room and had her slides going. She was even feeling that tingle of anticipation she always got on sales pitch day. Unfortunately, her potential customer was not nearly as energized as she was.

The director and a few lab techs who weren't too busy had come in to watch Shelby do her thing, but they looked bored now they'd already eaten the free bagels. Only one tech looked engaged, taking notes about the instrument in a well-worn notebook and hanging on Shelby's every word.

Shelby found herself directing her entire presentation to this one engaged lab tech who had no purchasing authority and probably wouldn't even be asked her opinion on the different options. Still, the tech reminded her of the way Morgan described herself as a lab tech. The way she wanted to know everything there is to know about the instruments and still had at least a low-burn excitement about her work. Half of her mind was on the presentation, the other half wondered if this lab tech might be interested in joining a sales team one day, just like Morgan. She made a mental note to chat with her about her career aspirations after the presentation was over.

Once Shelby finished her part, her colleagues took over. First up was Jessica, who was as peppy with customers as she was at the happy hour they went to together the night before. After they'd met up for wine and salads the day Shelby got home, they'd struck up a friendship she hadn't really been prepared for. But Jessica was sweet and genuine and seemed to need the girl time with Shelby to decompress from the job and her two-year-old at home. And when they were out together, Shelby wasn't pretty and generic. She was Shelby. It felt nice. This was the first time they'd teamed up for a sales call in the week since Shelby had been back, but they had several more joint calls planned. It was surprisingly great to be real friends with a colleague.

After Jessica came someone from their contracts department talking about the long-term maintenance for the instrument and then the local field service engineer who would be the one to respond to repairs should they choose to buy. Shelby hadn't met the engineer before and he seemed as bored as the audience, but he was nice enough and he talked to the mostly female staff with respect—a rare enough occurrence. A call for questions at the end resulted in a long stretch of awkward silence as usual. Potential customers rarely asked questions at this stage.

All in all, the trip went just about as well as it could've. Still, Shelby was relatively sure they had no chance of winning this sale. She couldn't say why exactly, but the general energy of the room was low and that never boded well.

As people slowly gathered the last few bagels and headed back to work, Shelby caught the lab director to chat. She was cordial but noncommittal and Shelby handed her quickly off to Jessica. She tried to catch the lab tech who had been so engaged, but she had made a beeline for the field service engineer and was peppering him with questions. So no sales interest, but maybe she could be a fit for the engineer staff. If she didn't hear the engineer bring it up, Shelby would mention to the tech about their opening in the service department. No one that engaged should be allowed to slip away.

"We appreciate your time and the bagels. Thank you," the lab manager said.

Shelby noted that the engineer was now packing up her demonstration unit under the close scrutiny of the interested lab tech.

"It's our pleasure. You have a wonderful lab here and I'm pleased so much of your staff was able to join us."

"They're probably just trying to take a break from the monotony out there," the lab manager said with a conspiratorial smile.

"Nothing wrong with that. Do you have many more presentations before you make a decision?"

"Just Pulsar later today. We should have an answer for you by the end of the week."

Shelby smiled her way through the rest of the good-byes. So, Pulsar would be there later that day. Which probably meant Morgan would be there later in the day, standing in the same spot Shelby had stood for most of the morning. She wished she could stick around to see it. Had Morgan changed her style after their fight at the cabin? Shelby smiled, hoping it was true. Several things the lab manager said had hinted that she was keenly aware of the extra burden the Ashworth instrument would put on her staff. All the burdens Morgan's instrument wiped away. If she had taken Shelby's advice and relaxed into her work, this would be an easy sale for her. Even though it meant a loss for her, Shelby hoped Morgan could pull it out. It would mean the world for her confidence. And maybe if she was more confident, she would finally get around to looking up Shelby's number and calling her for a date.

"Ready to go?" Jessica asked.

"After you."

Jessica's body language as they walked to their cars seemed to indicate she knew they wouldn't land this one. Shelby felt almost as bad for Jessica as she felt good for Morgan.

Once they were out in the sunshine, Jessica turned to her. "What do you think about this one? I give it about a sixty percent chance to close."

"That might be generous, but hey, you can't win them all."

Jessica turned a knowing smile on Shelby. "I heard Pulsar is giving their pitch this afternoon."

"I heard the same thing."

"We could hang out in the cafeteria and maybe you'll get a chance to see Morgan."

"I should have never told you about that." Shelby laughed. "I have no idea how you talked me into that second glass of wine. I never would've spilled the beans if you hadn't liquored me up."

Jessica bumped her hip against Shelby's playfully as they walked. "I talked you into the second glass of wine because I am an excellent saleswoman."

"That you are."

They stopped in front of Shelby's shiny silver SUV and Jessica turned to her with a serious, thoughtful expression.

"You're a very good saleswoman, too, you know?"

"Thanks," Shelby said.

"You're such a good saleswoman that I bet you could convince a certain rival saleswoman that you'd make a good girlfriend."

"I probably could convince her." Shelby forced herself to smile, but it tasted bittersweet. "But is it too much to ask that she not have to be convinced? That she just wants to be with me for me, not because of an excellent sales pitch?"

"I doubt you'll have to do a lot of convincing."

"Well, if she wants me, it won't be too hard for her to track me down."

Honestly, Shelby was a little hurt Morgan hadn't done so already. She had resisted the urge to call first, forcing herself to give Morgan the space she needed. But it had been a week since they last saw each other, and Morgan hadn't reached out. Was Shelby really that easy to forget? Because she certainly hadn't been able to forget Morgan. She'd thought about her every day at least once. Every night when she lay down to sleep, she'd remembered the way it had felt with Morgan on top of her and her dreams had filled in the gaps of their interrupted rendezvous.

"She'll call," Jessica said. "Just give her time."

Shelby nodded, wishing rather than truly believing it was true. It felt less and less likely the more time passed, but she wouldn't give up hope just yet. She would give Morgan all the time she needed. Shelby had a feeling Morgan was worth waiting for.

❖

Morgan had been sitting in her car for twenty minutes, prepping for her first sales pitch since she'd been rescued from the cabin. She was nervous, sure, but she was also excited and that was a new feeling for her in this situation. She usually sweated right through her shirt at least once on sales pitch days. Today she was calm, almost eerily so.

The wild part was, she usually was only able to relax by squeezing her stone from Gail and remembering how important this was. But she didn't have Gail's stone anymore, and yet somehow, she still had Gail. While she was melting down in the cabin, she'd thought she would lose the gravity of her work when she lost that hunk of pink quartz. Instead, she'd found double the strength it had provided inside herself. And she'd found peace. A deep, resounding peace that made everything so much easier.

"Shelby was right," she said aloud to the empty car.

As though Morgan had spoken her into existence, Shelby appeared in front of her, walking through the hospital parking lot just a few feet away. Beside her walked a woman who looked remarkably similar. Same pale blond hair in a high ponytail, same simple suit with heels and a silk shirt, same black computer bag sporting the Ashworth company logo, same model-pretty face. A casual glance would make anyone think they were identical, but Morgan's glance was anything but casual.

The stranger lacked any of the essence that made Shelby impossible to miss in a crowd. Her smile was vapid compared to the charming depth of Shelby's. Her laughter was hollow compared to the bell-ringing clarity of Shelby's. Her beauty was surface while Shelby's was earth-shattering. Perhaps it wasn't kind of Morgan to diminish the stranger so much, but how could she not when she was standing next to one of the most striking women in the world?

God's sake, Shelby looked amazing. Morgan had seen her most often in baggy, borrowed sweatpants and threadbare flannel. A body like hers begged to be wrapped in designer labels and soft, flowing fabrics. She was more stunning today than she had been

• 223 •

at the trade show. More stunning even than she had been leaning across an old couch to kiss Morgan until her mind went blank. How lucky was this random stranger that she got to stand in the reflection of Shelby's magnificence? A pang of jealousy shot through Morgan. Not that she thought there was anything between them—the matching computer bags confirmed they were simply colleagues—but she got to stand there, laughing with Shelby. Leaning in and touching her arm as their conversation grew serious. Meanwhile Morgan was just an observer, trapped inside her steel and glass bubble of invisibility.

They stopped just a few spaces away, but angled so that they wouldn't be able to see Morgan waiting here in her car. She was thrilled and a little ashamed at how thrilled she was to be watching while she couldn't be seen. It felt illicit, but it also felt safe. Morgan had spent the last week desperate to call Shelby but frightened, too.

So much had happened in the cabin and now, back here in the bustling streets and constant stimulation of Washington, DC, the solace of the snow-bound cabin felt like a dream. A fantasy. Did it feel the same way to Shelby? Did she think about Morgan the way Morgan thought about her? The ache to see her again, to hear her voice, to touch that skin she'd barely had a taste of, was so desperate it felt feral. Morgan couldn't quite believe it was possible that Shelby felt the same way. After all, Shelby adapted to every situation like a chameleon. Was that what she had done in the cabin? And what about Morgan's actions? Had the pull to Shelby been real or had it been the result of forced proximity? Morgan was determined to keep them separate for a little while just to see. Just to be sure it was all real. That it wasn't cabin fever.

Still, the more Morgan watched Shelby right then, the more she noticed how at ease Shelby was. There was something different about the way she was holding herself as she spoke to her colleague than she was at the trade show. She was at work in that moment, but she looked like she had in the cabin. Like she was being the real Shelby with her coworker the way she had been with Morgan. She couldn't put her finger on what exactly it was she saw, but it was unmistakably there.

Morgan's heart thudded uncomfortably in her chest. She couldn't tell if it was jealousy that Shelby might be interested in this woman—which her body language didn't really suggest but was still a terrifying possibility—or if she was excited at the possibility that Shelby might've taken her advice. It shouldn't have been such a surprise. After all, Morgan's hands had what felt like permanent blisters from the tools she'd been wielding nonstop in her attempt to commit to this job. Her house was full of new furniture and that furniture felt like roots she was putting down. She'd even bought a potted plant the day before.

As Shelby climbed into her car, looking suddenly a little sad, Morgan wondered if Shelby was interested in committing to a relationship the way she was committing to her career. It was a big leap to go from a week stranded in a cabin with someone to dating them, and maybe she didn't have the same lingering feelings Morgan did. She would never know unless she gave Shelby a call, but that felt like a bridge too far right now. An IKEA end table was one thing, asking Shelby out was another thing altogether.

Once Shelby had pulled out of the parking lot, Morgan sighed and pushed open her car door. There was no time to worry about this now. Right now, she needed to get inside that hospital and convince them that her instrument was the right one for them.

Chad was waiting for Morgan outside the lab when she arrived. She wondered if he'd seen Shelby. Had he talked to her? Had Shelby mentioned her? But then he turned to see her and she put her worries aside in the warmth of his fatherly smile.

"Ready to reel another one in?" Chad asked.

"You bet, boss."

"Boss?" He said the word with a bark of laughter. "I'm nobody's boss. Bosses have too much work to do. Plus they're traveling all the time. You know I hate that. Remember how grumpy I was when we went on that call down in Raleigh?"

He shuddered at the memory, but Morgan was focused on a different memory than her mentor fussing about lukewarm eggs at the breakfast buffet. All she could think about was strip mall empanadas.

"Hey, Chad." He'd been reaching for the door handle but stopped when she spoke. "What's your favorite food?"

"Ice cream," he said without hesitation.

"Too generic. What's your favorite ice cream?"

"Flavor or producer?"

His eyebrows knitted together in concentration and Morgan couldn't help loving this guy a little more every time he spoke.

"Either."

He squinted at her and asked, "What's this all about?"

"Just wondering if you have a food memory. A meal you have an emotional connection to."

"I know what you mean by food memory." He gave her a searching look, then a slow smile spread across his face. "I tell you what. Come to the house for dinner with me and the wife this weekend. You bring the ice cream."

"What kind?"

"Don't you worry." He pulled the lab door open and held it for her. "I'll give you all the details after you make this sale."

Chapter Twenty-one

Shelby rolled her shoulders and tucked one leg underneath the other, then went back to typing what she sincerely hoped was her last email of the day. She'd spent the day working from home and, though she had embraced those days since her time in the cabin, she still missed people time. It really only worked for her because of the budding friendships she'd been forming.

It wasn't just Jessica, although nights out chatting with her were still Shelby's favorites. Tonight she had a Women in Business get-together and she was seriously looking forward to it. She and Jessica had gone together the week before and had a blast. What a wonderful new experience it was to complain and celebrate in equal measure with other women. Of course, it was a networking opportunity, but for right now she was embracing it as a group of people with common interests just hanging out. Last week she'd had to force herself not to fall back into her old people-pleasing habits once or twice, but the fact that she'd managed to stop herself showed progress and she was happy with that.

When her work cell phone rang, it only took one glance to make Shelby groan. She'd hoped to avoid talking to Joshua for a long while after the trade show, but he was the bad penny that always turned up when you least wanted them. Especially as her reformation was so new. He was a backslide just waiting to happen. She answered on speaker phone both in the hopes that he would hear her clacking away on the keyboard and keep the conversation short and also because she didn't want to put a phone with him on the other end that close to her face.

"Hey, Joshua."

"How's it hangin', smoke show?"

Shelby's lip curled. He loved to give her a new, disgusting nickname each time they spoke, but this one was both stupid and gross. She took a moment to ponder whether ignoring things like that was cowardly. It probably was, but she wasn't sure exactly how to respond so she didn't.

"Nice of you to give the rest of us a chance by taking a week off," he said.

"My pleasure."

"I doubt it. I heard you got stuck in some cabin with no electricity and only that cold fish from the show for company."

"What did you say?" Shelby's annoyance flashed into anger.

"She was wound up pretty tight, but I bet you didn't have any trouble getting her to warm up, did you?"

Disgust flooded through Shelby, but it was only half about Joshua. Of course he would say something like that about Morgan, but this was exactly the kind of thing she went along with in the past. She would laugh and maybe even say something disgusting in return because joking together like this meant he liked her. When had everyone else's approval become so important to her that she would want a slimeball like him to like her? She didn't need a psychologist to answer that one, but it was time she stopped blaming things on her parents. This was the change she needed to make.

"You know what?" Shelby took a deep breath, closed her eyes, and dove in. "It's not okay for you to speak about Morgan like that. In fact, it's not okay to speak about any woman like that."

There was a moment of ringing silence before he said, "Huh?"

"Look, I know I went along with shit like that in the past. Hell, I can admit I even encouraged it, but it was wrong and I'm not doing it anymore."

"What the fuck? I thought you were cool."

"I thought you were cool, too, but apparently not if that's how you talk about women." Shelby was warming to the conversation with every new defense.

"Like you didn't talk about women like that. You're such a fake."

"I was a fake before, you're right. I admit I was an asshole, but I'm turning a new leaf."

"Oh great. Another hot woman going all woke on me," he said.

"You can call it anything you want, as long as you know where I stand."

"Yeah, I know exactly where you stand." He was starting to growl through his words now and Shelby was extremely happy she took this step over the phone rather than face-to-face. "You're looking to make trouble and be the HR hero or whatever. Fine. I don't care, but I'm keeping my distance because I don't want to be part of your feminist rampage. I don't need you to do to me what you did to Eric. He nearly lost his job because of you. I'm not losing my job for you or anyone."

The line went dead and it was honestly the best outcome. He could think whatever he wanted about her, but she wasn't going to validate his misogyny any more than she already had. He probably would lose his job, but not because of her. Both he and Eric were living on borrowed time with their outdated behavior. She was thrilled to have nothing more to do with either of them. Especially since she was going to spend the evening with a bunch of extraordinary women. Sometimes the group told stories about nightmare dealings with men like Joshua and Eric and she would inwardly cringe, knowing she had been part of the problem. Well, no more. She could walk into that group with her head held high tonight.

She let out a quiet laugh, shaking her head at herself. She hadn't done that for the Women in Business group. She'd done it because he said those things about Morgan. She stood up to Joshua for herself, of course, but maybe it was a little bit for Morgan, too. Another chance to prove she could be a better person. A person Morgan might call one of these days.

She was just closing her email so she could dress for her evening out when the screen pinged with a new email. Worried it might be another rant from Joshua, she pulled it up so she could keep all the drama confined to one day. As she read, she felt the corner of her mouth turn up.

Dear Ms. Howard,

I'd like to thank you and Jessica for your time last week, introducing my staff to the Ashworth ID-Flow 1500. While your presentation was compelling and the instrument was a top contender, we've decided to purchase an instrument from another company. Our priorities of ease of use for our laboratory technicians was the deciding factor, and while the ID-Flow performs well, it simply puts too great a burden on our hardworking staff.

Thank you again,
Sandra Goddard

Shelby laughed as she closed her laptop and plugged it in. Marching off to the shower, she made a mental note to congratulate Morgan on her sale the next time they spoke. Maybe it was wishful thinking, but it helped to convince herself she and Morgan would speak again. It gave her something to look forward to.

❖

Morgan parked her SUV in front of a ridiculously cute craftsman house at the end of a cul de sac. The grass in the front yard was so vividly green and neatly trimmed it looked otherworldly. Tidy flower beds with pristine red mulch and a few late season plants wrapped around the house to meet a brand-new privacy fence. If she knew Chad at all, there was a brick patio behind the fence, complete with a meticulously clean grill and probably a hammock stretched between a couple of the trees whose bare branches she could see over the fence. It was so picture-perfect she expected animated woodland creatures to pop out of the edges to sing a Disney-style song.

She grabbed the pie she'd baked that afternoon and the carton of vanilla ice cream Chad had insisted she bring.

"It's not a pie without ice cream," he'd said.

"Don't you want to know what kind of pie I'm making before you decide?"

"No need. Vanilla ice cream goes with every type of pie," he'd said in his usual mentor tone.

He really was a sweet man. Ever since her ordeal in New York, he'd been treating Morgan like a daughter. Honestly, she loved the feeling. She missed her parents. She hadn't realized quite how much. She really should go visit them more. Richmond was only a four-hour roundtrip drive, and it was worth it to get more time with them. When she couldn't visit, however, it didn't hurt to have a backup close at hand.

Chad and Cheryl opened the front door hand-in-hand about three seconds after Morgan rang the bell. Chad grabbed the ice cream while Cheryl wrapped her in a hug that smelled of floral perfume and warm spices. A lump of emotion formed in her throat, and she had to fight hard to keep the tears out of her eyes. These two were sweeter than the cherry pie she'd made from scratch.

They took her on a tour of their home before dinner. It was a modest size but in a lovely neighborhood and was worth a small fortune. They'd moved in twenty years before, but had obviously kept up on renovations because it felt modern in a cozy way. As she passed a bank of windows overlooking the backyard, Morgan could see her assessment was spot-on. There were actually two hammocks, hung side-by-side in the corner of the yard and the grill was protected under a tight-fitting wrap.

Morgan hid her smile behind an upraised hand. She'd never taken the time to read people before, but maybe she learned a thing or two from Shelby after all. Shelby would rub it in the next time they saw each other. The thought caught her by surprise, but then she remembered that feeling of walking down the hallway to the bedroom in the cabin. The inevitability of their intimacy. Now there was the inevitability of their reunion. Somehow, she'd known the moment they parted that it would be up to her to reach out when she was ready to start something real. Not because Shelby didn't want anything between them or wouldn't put in the effort, but Shelby knew she would need time. Of course she knew. She knew everything about everyone. She knew everything about Morgan. Even with her one-word answers and her evasions, Shelby had read her as easily as the cheap paperback thrillers on the bookshelf. Morgan was so grateful she had.

"What are you over there grinning about?" Chad asked.

"Oh, I just love your house. It's so charming and cozy."

The compliment made Chad puff up and he started prattling on about how much of the work he did himself. Cheryl interrupted occasionally with reminders about which contractor did this and which did that, but Morgan wasn't really listening. In fact, she allowed their loving and familiar banter to wash over her most of the evening. She was charmed by their deep affection and contentment with each other, so she had a lovely evening. Better than any she'd had in a long time, in fact. Still, her mind was fixed firmly on Shelby. At some point during the evening, she'd realized it was time to make the call and the thought had her both nervous and excited.

After dinner, Morgan and Chad lounged in bright red Adirondack chairs on the back patio with a second slice of pie each. More accurately, Chad's slice of pie was minuscule compared to the massive scoops of vanilla ice cream on his plate. She watched as he scooped up a mound of slightly melting ice cream and slid the spoon into his mouth with a groan of ecstasy.

"My wife never lets me keep ice cream in the house." He spoke with his eyes still blissfully closed. "She has this weird thing about wanting me to be healthy so I live longer. But what's the point of living a long life if it isn't full of vanilla ice cream?"

Morgan agreed with the sentiment, if not the object, and scooped up a big pile of baked cherries and flaky crust.

"How long have you two been together?" Morgan asked.

"She'll tell you forty-three years, but it's actually only been forty-two. She didn't want her folks to know how quick we rushed into getting married, so she bumps back the date by a year."

He looked over his shoulder to where Cheryl was just visible through the kitchen window, washing dishes and singing along to some classic rock playing through the stereo speakers. There was a tenderness in his gaze Morgan had seen several times tonight. There was a twinkle in his eye when he looked at her. Like she was what really mattered in his life. Cheryl looked at Chad that way, too. Like

• 232 •

he could lose everything and she would still love him. And that was true, of course. Chad had told her that's what she said when he was struggling early in his career. She would love him the same if he was working in a factory making telephones or if he was CEO of Pulsar. He was what mattered, not his job.

That's the way Morgan needed to look at life. She needed to ignore the trappings of professional success and just live the life she wanted. Live a life where she had someone at home to nag her about how much vanilla ice cream she ate and look at her like the sun rose and set behind her eyes.

Chad leaned forward and set his empty plate on the wicker table in front of him, "So did the ice cream give you the food memory you were looking for?"

"It's very good." She set her plate next to his and gathered all her courage. "But I'm actually stuck thinking about a different meal. Chad, can you give me Shelby's phone number?"

A smile grew slowly on his face. "I've been waiting for you to ask."

Chapter Twenty-two

Shelby ran as fast as she could manage in her spike heels and tight skirt, her purse banging against her hip as she dodged around a small group who'd stopped in the center of the sidewalk. She was never late. She hated to be late. Beltway traffic had been its usual snarled mess, though she wouldn't necessarily expect it to be so bad on a Wednesday evening. Fortunately, the restaurant was in sight.

After navigating the stuttering movement of the revolving door, she finally burst into the restaurant and immediately spotted her friends. Jessica waved and saluted with a very full glass of wine from a high-top against the window. Claire and Beth held up their glasses, too, and there were smiles all around. Shelby puffed out a relieved breath. Her friends weren't mad at her for her tardiness and she could relax into the evening.

As she crossed the bustling restaurant, Shelby marveled at the state of her life. Just a month ago, a scene like this would be unbelievable. Back then she would have made sure she was the first one here, aligning her work schedule to ensure it if necessary. She also would have made sure she was on the phone with a client when they arrived. She would have been overly friendly with the client and laugh the way some of the women farther down the bar right now were laughing at the bad jokes from their male companions.

Once her colleagues were seated, she would have finished the call, rolled her eyes, and made a joke about how these clients never gave us a break, did they, gals? The whole exchange would have been a way to establish camaraderie but also subtly establish dominance. A way for her to make them feel insecure about why they weren't on a call with clients right up until happy hour started. They would chat for forty-five minutes about work and complain about customers, and then Shelby would drop a question about one of their love lives, which would take another forty-five minutes. At the ninety-minute mark, she would have groaned and said she had to head home, confident that the other women would respect her, but she wouldn't gain anything else from the encounter.

Instead of that carefully choreographed evening, new Shelby truly looked forward to chatting with her friends. She dropped onto her stool, late, apologetic, and completely real. She ordered a glass of wine and then asked Beth about her new puppy and teased Claire about whether her boyfriend had finally proposed. They chatted about work a little, but mostly about their lives, and it was wonderful. She truly enjoyed their company and had no motivation in her questioning other than a genuine interest in their lives. She had real, important friends for the first time in years.

"Okay, ladies, bruschetta or buffalo cauliflower bites?" Jessica asked.

"No cauliflower for me," Claire said.

"Oh, Roger must be coming over tonight." Shelby gave a teasing laugh.

Claire blushed in her usual adorable way whenever her boyfriend was mentioned and elbowed Shelby.

"I can't handle the spice either. How about spinach artichoke dip?" Beth asked, ever the peacekeeper.

"As long as there's more wine, I'll eat anything," Jessica said.

They clinked empty glasses and laughed too loud, but every guest was too loud, so they didn't garner any attention. The waiter had taken their order and the empty bottle of wine when Shelby's phone vibrated on the table. She was going to ignore it in favor of her friends, but she glanced at the caller ID by habit. She hadn't realized she'd gasped out loud until she looked up to find the other three women staring at her, grasping each other's arms and identical expressions of barely contained excitement on their faces.

"It's her, isn't it?" Jessica asked.

Shelby nodded, a bubble of anticipation blocking her throat. The phone rattled a second time, but Shelby was stuck staring at it.

"Oh my God, answer it quick before she loses her nerve," Claire said.

That caught Shelby's attention. It had taken Morgan three weeks to finally call. There was every chance she'd chicken out and end the call if Shelby waited too long. She leaped off the barstool and snatched the phone, running toward the patio door.

"Hello?" Shelby was out of breath as she answered the call and burst out into the December cold.

"Um, hi."

Those two syllables made blood roar in Shelby's ears so loud she could barely hear. "Morgan? Is that you?"

"Yeah. It is. Hi."

"Hi."

"I got your number from Chad. I hope that's okay," Morgan said.

The awkwardness and hesitation were so cute it made Shelby's confidence soar.

"Of course." Shelby had asked Chad for Morgan's number a few days after returning, knowing she wouldn't be the first one to dial it, but also wanting to know who it was when the call finally came in. "I was wondering if I'd hear from you."

There was a long silence on the other side of the call and Shelby knew Morgan was deciding how to respond to that comment. Apparently, she decided to ignore it.

"How are you doing? Adjusting to being back at work?" Morgan asked.

"I'm trying, but I do miss all that free time and…" Shelby let a short, pregnant silence grow. "The roaring fire and a good book."

Shelby paced the patio, her heels clicking on the bricks. She hadn't flexed her flirting muscles in a long while, but it sure was fun.

"I miss that, too," Morgan said, her voice low.

Shelby's heart soared that Morgan had picked up on the flirting. It gave her hope. She turned in her pacing and saw her friends pressed to the window. They were all grinning from ear to ear and they gave her thumbs-ups. Beth held out a bottle of champagne they'd apparently ordered after she'd left. Shelby couldn't help but laugh at their jumping up and down and encouraging her.

"What's so funny?" Morgan asked.

"You. I never thought you'd miss…the fireplace."

"I like surprising you."

Shelby's heart was thudding again and her senses swam. She had to stop walking to keep from falling over. "This call is a surprise," Shelby said. "For a while there I thought you were bored of me."

"I can't imagine anyone getting bored of you."

Shelby closed her eyes as her cheeks ached from her smile. She took a long breath, reminding herself not to try controlling the situation. She wanted something to happen here, but she didn't want to dictate it. That's what old Shelby would do, but new Shelby wanted Morgan to set the pace. She could be patient. Morgan was worth being patient and letting go.

Morgan cleared her throat and launched into what was obviously a prepared speech. "I realized when I unpacked that I ended up with a few items that don't look familiar. I'm not sure if they're yours or if I accidentally stole from our host. If they're yours, I'd like to return them. Plus, I owe you dinner for helping me when I hurt my ankle. Are you free to come over to my place Friday night?"

"I am free Friday night and I'd love to come over."

"Great," Morgan said.

"On one condition."

"Oh?"

"You have to cook me fresh vegetables. And no canned meat," Shelby said.

"Deal." Morgan's voice was a little breathy.

"In that case, I'll see you Friday night."

Shelby wasn't entirely sure how she managed to finish the conversation so calmly. By the time they hung up, she was lightheaded with joy and not a small amount of relief. She took a moment to bask in the glow before turning back to the bar. Her friends were still there at the window, this time holding up glasses of champagne and cheering so loud she could hear it outside. The manager would be over soon to make them calm down, but it was worth it, right?

She marched inside to claim her glass of champagne, only dimly hoping she wasn't celebrating too soon. She downed the bubbly in one the moment her butt hit the stool.

"Well?" Jessica's voice shook with suppressed excitement. "Don't keep us in suspense. What did she say?"

"I'm going to her house on Friday for a thank-you dinner." The other three squealed and high-fived each other, but she forced herself to say, "It's not a date. Just a thank you."

"Oh sure." Claire scoffed.

"Seriously, I'm not going to force anything."

"You don't have to force it. It's definitely a date," Beth said.

"It's one hundred percent a date." Jessica refilled her champagne flute.

Shelby grabbed the glass. "God, I hope so."

❖

Morgan was so nervous cooking dinner that she nearly chopped her finger off while slicing red bell peppers for the salad. She set the knife down and took a deep breath, reminding herself she didn't want another romantic evening with Shelby to end in the ER. Suddenly, she remembered she'd forgotten to chill the ridiculously expensive bottle of wine she'd picked up for dinner.

After putting the wine in the fridge, she wandered around the living room, fluffing new pillows and adjusting the massive print over the couch. It wasn't until she looked around for something else to futz with that she remembered she hadn't finished making the salad. On her way back to the kitchen, however, the timer dinged and she had to detour to take the bread out of the oven.

"Just relax," she told herself as she finally got back to the salad. "It'll be just like in the cabin with Shelby. So what if we're back to our regular lives? She's still the same person."

Morgan wasn't sure if that was true exactly. After all, she wasn't the same person she'd been out there and that was a good thing. Still, Shelby had been quick to agree to dinner, so she wanted to be there. Of course, Morgan wanted this to be more than a thank-you dinner. She wanted this to be a date and she had no idea if that's what Shelby wanted. She was too afraid to ask. She was too afraid to go after something and miss.

Forcing herself to put the knife down again, Morgan reached for the stone in her pocket. She was met with only empty fabric. It wasn't the first time she'd reached for the missing stone since she'd come home. There had even been one bad Saturday when she had cried harder than she had since Gail's memorial. There hadn't been a funeral, of course. No one got a funeral in those early days of COVID, but the lab staff had come together in the hospital courtyard to reminisce at a safe distance. Morgan hadn't thought about that depressing farce of a memorial in a long time because she had Gail's stone to console her.

Morgan forced her thoughts away from what she had lost to what she had gained. She looked into her living room at the new decor and the potted plants dotting the windowsills. These were her new talismans. Her new reminders that negative thinking wasn't helpful and she had to stop with it. She was done making herself miserable in the off chance she would fail. She would apply that to this evening. If things didn't work out with Shelby, that was okay. At least she had tried. The thought of things not working out with Shelby freaked her out, but she forced herself not to dwell on it. She wouldn't sabotage this night before it started. She would put herself out there.

Morgan had finished the salad and washed both the knife and the cutting board by the time the doorbell rang. She took a deep breath and checked the security camera display on her phone. Shelby stood on her stoop, shifting her weight from one foot to another. Honestly, she looked a little nervous, too, and that gave Morgan hope.

"You can do this," Morgan repeated to herself as she crossed to the front door.

When she opened it, she froze in her tracks. Shelby was absolutely breathtaking. She had clearly come straight from work.

She wore a cowl neck sweater the golden-brown of autumn leaves, and black trousers with a high waist and flowing legs that covered up all but the very tip of her high heels. A gunmetal gray peacoat that stretched to her knees hung open and a bulging computer bag with the Ashworth Diagnostics logo pulled down one shoulder. But it was her flowing, slightly windblown blond hair and shimmering blue eyes that captured Morgan's attention. Perhaps she'd imagined the nervousness through the doorbell camera, because standing in front of her now was the same light, confident woman who had captured her eye in Rochester a month ago.

"Hi there." Shelby held out a bottle of wine.

"Hi." Morgan took the bottle in numb hands without really feeling its weight. She cupped one hand underneath it to make sure she didn't drop it, since she couldn't quite bring herself to tear her eyes away from Shelby's smile. After a few seconds, Morgan remembered to step back and invite her inside.

Shelby dropped her bag in the entryway and shed her coat, staring around at the townhouse with obvious interest. Morgan awkwardly hung the coat in her closet one-handed, but Shelby was gone when she turned around.

"I love that print."

Morgan followed the sound of her voice into the living room. She was admiring the massive frame over the couch, depicting a vividly green forest with a wooden footbridge in the distance. Morgan had been struck by the image immediately and couldn't leave the store without it. She knew it was because it reminded her of the cabin—minus the mounds of snow—and she chose not to examine her interest in a piece of art that evoked the memory of her dalliance with hypothermia.

"It's beautiful, isn't it?"

Morgan was just able to flick her eyes from the way Shelby's trousers cupped her butt perfectly to the print before she was caught staring.

"So beautiful that I forgive you for lying to me," Shelby said with a teasing grin.

"Lying to you?"

"You said you hadn't decorated your place at all, but here I am in a super cozy, super adorable townhouse. I see art and even plant life."

Shelby's heels clicked on the hardwood as she slowly marched across the living room. The closer she got, the less Morgan was able to string together coherent thoughts.

"I wasn't lying. I've just made a lot of changes since I got home."

Morgan's face went numb as Shelby drew level with her. The intensity in Shelby's gaze, the fire and the shameless interest, were intoxicating. But Morgan's statement seemed to catch her up short. She stopped and stared at Morgan thoughtfully, even reaching up to tap one of her short, French-tipped nails against her own chin.

"I made a lot of changes after our time together, too."

There was a breathy intensity in her voice and she grabbed Morgan's gaze and held it fast. Any thought of asking Shelby what those changes had been or really speaking at all fled in the face of that sizzling eye contact. In a heartbeat, she was back on that worn-out, decades old couch, a fire crackling over her shoulder and the taste of Shelby's breath on her tongue. In truth, she had never really left that moment. Or at the very least that moment had been a fulcrum point in her life. She had been someone else, then she leaned forward and her life had pivoted like a see-saw. She'd never be able to set her feet back down on the ground she'd left when Shelby kissed her.

A timer buzzed in the kitchen and Morgan jumped, her toes actually leaving the ground for a moment. She'd forgotten pasta was boiling away on the stove and a pork loin sizzled in the oven. She'd forgotten there was a world outside those sapphire eyes and that crooked, knowing smile. Shelby had the strangest power to make the world melt away.

"Dinner," Morgan said in a thin voice.

She didn't invite Shelby to follow her, just hustled off to make sure her distraction hadn't ruined their dinner. She didn't hear the click of Shelby's heels behind her and she was relieved. She needed a moment to get her feet back underneath her. Based on that intense stare, she was pretty sure this was a date, but that somehow only made her more nervous.

Morgan was just pouring the newly drained pasta into her pan with caramelized onions, garlic, and white wine when she finally heard Shelby enter the kitchen. She tried to act cool and stir the pasta rather than turn around, but she was pretty sure Shelby could tell she was holding her breath.

"Have you finished all your knife work?" Shelby asked.

"Yep. Just a couple minutes until dinner."

"Great, then you are allowed a glass of wine. Where do you keep your corkscrew?"

Morgan indicated a drawer as she flipped the contents of her frying pan with a few flicks of her wrist. She was hoping to impress Shelby, but her focus was on opening the bottle of red wine she'd brought.

"I didn't know what you'd make, but Granny Reeves said always bring a gift when you visit someone's home," Shelby said.

"I'm not a connoisseur or anything. I had to get a recommendation from the guy at the wine store."

"Cheap stolen whiskey is more your style, huh?" Shelby slid a generous glass of red wine along the counter to settle next to the stove.

"The cheaper the better."

Shelby laughed and it became Morgan's new goal in life to make her repeat that incredible sound as often as possible. They tapped their glasses together and sipped, maintaining eye contact that crackled with the same heat as the look they'd shared in the living room.

"Hey, Morgan." Shelby leaned close.

"Yeah?"

"Your onions are burning."

"My onions are…oh fuck."

Morgan shook the pan hard and Shelby laughed just as hard. When heat crept up Morgan's neck, she knew she was blushing. She focused back on her task before she really embarrassed herself, but Shelby was too sweet to make her sweat. She hopped up on the counter well out of Morgan's way, but still close enough they could chat, and sipped her wine.

"It's been harder than I thought it would be to get back into my work routine after so many days of rest," Shelby said.

"I thought you lived for work?"

"I did. That's why it's such a shock. I should probably take more vacations so I get used to the feeling."

It was easier to relax when Shelby was so casual. She crossed her legs and leaned back into the cabinets as they chatted about nothing of real consequence. It was wonderfully domestic. Time and wine flowed by until they were nearly finished with Shelby's bottle and the pork had sufficiently rested.

"Are you ready for dinner?" Morgan asked.

Shelby leaned closer, inspecting the plates. "Why does this look familiar?"

"Well, I didn't have your recipe, of course, but it's sort of a fresh version of the pasta you made me our first night in the cabin. With fresh peas rather than canned and marinated pork tenderloin rather than SPAM."

When she saw Shelby's eyes were shining with unshed tears, Morgan thought she might have made a mistake. She should wait to explain the whole food memory thing just in case it was too much. Shelby's smile was wide and genuine, though, and she hopped right down off the counter, landing more gracefully than Morgan thought she could wearing spike heels.

For dinner, Morgan presented the Sancerre suggested by the man at the wine shop in town. Shelby's eyebrow rose at the label, and that seemed to be a good thing because she eagerly swapped out her glass of red. The pasta, too, seemed to be a hit. Shelby's eyes rolled back at her first bite, and she let out a moan that had Morgan biting the inside of her cheek.

Honestly, Morgan still preferred Shelby's version of the pasta, but it was pretty good. Shelby seemed to like it and that was all that really mattered. As the meal progressed and the wine glasses slowly emptied, Morgan realized the first date nerves had fully dissipated. More than that, she realized the easy rapport they'd built in the cabin was still going strong. Maybe it wasn't cabin fever after all. Maybe this thing between them was real? Shelby seemed to think so, too, because she leaned in closer and closer as dinner progressed. By the time they pushed their plates away, their faces were only inches apart and Morgan was thinking about the taste of Shelby's lips again. Did Shelby want to be kissed? Had she come here expecting to go to bed with Morgan? Morgan hoped rather than expected it to be true.

"I should get these." Morgan grabbed their empty plates.

"I'll help."

Shelby grabbed the salad bowls and followed, standing close while Morgan deposited the dishes in the sink. Morgan tried hard to convince herself that Shelby was just tipsy, not flirting, so she wouldn't put expectations on the night which might be disappointing. That was until she turned off the kitchen faucet and felt Shelby slide up behind her.

"Do you know what I can't stop thinking about since the cabin?" Shelby whispered against the back of her neck.

Morgan turned, locking eyes with Shelby. "What?"

Shelby's eyes burned and she leaned in as though to kiss Morgan, but she stopped a breath away from her lips.

"You on top of me." When Morgan's breath caught, Shelby smiled. "Have you been thinking about it, too?"

Morgan couldn't speak. All she wanted was Shelby's lips to finish their push forward and lock with hers. She wanted Shelby's hands to slide up her sides. She wanted to run her tongue from the base of Shelby's neck to the hinge of her jaw. She wanted to spend the rest of the night with her tongue and fingers buried deep inside Shelby.

"Every night," Morgan said.

"Glad to hear it." Then she finally leaned in. She caught Morgan's lips with hers and slipped her tongue into Morgan's mouth. That kiss that had haunted her dreams was nothing compared to this one. She knew for certain this kiss wasn't born of boredom or lack of options. This was a kiss they had both craved for weeks and they wouldn't be denied.

Morgan had no fears about appearing desperate. She was desperate and she was fine with it. She threw her arms around Shelby. Shelby's arms tightened around her, fingers clawing into Morgan's back and making her mind go blissfully blank.

Morgan was fully prepared to throw Shelby back on the counter or, even better, on the kitchen floor, but Shelby pulled back far enough to pant until she caught her breath.

"Where is your bedroom?" Shelby asked.

Chapter Twenty-three

Shelby walked into every room like she owned it, and that included Morgan's bedroom. She didn't turn on the light or wait for Morgan to invite her in. She just marched to the foot of the bed, turned to sit on the edge of the mattress, then crooked her finger in Morgan's direction with a smoldering look that could have melted the paint off the walls.

Morgan forgot about the way her button up had twisted in the waistband of her khakis while they were making out. She forgot how she smelled like garlic and wine. She forgot that Shelby had only ever seen her naked body broken and bruised. When a woman like Shelby looked at you the way she was looking at Morgan right now, there was no room to be self-conscious. When a woman like Shelby looked at you like that, you were bulletproof.

Shelby spread her legs and Morgan knelt between them like a supplicant. She didn't wait to be invited or ask what Shelby wanted. She ran her hands greedily through that goldenrod hair and dragged those ruby lips to meet hers. Morgan bathed in her. Devoured her. Worshiped her. When Shelby's legs wrapped around her back and the heel of her pumps scraped against Morgan's back, she lost herself in the sensation of their joining.

As they kissed hungrily, Shelby crawled toward the pillows, dragging Morgan on top of her. Morgan pushed the thick, cabled sweater up to expose Shelby's stomach. She slid her tongue up and down that pale skin she'd barely tasted before. A glimmer of doubt flashed in the back of her mind, waiting for the angry bumblebee buzz of snow mobiles to interrupt them again. But they were hundreds of miles from that snowbound cabin and she had Shelby all to herself. She could spend all night right here on top of her, exhaustion the only barrier to an endless sea of shared ecstasy.

"Please, God, Morgan. I need you. Please don't make me wait."

In that moment, Morgan discovered her two new favorite sounds in the world. Shelby breathing her name like that and Shelby begging. She would do just about anything to hear them again, over and over, all night long.

Fortunately for Shelby, Morgan was just as desperate. She slid her hands up Shelby's side until they encountered thick lace and ample breasts. She made quick work of the sweater, but she left the lace bra in place a while longer. Shelby made the most incredible noises as Morgan teased her through the lingerie, but it was nothing to the sound she made when Morgan's lips wrapped around the already rock-hard bud of her nipple. Shelby arched up into her, searching for contact, and her thigh slipped between Morgan's.

The pressure where Morgan needed it most nearly got the best of her, but she recovered quickly. Holding Shelby's body down against the mattress with her own, Morgan lavished attention on first one nipple, then the other with tongue and teeth, but there were places far more tempting for her mouth to venture.

Shelby's eyes flashed dangerously in the moonlight when Morgan slipped off her trousers and panties but left the heels in place. Morgan hadn't been aware of how sensual it could be to feel the scrape of patent leather against her back until that night, but she had a feeling she wouldn't get over the fetish any time soon. She made sure to strip naked so she could feel them against her skin before she lowered herself between Shelby's legs.

Morgan started with a teasing flick of her tongue. She caught just the barest taste of Shelby, but it was enough to drive her wild with craving. She wanted to linger. She wanted to tease out tiny exclamations and build Shelby slowly to release, but her impatience got the better of her. She swiped the flat of her tongue hard against Shelby's clit over and over. Soon Shelby was swearing and repeating her name in sharply increasing octaves. Within moments, Shelby's back arched off the bed and she screamed her pleasure into the night air. But Morgan hadn't had enough of either her pleasure or her taste, so she didn't slacken her pace through Shelby's first orgasm or her second. By the third, Shelby was begging for a break and Morgan reluctantly agreed.

She slid along the sweat-sheened length of Shelby's panting form, caressing every inch of flesh she encountered on the way up. The moment she was within reach, Shelby grabbed her and buried her face in her neck, a quiet sob stifled against Morgan's skin. The emotion shocked her at first, but it felt so good to hold Shelby close—to comfort her as she processed the sensations that overwhelmed her—that she couldn't bring herself to feel anything but gratitude.

Even before Shelby's breathing calmed, her body was moving. She pressed up into Morgan, her nipples tight and hard against her overheated skin. Morgan's body quivered with anticipation and she couldn't stop her hips from bucking forward. Shelby slid a thigh between hers and the pressure was deliciously perfect.

"Will you stay on top of me?" Shelby asked against her ear. "I need your weight holding me down."

Morgan's voice was lost as Shelby rocked her hips up and all she could do was nod. In truth, there was nowhere else she wanted to be. She'd dreamed of this so many times. Shelby's body beneath her just like this. Her nails scratching into her back as she pressed her thigh against Morgan's clit. Burying her face in the pillow next to Shelby's neck as her orgasm ripped through her, throwing her rhythm into a frantic staccato. But her dreams had not prepared her for the glory of collapsing, spent and overwhelmed, into Shelby's welcoming arms. Nothing could have prepared her for how right that moment felt. How they melted into one.

They spent the rest of the night in each other's arms, giving and receiving pleasure over and over, and each time they shared the same overwhelming emotion at having found their way into this moment together.

❖

Shelby had never really appreciated the benefits of a padded fabric headboard. Her own bed had a nice wooden headboard that was pretty, but not nearly as comfortable as Morgan's to lean against while working in bed. Of course, she never lingered in her own bed to work. Normally she got right up, made a pot of coffee, and got straight to work either in her home office or by hitting the road. Even on the weekends, she didn't linger. As she snuggled a little deeper into the firm but cushioned headboard, she decided this would be another thing she would change.

It didn't hurt, of course, that she had slipped into one of Morgan's old T-shirts that was butter soft and carried the lingering scent of the woman herself mixed with lavender laundry detergent. Added to that were the adorable little cooing noises Morgan made in her sleep every so often, and Shelby had never had a better Saturday morning. Even as she thought about it, Morgan made another little contented sigh and snuggled deeper into her pillow. It was so cute Shelby fully turned her attention away from her laptop.

While she watched Morgan, she wondered if she'd ever had a morning like this. She couldn't think of a time. Certainly not recently. It had been many years, possibly over a decade, since she'd had a girlfriend for longer than twenty-four hours. It wasn't that she hadn't tried at all, it was just that she'd hadn't felt like this with anyone in recent memory. Like she was completely relaxed and content with a woman but also kind of wanted to jump her bones constantly. Maybe this is what it was supposed to feel like? She wasn't sure, but she hoped Morgan would be interested in figuring that out together.

A little while later, Morgan began to stir. She was slow to come awake, rolling over and grumbling and then slowly blinking her eyes open. She had such an open face. Shelby could see everything she was thinking as she worked herself into consciousness. Her eyes searched around, then landed on Shelby. A slow smile spread on her face as she looked up.

"Hey, you." Morgan's voice was gravelly with sleep and did a number on Shelby's hormones.

"Good morning, sleepyhead."

"Not my fault. Someone kept me up past my bedtime."

"Oh, babe, I had you in bed pretty early in the evening if I recall correctly," Shelby said.

"Yeah, you did." Morgan's eyes sparkled and Shelby could tell she was replaying some of their greatest hits in her mind's eye. She even looked like she might request a reenactment until her gaze landed on Shelby's laptop. She sounded much more awake when she asked, "Are you working?"

"I sure am. I'm a morning person and I felt like a creep just sitting here watching you sleep."

"Sorry, I'm not a morning person."

Shelby closed her laptop and set it on the nightstand before sliding down into the sheets and pressing her whole body against Morgan's. The shiver she felt run through Morgan was incredibly satisfying.

"I remember." Shelby nibbled on Morgan's ear. "I was always up before you in the cabin. Remember that first day when you caught me coming out of the shower?"

Morgan answered with a lingering, searing kiss and wandering hands. She seemed to appreciate Shelby's decision to wear a T-shirt and nothing else, but when the hem of the shirt got pinched between their bodies, Morgan growled in frustration.

"Are you wearing my shirt?" Morgan asked.

Shelby leaned up and plucked at the fabric. It was a bright, sunshine yellow and had the words "Heroes Among Us, Lab Week 2019" emblazoned across it. She'd found it in the first drawer she'd checked in Morgan's dresser and didn't want to keep searching and possibly wake Morgan.

"I like it. It smells like you," Shelby said.

Morgan stuck out her bottom lip in an adorable little pout. Shelby dropped a kiss on her extended bottom lip, but Morgan kept up her pout.

"Oh no, am I wearing your favorite shirt?" Shelby asked in mock horror.

"It's not the specific shirt, it's more that you're wearing a shirt at all when you could be naked. Like me. We could be naked together."

"But you have to tell me what this heroes thing means."

Shelby pulled the shirt tight, trying to read the words, but noticing that her nipples showed rather prominently through the thin fabric. She liked the way Morgan's eyes went all hungry and hazy and the way she couldn't seem to make herself look away. She bent and slowly, sensually kissed Morgan, making sure to show in no uncertain terms how much she appreciated that desire.

"As much as I want to give you everything your little heart desires, I'm going to need at least one meal and three cups of coffee before you can seduce me again. Last night wore me out." Shelby rolled back to her side of the bed.

"I'd love to argue, but I feel the same way." Morgan laughed and flopped back onto her pillow. "Did you borrow anything else of mine while I was asleep?"

"Yes, actually. The coffeemaker."

Shelby nodded across at the other nightstand where Morgan's laptop sat next to a mug that had just about stopped steaming. Morgan did a double take, then sat up abruptly in bed.

Her reaction made Shelby worry. "Did I overstep? I'm sorry, I am a bit of a caffeine addict."

"Wait." Morgan stared incredulously at Shelby. "Do you expect us to spend our entire Saturday working?"

Shelby's stomach dropped and the lingering taste of Morgan's kiss soured on her tongue. "No, not exactly. I just…it was a dumb idea. Sorry."

Morgan reached out and tilted her chin up to meet her eye. Shelby's stomach still squirmed uncomfortably, but there was something unreadable and almost sweet in Morgan's expression. Not to mention, her voice was gentle and kind. "Tell me. Please?"

"Like I said, it's dumb." Morgan didn't release her chin, so Shelby took a deep breath and took the plunge. "It's just that I've always wanted one of those relationships you see in sitcoms and rom-coms. With lazy weekend mornings in bed with coffee and a newspaper. But we spend our weekends working, so I thought, well, no one reads a newspaper anymore anyway. I thought we could have some coffee and work in bed for a little while."

Morgan laughed quietly and dropped Shelby's chin. "How domestic."

Shelby's chest tightened and she realized it was now or never. Morgan was the brave one to reach out for a date. This was Shelby's time to be brave. Shelby's time to ask for what she wanted even with the threat she may never get it.

"Is that something you might be interested in?" Shelby asked. "Being domestic? With, um, me?"

Morgan studied her for a long moment. Her expression changed to thoughtful, almost frightened. It was something Shelby had come to call her "scientist face." Where her brain worked through all the possible outcomes of the experiment to determine a risk versus reward calculation. It was the same one she had when Shelby first pointed out the cabin porch light in the distance after the crash and when she realized one of them would have to go back to the road to clear the snow off the car.

She wasn't exactly excited to see the calculations happening. Shelby knew she was a risk for Morgan and she had no idea if she represented enough of a reward. She never really had been for anyone in the past. Of course, that had never bothered her before. Maybe she had done her own calculations in those past relationships and she had never closed the deal long-term with girlfriends before. But she hadn't wanted them like she wanted Morgan. Not just the sex, but she really, really wanted to have coffee in bed with her on the weekends.

"I'm willing to take a look at your offer." Morgan rubbed her chin. "How soon can you work up a quote for me on this whole being domestic with you thing?"

A string that had been pulled too tight for too long in Shelby's chest snapped. A gurgle of laughter bubbled up in her throat, and it was half humor, half disbelief.

"Did you just make a sales joke about dating me?" Shelby asked.

"I sure did." Morgan laughed and pulled Shelby into her lap, silencing her laughter with a sweet, hungry kiss. "I'd love to drink coffee and catch up on work in bed with you, but, sweetheart? Not right now."

Morgan surged forward, knocking Shelby onto her back and slipping between her legs. Shelby's heart rate tripled at the feel of their naked skin pressed together. Maybe she didn't need a meal or coffee after all.

"Right now," Morgan said. "I'm going to have to take my shirt back."

Epilogue

"Take it all in, kids. You've arrived."
Morgan still didn't think she qualified as a kid and she still didn't think anyone had ever truly "arrived" by walking into the Joseph A. Floreano Riverside Conference Center in Rochester, New York, but she would never take this moment away from Chad. She also held a special place in her heart for Rochester and for this conference center in particular, so she wouldn't besmirch its name. Most importantly, however, was the fact that she would never embarrass Chad in front of his new protege.

"Wow, this place is huge," Mateo said in an awed murmur.

"Don't be intimidated. Morgan and I will show you the ropes. Maybe even introduce you to some of the rock star sales types from other companies."

Chad shot Morgan a conspiratorial grin, but Mateo looked aghast at the very thought of meeting competitors. In fact, Mateo looked aghast a lot. And scared. And nervous. And pretty much every other emotion. Maybe it was because he was so young, maybe it was just his personality, but every single emotion he felt was splashed like a neon billboard across his face. It was endearing in a way, but it didn't do him any favors to look like a frightened rabbit when a customer asked a question he didn't expect.

Still, Mateo was a sweet kid and he had a lot of potential. All he needed was a little confidence, and Morgan knew a thing or two about that. After all, last year at this time she had been exactly in

Mateo's spot—the invitee of a benevolent mentor to an event that could be her big break. This year, she'd made the trip on her own merit, having landed a massive contract with a chain of doctor's offices that stamped her ticket.

"There's always something to learn from our competitors," Morgan said. "And these shows are all about networking."

"Is that what these shows are all about?"

The silky purr of Shelby's voice against her earlobe made a burst of goose pimples flash across Morgan's neck. Fortunately, Chad had dragged Mateo off to a nearby booth for the latest model of refrigerated centrifuges, so they didn't hear her stifled groan.

"You love sneaking up on me, don't you?" Morgan said over her shoulder.

"Sometimes I'm lucky and it makes you squeak like you've seen a mouse."

"You're never going to let me live that down, are you?" Morgan couldn't wait any longer, so she turned to take in Shelby's dazzling eyes and smug grin.

"It was just so cute."

"It wasn't cute. It was embarrassing."

"Oh, sweetie." Shelby wrapped her arms around Morgan's neck, flagrantly violating the no-touching-while-working policy they'd had to enact after an illicit meeting in a client's bathroom. "Nothing you could ever do is embarrassing. You're endlessly sexy and charming."

"Don't try to flatter me. You're the charming one and you know it."

"Baby, you could charm the skin off a snake," Shelby drawled.

Over the last year, Morgan had discovered a weakness for North Carolina accents and strange, undecipherable Southern aphorisms. Whenever Shelby was feeling particularly amorous, she pulled out one or the other, but to pull out both at once was overkill.

"Did you do something that's going to make me mad?" Morgan squinted at her with suspicion.

"Me? What could I possibly have done? Why, I'm innocent as the child unborn."

Before Morgan could do any more than wonder, she looked up to see Joshua and Eric walking across the conference center lobby staring daggers through the two of them. When they realized Morgan was looking at them, they changed course so they would cross farther away. Shelby spotted them as they passed and rolled her eyes, letting her arms drop from around Morgan's neck.

"Damn, I was hoping they'd get the hint and clear out," Shelby said.

"Did you talk to them?"

"God no. But I saw them picking up their name badges and figured I ought to distract you."

One night while they were stuck in Shelby's condo during a fierce spring thunderstorm, Morgan had finally gotten Shelby drunk enough that she confessed all the sordid, terrible things Joshua had said to her over the years. The ways they had discussed clients together and, finally, how Shelby had finally told him to drop dead when he'd said some of those things about Morgan. She'd also told the whole Eric making a pass story in more detail. Apparently, Shelby had been worried Morgan would judge her for her complicity. Instead, Morgan had been outraged that both men been such garbage people and had dragged Shelby down with them. She'd threatened to punch them both on the nose when they saw each other again, and Shelby had taken her at her word, even though she knew full well Morgan had never punched anyone in her life.

"Okay, you two. Less kissing, more selling." Chad's voice from just over her shoulder made Morgan jump and, embarrassingly, squeak loud enough for Mateo to jump and squeak, too. The high five Shelby and Chad shared was so endearing, Morgan couldn't even be mad at them for it. With a final peck on Morgan's cheek, Shelby released her in favor of Chad's arm. They marched off into the melee on the main floor, leaving Morgan to smile wistfully after them.

"Any last-minute advice?" Mateo straightened his tie.

"Yeah. If it starts to snow, make sure to book yourself a rental car. You might just drive off with the love of your life."

About the Author

Tagan Shepard (she/her) is an author of women-loving-women fiction, including the 2019 Goldie award-winning *Bird on a Wire*. Her work has ranged from contemporary romance to science fiction to action. But all of her work has one thing in common: it centers around extraordinary women falling in love with other extraordinary women.

Tagan is an avid reader, a cat lover, and a gamer. She also loves cheese. And wine. And bread. Pizza. French pastries. Look, if it has too many calories and doctors say you should limit your intake, she's a fan. www.taganshepard.com

Books Available from Bold Strokes Books

A Heart Divided by Angie Williams. Emmaline is the most beautiful woman Jackson has ever seen, but being a veteran of the Confederate army that killed her husband isn't the only thing keeping them apart. (978-1-63679-537-9)

Adrift by Sam Ledel. Two women whose lives are anchored by guilt and obligation find romance amidst the tumultuous Prohibition movement in 1920s California. (978-1-63679-577-5)

Cabin Fever by Tagan Shepard. The longer Morgan and Shelby are stranded together, the more their feelings grow, but is it real, or just cabin fever? (978-1-63679-632-1)

Clean Kill by Anne Laughlin. When someone starts killing people she knows in the recovery world, former detective Nicky Sullivan must race to stop the killer and keep herself from being arrested for the crimes. (978-1-63679-634-5)

Only a Bridesmaid by Haley Donnell. A fake bridesmaid, a socially anxious bride, and an unexpected love—what could go wrong? (978-1-63679-642-0)

Primal Hunt by L.L. Raand. Anya, a young wolf warrior, finds herself paired with Rafe, one of the most powerful Vampires in the Americas, in an erotic union of blood and sex. (978-1-63679-561-4)

Puzzles Can Be Deadly by David S. Pederson. Skip loves a good puzzle. Little does he know that a simple phone call will lead him and his boyfriend Henry to the deadliest puzzle he's ever encountered. (978-1-63679-615-4)

Snake Charming by Genevieve McCluer. Playgirl vampire Freddie is on the run and a chance encounter with lamia Phoebe makes them both realize that they may have found the love they'd given up on. (978-1-63679-628-4)

Spirits and Sirens by Kelly and Tana Fireside. When rumored ghost whisperer Elena Murphy and very skeptical assistant fire chief Allison Jones have to work together to solve a 70-year-old mystery, sparks fly—will it be enough to melt the ice between them and let love ignite? (978-1-63679-607-9)

A Case for Discretion by Ashley Moore. Will Gwen, a prominent Atlanta attorney, choose Etta, the law student she's clandestinely dating, or is her political future too important to sacrifice? (978-1-63679-617-8)

Aubrey McFadden Is Never Getting Married by Georgia Beers. Aubrey McFadden is never getting married, but she does have five weddings to attend, and she'll be avoiding Monica Wallace, the woman who ruined her happily ever after, at every single one. (978-1-63679-613-0)

Flowers for Dead Girls by Abigail Collins. Isla might be just the right kind of girl to bring Astra out of her shell—and maybe more. The only problem? She's dead. (978-1-63679-584-3)

Good Bones by Aurora Rey. Designer and contractor Logan Barrow can give Kathleen Kenney the house of her dreams, but can she convince the cynical romance writer to take a chance on love? (978-1-63679-589-8)

Leather, Lace, and Locs by Anne Shade. Three friends, each on their own path in life, with one obstacle…finding room in their busy lives for a love that will give them their happily ever afters. (978-1-63679-529-4)

Rainbow Overalls by Maggie Fortuna. Arriving in Vermont for her first year of college, an introverted bookworm forms a friendship with an outgoing artist and finds what comes after the classic coming out story: a being out story. (978-1-63679-606-2)

Revisiting Summer Nights by Ashley Bartlett. PJ Addison and Wylie Parsons have been called back to film the most recent Dangerous Summer Nights installment. Only this time they're not in love and it's going to stay that way. (978-1-63679-551-5)

The Broken Lines of Us by Shia Woods. Charlie Dawson returns to the city she left behind and she meets an unexpected stranger on her first night back, discovering that coming home might not be as hard as she thought. (978-1-63679-585-0)

Triad Magic by 'Nathan Burgoine. Face-to-face against forces set in motion hundreds of years ago, Luc, Anders, and Curtis—vampire, demon, and wizard—must draw on the power of blood, soul, and magic to stop a killer. (978-1-63679-505-8)

All This Time by Sage Donnell. Erin and Jodi share a complicated past, but a very different present. Will they ever be able to make a future together work? (978-1-63679-622-2)

Crossing Bridges by Chelsey Lynford. When a one-night stand between a snowboard instructor and a business executive becomes more, one has to overcome her past, while the other must let go of her planned future. (978-1-63679-646-8)

Dancing Toward Stardust by Julia Underwood. Age has nothing to do with becoming the person you were meant to be, taking a chance, and finding love. (978-1-63679-588-1)

Evacuation to Love by CA Popovich. As a hurricane rips through Florida, so too are Joanne and Shanna's lives upended. It'll take a force of nature to show them the love it takes to rebuild. (978-1-63679-493-8)

Lean in to Love by Catherine Lane. Will badly behaving celebrities, erotic sex tapes, and steamy scandals prevent Rory and Ellis from leaning in to love? (978-1-63679-582-9)

Searching for Someday by Renee Roman. For loner Rayne Thomas, her only goal for working out is to build her confidence, but Maggie Flanders has another idea, and neither are prepared for the outcome. (978-1-63679-568-3)

The Romance Lovers Book Club by MA Binfield and Toni Logan. After their book club reads a romance about an American tourist falling in love with an English princess, Harper and her best friend, Alice, book an impulsive trip to London hoping they'll each fall for the women of their dreams. (978-1-63679-501-0)

Truly Home by J.J. Hale. Ruth and Olivia discover home is more than a four-letter word. (978-1-63679-579-9)

View from the Top by Morgan Adams. When it comes to love, sometimes the higher you climb, the harder you fall. (978-1-63679-604-8)

Blood Rage by Ileandra Young. A stolen artifact, a family in the dark, an entire city on edge. Can SPEAR agent Danika Karson juggle all three over a weekend with the "in-laws," while an unknown, malevolent entity lies in wait upon her very skin? (978-1-63679-539-3)

Ghost Town by R.E. Ward. Blair Wyndon and Leif Henderson are set to prove ghosts exist when the mystery suddenly turns deadly. Someone or something else is in Masonville, and if they don't find a way to escape, they might never leave. (978-1-63679-523-2)

Good Christian Girls by Elizabeth Bradshaw. In this heartfelt coming of age lesbian romance, Lacey and Jo help each other untangle who they are from who everyone says they're supposed to be. (978-1-63679-555-3)

Guide Us Home by CF Frizzell and Jesse J. Thoma. When acquisition of an abandoned lighthouse pits ambitious competitors Nancy and Sam against each other, it takes a WWII tale of two brave women to make them see the light. (978-1-63679-533-1)

Lost Harbor by Kimberly Cooper Griffin. For Alice and Bridget's love to survive, they must find a way to reconcile the most important passions in their lives—devotion to the church and each other. (978-1-63679-463-1)

Never a Bridesmaid by Spencer Greene. As her sister's wedding gets closer, Jessica finds that her hatred for the maid of honor is a bit more complicated than she thought. Could it be something more than hatred? (978-1-63679-559-1)

The Rewind by Nicole Stiling. For police detective Cami Lyons and crime reporter Alicia Flynn, some choices break hearts. Others leave a body count. (978-1-63679-572-0)

Turning Point by Cathy Dunnell. When Asha and her former high school bully Jody struggle to deny their growing attraction, can they move forward without going back? (978-1-63679-549-2)

When Tomorrow Comes by D. Jackson Leigh. Teague Maxwell, convinced she will die before she turns 41, hires animal rescue owner Baye Cobb to rehome her extensive menagerie. (978-1-63679-557-7)

You Had Me at Merlot by Melissa Brayden. Leighton and Jamie have all the ingredients to turn their attraction into love, but it's a recipe for disaster. (978-1-63679-543-0)

BOLDSTROKESBOOKS.COM

Looking for your next great read?

Visit BOLDSTROKESBOOKS.COM
to browse our entire catalog of paperbacks, ebooks,
and audiobooks.

Want the first word on what's new?
Visit our website for event info,
author interviews, and blogs.

Subscribe to our free newsletter for sneak peeks,
new releases, plus first notice of promos
and daily bargains.

SIGN UP AT
BOLDSTROKESBOOKS.COM/signup

Bold Strokes Books
Quality and Diversity in LGBTQ Literature

Bold Strokes Books is an award-winning publisher
committed to quality and diversity in LGBTQ fiction.

Milton Keynes UK
Ingram Content Group UK Ltd.
UKHW020659070524
442340UK00001B/64